ONE WHO
HAS BEEN HERE
BEFORE

Advance Praise for
One Who Has Been Here Before

"A strong, confident debut novel about a complicated homecoming, peopled with characters you will remember and even almost recognize. Brimming with compassion, *One Who Has Been Here Before* explores family in all its forms, those we're born to and those we build, those we lose and those we find again."

–Rebecca Silver Slayter, author of *In the Land of Birdfishes* and *The Second History*

"Rebecca Babcock has done what most good writers do: taken an old story and made it new again. *One Who Has Been Here Before* is wonderfully written, evoking thought, questions, and ponderings long after the last page is read. First novel? I'm betting it won't be her last!"

–Donna Morrissey, award-winning author of *The Fortunate Brother*

"A contemplative and compelling novel about a young woman's fascination with a notorious Nova Scotia family. *One Who Has Been Here Before* is an artfully braided book about the power of storytelling, history, and, ultimately, belonging."

–Harriet Alida Lye, author of *The Honey Farm* and *Natural Killer*

"Many paths lead away from tragedy. What happens after an entire extended family is carted away amidst reports of abuse and neglect? From page one I was drawn into the ever-darkening woods of *One Who Has Been Here Before*. Rebecca Babcock's debut novel takes us beyond the whispers of scandal, humanizing a story of shame with fully-drawn characters, keen attention to detail, and superb pacing. It's a heartbreaking story of a shattered family rooted in Nova Scotia's not-so-distant past."

–Nicola Davison, award-winning author of *In the Wake*

ONE WHO HAS BEEN HERE BEFORE

∾

BECCA BABCOCK

Copyright © 2021, Becca Babcock

Vagrant Press is an imprint of
Nimbus Publishing Limited
3660 Strawberry Hill Street, Halifax, NS, B3K 5A9
(902) 455-4286 nimbus.ca

Printed and bound in Canada
NB1493

Editor: Stephanie Domet
Editor for the press: Whitney Moran
Design: Jenn Embree

Library and Archives Canada Cataloguing in Publication

Title: One who has been here before / Becca Babcock.
Names: Babcock, Becca, 1978- author.
Identifiers: Canadiana (print) 20210107405 | Canadiana (ebook) 20210107448 | ISBN 9781771089296 (softcover) | ISBN 9781771085663 (EPUB)
Classification: LCC PS8603.A255 O54 2021 | DDC C813/.6—dc23

Nimbus Publishing acknowledges the financial support for its publishing activities from the Government of Canada, the Canada Council for the Arts, and from the Province of Nova Scotia. We are pleased to work in partnership with the Province of Nova Scotia to develop and promote our creative industries for the benefit of all Nova Scotians.

On a day there comes once more
To the latched and lonely door,
Down the wood-road striding silent,
One who has been here before.

—Charles G. D. Roberts, "The Solitary Woodsman" (1897)

ℴℴ

Days, weeks, months, years
Afterwards, when both were wives
With children of their own;
Their mother-hearts beset with fears,
Their lives bound up in tender lives;
Laura would call the little ones
And tell them of her early prime,
Those pleasant days long gone
Of not-returning time:
Would talk about the haunted glen,
The wicked, quaint fruit-merchant men,
Their fruits like honey to the throat
But poison in the blood;
(Men sell not such in any town):
Would tell them how her sister stood
In deadly peril to do her good,
And win the fiery antidote:

—Christina Rossetti, "Goblin Market" (1862)

CONTENTS

THE WOODS ARE DARK

ONE

I've found the place. It took a long time, but here I am. At last. It doesn't look familiar at all. I'm both relieved and disappointed.

I wonder when the last time someone, a person, was here. How long did it sit, untenanted, waiting?

No. Not waiting. It wasn't waiting for anyone. I can see that. Its doors don't open properly now. They're not really doors anymore. The one at the back of the house is a measured gap, letting in smaller animals, birds and insects, squirrels and mice. Letting in curling limbs of snow that whirl on the warped linoleum, or leaves that clatter and swish. Letting in the tendrils of nightshade that curl up around the frame. The front door is closed, barring light and air and creatures, though some of the windows are smashed, and they're portals, too, for the life that wants in. The rest just admit light, letting the seeds root and grow in crevices between the floor and the wall.

The buildings aren't waiting. They're sighing, sinking, leaning back into the ground, letting themselves ease slowly into the soil. They're not surrendering to the seeds and the roots, the bird and mouse nests. They're opening up, offering themselves. They're not waiting at all. They don't need anyone. They don't need me.

Taylor Lake is just over an hour from my hotel, which sits in a corner of a commercial park just outside of Halifax. This morning, I programmed my destination into my cellphone's mapping app and headed out onto the highway to the South Shore. Taylor Lake is just east of New Russell, which *is more of a dot on a map than it is a town, and New Russell is just north of the quaint village of Chester. Of course, it shouldn't be called Taylor Lake at all. I don't know if it was ever labelled Gaugin Lake on the maps, but it was once called Gaugin Lake by everyone who knew it. I've heard that the old folks in New Russell and New Ross still call it Gaugin Lake. I've also heard that they won't go there.*

I turn off the paved road onto a well-graded gravel road that loops around the lake. Cottage country. The way is marked with handwritten, passive-aggressive signs admonishing drivers to slow down or else four-wheelers will no longer be allowed on this road. Sweet, self-consciously rustic cottages dot the forest on either side of the road. A few have lawns, but most are tucked within a cleared and tidied patch of the natural forest. My research has told me that this is one of the few areas that still boasts original Acadian forest: tall oaks, pines, stout sugar maples instead of the adolescent firs, the brittle spruce, the thin, weedy-looking red maples that cover the rest of the province. I've heard there is even ironwood growing in this forest. The bulk of the province was clear-cut by the logging companies in the last two centuries, and the forests are relatively new, populated with young, fast-growing tree species. But not Gaugin lands. And the Gaugins were here a long, long time. They were the ones to snatch this bit of forest from the Mi'kmaq.

The people in these cottages likely don't talk about the Gaugins. Or maybe they do. Maybe it's a joke, an insult. "God, Gordie! If you don't wash that pickup truck, people are gonna start to think you're a Gaugin!" Maybe they're a bedtime story to scare children. "Turn out that light right now or the Gaugins will come and take you!" Who knows. But if the Gaugins had not been here, had not been what they were, these people wouldn't own the most valuable lakefront property on the mainland of Nova Scotia.

When I reach the back of the lake, the farthest point from the paved road, I park my car. My app tells me this is the place here, through the forest. Newspaper articles pointed me in the right direction, and satellite photos from the mapping site let me piece together the directions. You can see it, a faint clearing, the buildings themselves greyish rectangles. Now that I'm here, I can see what once might have been a road of sorts. It's a parting of the big trees, and it looks like the ATVs and snowmobiles, under threat of expulsion by the community watch, have kept the trail open. I take a picture and I start my hike in.

After about four kilometres, the trail veers right, but I need to keep on straight, almost due north. I walk for an hour. It's June and the blackflies are vicious. I've coated my skin and clothes in Deet, but they still manage to tangle into my hair, chewing at the skin until trickles of blood alert me. Blackflies have a pain-numbing compound in their saliva. I won't feel the bites until later.

I stop to pee, crouching low and holding the seat of my pants away from the stream. My guess is that I can't be more than a kilometre away. The forest seems untouched. Nothing is familiar.

I am checking my position on the phone when I finally spot the house. When I first notice it, it startles me, as though it might be a wild animal and I've just interrupted its dinner. But it's just a house. Just an old, old house made of weathered boards. Two brick chimneys rise from its roof, and its windows stare blindly out at the forest surrounding it. The front door is tightly shut, but the glass in the window next to it is smashed.

I stare at the house, and something heavy and slow unfolds in my belly. I don't recognize the place—not at all—but still, I'm staring at it, and I feel a slow, creeping dread coming from somewhere deep down within me. My guts shift. I have to shit. I go back to the trail and find a clearing, some place I won't step when I return this afternoon, or when I come back later this week. My bowels empty and I feel lighter, cleaner. I am ready to go back and take some pictures.

I start with the house itself. I start at the front, the approach from what must have been the road. Later, I will need to compare these photos to pictures run in the newspapers twenty-five years ago. I work systematically, capturing the front of the house, the sealed front door with its rotted step, the broken panes of the main-floor windows. Then I take a picture of the chimneys, the pitch of the roof, the unbroken glass of the attic window. I keep my mind on the pictures themselves—the light, the depth of field, the composition. I cannot bring myself to think about the rooms beyond. Not yet.

Then I move around the side of the house. There is a thick mass of shrubs on the northeast side. Juniper, and caragana gone wild. Now, in the early summer, it is covered in yellow blossoms. *Without thinking, I pluck a flower and put it into my mouth, savouring the delicate yellowness of its flavour. Now when did I learn to do that? Who first put a caragana blossom on my tongue?*

An apple tree past its prime has sloughed off a heavy bough, probably the winter before. It lies, grey and dejected, under the early green leaves and tiny nubs of fruit. Here and there, withered petals still dust the earth and roots.

Beyond the shrubs, more buildings. I'll attend to those soon enough, but first the main house. Here, where the wall faces north, I can see that the boards were once painted white. Who painted them? Whose job was it to do that? How often did it have to be done? I wonder if there were maybe flowers then, too. (Of course, there had to have been a vegetable garden. I will try to figure out where it might have been.) Was there time for tending flowers? Or was that too frivolous? Maybe painting the house was practical, rather than decorative. Painted wood doesn't weather as fast as bare.

On this side of the house, most of the windows on the ground floor are broken. Upstairs, the dormer windows are intact. I photograph everything, then I move around to the back, to the east side. More white paint, more broken windows, a back door. This one is open slightly—enough to admit wind and birds and rodents, maybe a very svelte raccoon, but not wide enough for anything bigger.

The paint is all gone on the west side. The boards are weathered and cracking. One is missing, and I wonder whether the darkness that I see in the space where it should be is the inside of the house, or just the inside of the wall.

The outbuildings now. I count six. The largest is a barn. It is caved in, its roof a broken, sagging mare's back. It will not be safe for me to go in and get pictures. Two of the smaller outbuildings have also collapsed, but three are still standing. One even has a door on its hinges. They all have windows. What was kept out here? Food? Tools? Did children or more peripheral members of the family sleep here?

A rusted hulk that used to be a station wagon is rotting behind the buildings. And that's it. All that's left of the Gaugin home. The Gaugin farm. Compound. Of course, there are others. Other homes rotting away in this forest. Or there were. There were at least two long-abandoned places on the lakefront, but those have been swept away to make room for modern cottages. This is the main one. This is the one I have come to photograph. This is the one the reporters came to photograph almost three decades ago.

It's time to start hiking back to my car.

I feel relieved as I walk away from the house, but also a little frightened, as though something in the woods might be staring at me, crouched to pounce. I walk quickly, but I don't let myself run. Or look back. I'm relieved to be leaving.

But today's trip is momentous. Today is an occasion.

Today is my first time back here in twenty-eight years.

ॐ

THREE HOURS. THREE HOURS SURVEYING AND PHOTOGRAPHING THE house, the yard, the outbuildings, then Emma hiked back to her car, drove back through the forest dotted with comfortable cottages. Just three short hours. Somehow, that felt cheap. It should have been longer. It should have cost her more.

Emma took her time driving back to the hotel on the edge of Halifax. Before she pulled out onto the highway, she plugged her phone into the stereo. She cranked the music up and sang along to her Workout playlist. She was sure that drivers passing her must have thought she was having a great time, but really, she just wanted to make so much noise she couldn't think.

As she crossed the hotel lobby, the guy at the front desk said hello. He smiled at her when he said it, holding her gaze for a long second. He had dark, almost-black hair and light eyes. His cheekbones were sharp, his chin small. He was slight—thin, and not much taller than her. As she stepped into the elevator, she wondered whether she'd remembered to say "hello" back.

The electronic lock accepted her key card with a demure click. She stepped into her room, bolting the door behind her. She was thinking about the house, the way it seemed to be inhaling through its broken windows. She felt a rush of accomplishment. There. She'd made her first trip. She'd found the site, recorded her impressions of the place. She had taken pictures and made notes. She'd done that much.

That was the thing about places. They were simply there. You could always go find them, if you knew where to look. You didn't have to ask permission, wait for an answer that might just fell you.

As she stood in the entrance to her bland hotel room, her mind trailing over all that she'd seen, the shift crept over her. Familiar but always jarring. She tried to hold it back and redirect her thoughts—to dinner, to her parents, to her apartment at home. She was trying not to think of the house, of going back there, but it was too late. She felt the quaking in her thighs and the tightening in her chest. She pulled off her coat, shirt, bra, trying to get enough air into her lungs. She knew she should sit down, focus on her breathing, start one of the exercises her therapist had given her, but she was past all that now. She couldn't hold still. She walked to the window, back to the door. Fought the urge to put her shirt back on and run into the hallway, back down the stairs, out into the parking lot. She didn't know where she would go from there. Somewhere. Away. So instead, she rooted through her bag, her hands jerking uncontrollably until she found the pills. She took one, but there wasn't enough saliva in her mouth to swallow it dry. She didn't dare try to pick up a glass, so she ran to the bathroom and gulped water directly from the faucet. She looked at the clock, marking the quarter-hour it would take for the drug to kick in.

Distantly, she felt a burning in her arm. She looked down. There was blood above her elbow, blood under her fingernails. She'd been scratching at the blackfly bites, grating away the skin. She made herself drop her hands to her sides, made herself stop pacing the room, made herself concentrate on her fast, shallow breaths.

When the drug eased into her bloodstream and the world began to feel muffled and soft, she got into the shower. Small leaves fell out of her hair as she shampooed it.

When she got out, she stared at the outline of herself in the bathroom mirror. Her reflection in the steam was like her anxiety under the Lorazepam—still there, but soft, indistinct.

She should call her mom. She pulled on the thick hotel bathrobe and sat on the bed, squeezing her rope of wet hair into a towel. Turned on the TV, hoping the sounds would mask the droopiness in her voice.

"Sweetie! How was your flight?" Emma's mom asked as soon as she picked up. Julia never answered the phone with a simple "Hello."

"Fine. Got in last night, and I managed to find the site this morning. I got some good pictures, I think."

A pause. Damn. Julia could hear it in Emma's voice. "You okay?"

"Yup. All good."

"Did you meditate, or did you go right for the pills? Can you find a drop-in yoga place near your hotel?"

"I'm fine. Everything is fine. I'm just tired from the trip and a long day outside. Don't worry, OK?"

Emma could hear her mom breathing lightly. "I can still come out, you know," she said. "I'll stay out of your hair, but I'll be close if you need me."

"Mom. Don't fly out here. I'm a grown-ass woman. I can go on a research trip without my mommy."

Julia laughed a little. Emma told her she had to go, had to start sorting her photos, and they said good night.

"I can look up drop-in yoga studios in Halifax, if you want," Julia said, just as Emma was about to hang up. Julia did that so often—blurted out a question or a comment after she'd already said goodbye—that Emma knew to wait a few seconds before ending the call.

"I know how to google, Mom," Emma said. "Why else do you think they let me into grad school?"

"All right, all right, as long as you promise to look."

"Cross my heart, hope to die," Emma said. "Stick a yoga mat in my eye."

Yoga. Not something Emma would have ever seen herself doing when she was younger—in high school, for instance. It wasn't really even something she would keep up now, except for Julia. It was their thing, their mother-daughter thing. "Bonding through bending," Emma's dad called it.

The first yoga class they'd attended together, Julia hadn't even told Emma where they were going. "Wear comfy clothes," she said as she ushered Emma out to the car.

"Why?" Emma asked. "What are we doing? I don't want to go out." She needed a shower. She hadn't washed her hair for a couple of days. All she wanted was to eat popcorn and binge-watch TV until bedtime.

"Don't worry, we're not going out-out," Julia had replied. "You'll see."

She'd driven the two of them to the rec centre in their neighbourhood, a long, low building with chipping grey stucco. It was the kind of place that usually hosted Scouts and Brownies, or potluck fiftieth-anniversary parties. Emma turned to stare at her mom before she got out. What was this? Some kind of support group? She couldn't seem to find the energy to tell Julia she wasn't going in.

"Come on," Julia said, getting out of the car. Obediently, Emma followed her inside.

In the smaller hall just off the dated lobby with its chipped pine panelling, a woman was laying out yoga mats on the floor. Julia strode toward her.

"Mom," Emma said in a low voice. "No. This isn't my thing."

"How do you know?" Julia replied as she selected side-by-side yoga mats in the front row. "You haven't even tried."

At first, Emma had felt self-conscious, especially up at the front of the class, so near the compact, well-muscled yoga instructor. But doing the beginner poses was so new, so unnatural, that Emma had to turn her whole attention to moving and holding her body. And it was soothing, that kind of effort. It felt good to let everything else get pushed out of her head for a while.

"That wasn't bad," she conceded as she and Julia climbed back into the car afterward.

"So we'll come back next week?"

"Maybe," Emma said. "We'll see."

Julia nodded, and Emma could see a sliver of worry lift from her, too. It stung, suddenly, to realize how much Julia felt, how much she tried to carry for Emma.

"Okay, Mom. Next week."

In her hotel room, Emma flipped aimlessly through the television channels for a minute, then turned off the TV. She grabbed her phone again to do a quick search for local bars and restaurants. She wanted to be in a noisy place all of a sudden. She wanted the buzz of people talking and just being normal all around her. But there was nothing but fast food in this neighbourhood—nothing except the little bar off the lobby downstairs. She pulled on a pair of jeans and a T-shirt and took the elevator down.

In the corner of the bar, two thick-necked men in suits were watching a baseball game on TV. One of the businessmen turned and gave her an appreciative smile, almost a leer, really. She repressed the urge to flip them the bird—who knew how long they were staying here, how many times she'd run into them again—and gave them a tight smile instead, and then scanned the bar for a spot outside their field of vision.

Emma didn't see a waiter or a bartender. She picked an armchair next to the fake fireplace and thumbed through the menu on the table. She decided it had been long enough since she took her pill—she could have a beer. She had just begun to wonder how to order when the guy from the front desk rounded the corner.

"What can I get you?" he asked.

"I thought you worked the front desk," Emma said.

"What, I can't do both?" he asked. He had the rounded-vowel regional accent.

"You can do anything you put your mind to, I guess."

He smiled. "We were short-staffed this afternoon. I was just covering the desk."

"Ah." There was a pause, and Emma realized he was waiting for her to order. "What's a good beer?"

"That one," he said, pointing at a pricey local selection.

"Let's do it," she said. "And some fries."

He nodded and disappeared, taking the menu with him.

Emma stared into the gas-fuelled flames of the fireplace next to her while she waited. She breathed slowly as she went over the day's trip in her mind, trying to match the image of the crumbling house and outbuildings with something from her memory, but there was nothing. When she pressed her thoughts far, far back, she remembered the scratchy velvet-like fabric of a couch patterned with gold- and deep-green-coloured flowers. The feel of bare wood stairs under her feet. She recalled a bigger hand tugging on hers, leading her out to play in the even deeper green of the shrubs and grasses. There was a softness to these memories, a comfort. The ghost of an old feeling, one she hadn't lingered on in—how long, really? She couldn't remember. She braced for the shift to come over her again. It didn't.

The bartender-waiter-desk clerk plunked the beer down on a cardboard coaster in front of Emma, startling her. She murmured a thanks, and he smiled in reply.

"You're not going downtown tonight?" he asked.

She shook her head. "I'm here to work," she said, and immediately realized she sounded horribly prim. She took a swallow of the beer to avoid having to elaborate. But he wasn't going away. He was still smiling at her.

"People from here usually leave to work out west, not the other way around," he said. "What do you do?"

She considered an outlandish reply. *I'm a locations scout for adult films.* Or *I'm here to invest in bio fuels made from lobster carcasses.* She wasn't even sure what reaction she hoped for by saying something like that—did she want him to go, or stay? Instead, she offered the truth. "I'm doing some research on old South Shore families." Well, part of the truth, anyway.

He nodded. "Sounds interesting."

She raised her eyebrows. "It does?" She remembered to smile a little. She sometimes forgot to smile when she was joking. It unsettled people.

He smiled back, stuck out his hand. "I'm Glen."

"Emma," she replied and considered giving him her last name.

She wondered which last name to give him. But she didn't offer either. Just Emma.

"Nice to meet you, Emma," he said. He had a nice smile. "Your fries will be up in a minute."

TWO

EARLY SUNLIGHT WAS JUST BLEACHING THE HOTEL CURTAINS WHEN Emma awoke. If she could fall back asleep, she'd have another hour and a quarter before her alarm woke her. She'd gone to bed before ten the night before, not because she was tired but because she was bored. She'd lingered in the bar as long as she could, drawing out her fries and two hoppy beers before retreating to her room and the blue light of the TV. She typed up her account of her visit to the cabin, wondering how much of her writing she'd have the courage to submit to her supervisors when she got back, when she'd really had the chance to go over her work. She considered just sending it to them now, when it was fresh and she was brave. But she knew they didn't want her raw, unsorted notes. So. What would she manage to send once she'd had a chance to put it together, to polish it? How much would she chicken out? How much would she cut, delete, bury forever?

And if she did send it all, how would she manage to meet with them when she got back? It wouldn't do any good to try to joke and swagger her way through it, to deflect their questions with crude remarks. If this was to be her thesis, she'd have to actually talk it over with them, seriously. She'd need to let Dr. Melnyk and Dr. Fuentes, and two more professors, too, read her work and demand that she defend it. A thesis had to be defended.

And what would she be defending exactly? The Gaugins themselves? What could she leave in, then? What *could* she defend?

She'd leave in the part about taking a shit in the woods, for sure. That was exactly the kind of visceral detail that would get a notation of *Nice!* in the margin. Professors were easy to please that way.

Sometimes, when she caught herself scrabbling for the approval of her professors, her teachers, her bosses, she thought of Elaine. They had been best friends through most of their teen years, though they lived in different parts of Edmonton and attended different schools. Emma sometimes wondered if Elaine would have liked her as much if they'd gone to school together, if Elaine had seen her with adults other than their parents.

One time, Emma and Elaine had gone to see a movie together. It was the summer after Emma's grade eight, and they'd decided on a midweek matinee at the mall near Elaine's house. The theatre there showed movies that had already gone through the major cinemas, and admission was only a loonie.

They went to see a comedy, a cop-buddy movie, and the only other people in the audience were a group of boys about their age who had laughed and made rude jokes at the screen. When the boys' jokes were funny, Elaine would chuckle, and when they weren't, she'd grumble "Shut UP." Not shout it, just say it loud enough that they'd hear. And for a moment, they would. They'd shush and whisper dramatically before their mirth boiled up again.

As the end credits rolled, the boys started a popcorn fight with what was left in their buckets. Elaine and Emma shuffled past them toward the exit when an employee bustled through the door and up the aisle. He was carrying a broom and a long-handled dustpan and his face was pulled down in a scowl.

At the time, he had seemed intimidating, terrifying even, to Emma. Much later, Emma realized that he couldn't have been more than seventeen or eighteen. He was thin and not much taller than Elaine. His patchy goatee the epitome of part-time-job authority.

He thrust the broom and dustpan out to Emma, who was closest. "No way am I cleaning this up!" he shouted, loud enough that the boys' laughter faltered. "Every piece of popcorn had better be gone, or you're *banned*."

Instinctively, Emma had started toward the boys, broom and dustpan in hand, but the flat tone of her friend's voice arrested her.

"That's not our problem," Elaine said, looking him coolly in the eyes. "We weren't the ones throwing food."

The theatre employee drew himself up. "Far as I'm concerned, it is your problem," he said. "Unless you want a lifetime ban." And Emma started again toward the mess.

"Don't listen to this guy," Elaine said, her voice calm, matter-of-fact, but Emma thought she detected something else. Pity, perhaps, for Emma's obvious distress at being banned, or perhaps even disdain. "They're the jerks who made the mess, they clean it up."

That's when Emma realized they were all looking at her—the teenaged employee, Elaine, and the boys. She felt the weight of the cleaning tools in her hands. "It's okay," she started to say—she didn't mind helping to clean up.

Elaine looked at her hard, then shrugged. "Your call," she said, pushing past the employee, who was still staring at Emma, still watching to see what she'd do. Elaine walked out of the theatre.

Emma stood for a moment, feeling as if a cord were tied around her middle, one end held by Elaine and the other by the employee and the boys. She felt momentarily paralyzed, then with a sudden lurch, she worried she would lose Elaine in the mall if she didn't hurry up. She set down the broom and dustpan. "Sorry, sorry," she said as they fell down with a clatter and she raced to catch up with her friend.

Elaine was standing outside, waiting for her. She shook her head when Emma emerged. "Guys like that just want you to think they're something," she said. "Let's go get a slushie."

Emma's hotel windows looked out over the parking lot. She could just see the back of her rental car from where she lay. The sight of it felt like a nudge to get up, get going. If she got up now, she could get back out there early, spend a full day looking for the original cabin in the woods north of the old house. She knew to look for some foundation stones and part of the stone hearth. The original cabin had crumbled decades ago, but still, she wanted to photograph it. If she left the hotel early, she stood a good chance of finding it, maybe even going back and getting into the main house today. She could get in a good day today—finish up at the compound, move on to the next thing.

But then what?

What if there was nothing more to find?

She reached for her phone, pulling the plushy duvet back around her as she scrolled through Yelp reviews of Peggys Cove. There was an artisanal ice cream place there. She could sleep in, then later on get a selfie at the Peggys Cove lighthouse. Her mom would like that. She could keep Julia happy, keep the prospect of failure at bay another day. She had enough grant money to spend two weeks here. Two weeks of hotels, rental car, gas and fast food, and the occasional real meal in a restaurant. And when her time was up, she had to take her research back to Edmonton, to her supervisors in the History and Anthropology departments with archival and anthropological stones left unturned, and her whole flimsy house of cards in a tattered heap. A wave of uneasiness overtook her.

No. No Peggys Cove.

She pressed her face into the mushy hotel pillow. Mapping and photographing the site, searching the newspaper archives, checking out the historical society in Lunenburg, trying to find reporters or social workers or police who were there that day to interview. It was a mountain of research—a whole mountain range, even. Better get climbing.

She rolled onto her back, closed her eyes, and focused on the top of her head. She imagined a calm relaxing feeling pouring down her body like liquid. She breathed into her belly, her chest, where the anxiety was a physical weight. She imagined her breath vaporizing the weight, imagined blowing it out through her nose. Her chest eased and her skin stopped burning. But she couldn't get back to sleep.

In the hotel gym, the TV was showing a kids' cartoon. An animated dog flew a helicopter around the Arctic while she pounded her feet on the treadmill.

Today, she'd visit the archives instead of the site. One of the universities in Halifax had all the local newspapers on microfiche, going back over almost ninety years. The idea of flicking through old files, scanning for the name Gaugin, carefully logging and categorizing and filing everything gave her a small surge of energy. She checked the library website on her phone—it opened at 8:30. More than enough time for breakfast and a shower.

The day was shaping up warm and sunny as she drove into Halifax. It seemed kind of stupid now, wasting a beautiful sunny day in the library.

Oh well.

The university was more compact than the University of Alberta back home. The older buildings were clustered at the end of a boulevarded street that was lined with the academic structures built over the last century. The library was a formidably ugly fortress on the corner between the charming old stone architecture and the strident new buildings.

Emma considered dropping by the departments of Anthropology and History to introduce herself. Her own study was interdepartmental: she was performing a historical auto-ethnography of the Gaugin clan. Her two supervisors, Dr. Fuentes and Dr. Melnyk, were married to each other. Dr. Fuentes had suggested Emma stop in to meet some of her own colleagues from her grad school days in the History department, and Dr. Melnyk recommended Emma meet some of the current PhD students in Anthropology.

But Emma dreaded the idea of explaining her research topic. She was always vaguely nervous that academics would see through her, call her out as a fraud, or that they'd reveal her trendy research field had been recently debunked and she hadn't heard about it yet.

Historical auto-ethnography had not been Emma's idea. In fact, she had wanted to stick to a fairly pedestrian topic in the History department. In actual fact, she had never wanted to apply to the graduate program at all. A Bachelor's degree had been more than she'd ever aspired to. But somehow—she still struggled to piece together exactly how it had happened—she'd gotten tangled up in the program, and now here she was, a Master of Arts student in the Department of Anthropology at the University of Alberta, on a university-funded thesis research trip in Nova Scotia.

She had been, officially, a fourth year Bachelor of History student (though she had actually been chipping away at her degree for six years), working with Dr. Fuentes on a grad school proposal to study Canadian women in the First World War when Dr. Fuentes and Dr. Melnyk invited all of their grad students to a cocktail party at their home. Emma didn't want to go—she wasn't even a grad student yet—but Dr. Fuentes had insisted.

"If you're going on to grad school, you're going to have to learn to network," she'd said. "Talk about your research, learn what other people are working on."

Emma could see no advantage in talking about her embryonic undergraduate ideas with a room full of fully-fledged graduate students—who were, for the most part, younger than her, and yet already so much more academically sophisticated. This was the worst part of being a mature student. Having to defer to the intellectual superiority of students six years her junior. Students who had no idea what it was to pay rent.

After high school, Emma had taken a gap year at her parents' insistence. She was supposed to read and travel. Her parents had been saving money to send her on a trip to Europe or India or to climb Machu Picchu so she could expand her horizons, read the great novels in hostels, prepare for the intellectual enlightenment of university. But Emma kept putting off her departure. And her trips to the library. She slept in, watched daytime TV. She got a job in a café, getting up for work at 4:30 in the morning and going to bed at 9 in the evening, then in July, three months after she was supposed to have been finishing her first year at university, she enrolled in a six-month IT course at a local private college.

"I don't know what I want to study in university," she explained to her parents. The idea of selecting a major, a program of study, a career, an entire future almost crushed the breath out of her. "I don't even know for sure that I want to go. If I get this IT certificate, I can at least make some decent money while I decide."

Of course, tuition for the IT program was exorbitantly high. She had waited too long to apply to the community college, though the private colleges still had spots open for September. The half-year program cost almost the equivalent of two years of university tuition, but after graduation she got a job right away, working for a transnational frozen seafood company whose head offices were inexplicably stationed in downtown Edmonton, over a thousand kilometres from the nearest ocean. Emma worked on the twelfth floor of an office building downtown, at a six-person cubicle that looked like a spaceship component. She answered phones and chat-messages from employees all across North America who couldn't get YouTube to stream on their office computers.

Over the next year and a half, her parents launched a subtle but persistent psychological attack meant to motivate her to enroll in university.

"You need some time away from Edmonton," her mother said over dinner. "Why don't we three spend some time studying yoga and meditation at the ashram near Bangalore. The one Gwyneth Paltrow visited last year."

"That wasn't Gwyneth Paltrow. That was Uma Thurman," Emma's father interjected, spearing a piece of tempeh on his fork.

"Are you sure?" her mother asked.

"No one ever talks about Uma Thurman anymore," Emma commented, hoping to steer the conversation away.

No luck. "If you don't want to go with us, go on your own. It'll be good for you. Get you ready for university."

"It could help you handle the pressure of classes and assignments and deadlines a lot better," said her father.

Emma's mother threw him a sharp look. "An anxiety disorder is an *illness*," she said. "It can't be helped."

"No, but it can be managed."

"Electric shock therapy is making a comeback," Emma offered, widening her eyes innocently. "Maybe I should look into it."

Her mother shook her head quickly, almost a shudder. "You're not as funny as you think you are, Em."

Her father chewed, considering. "I don't think your symptoms are severe enough to warrant a treatment that invasive," he said. "Perhaps a lobotomy, though?"

Julia cast her husband a look of gentle remonstrance. She'd never been fond of what she lightly called Emma's "sass," and she especially didn't appreciate what she saw as his encouraging it.

Emma could remember the first time she'd tested out her swagger with her parents. She'd just brought home her Grade Eight fall report card. Her teacher, Mrs. Montgomery, had made some kind of note in the comments about Emma's unwillingness to speak up in class. Mike had read it with an arched brow.

"Your teacher seems a little critical," he said. He was always careful not to criticize other adults in front of her, but Emma had learned to spot the signs that he disliked someone. "Is she singling you out?"

"No," Emma replied. And it was true. Mrs. Montgomery was distinctly unpopular among her students. The consensus at school was that she hated kids. She shouted more often than she talked, her index finger always stabbing the air angrily in the direction of one student or another, and she'd often send some of the boys to stand out in the hallway with next to no provocation. It was true that Mrs. Montgomery didn't seem to have any particular affection for Emma, but Emma hardly felt singled out.

"Are you sure?" Julia asked. She had that soft worried look she'd worn so often in the first years that Emma had lived with them. She'd fix Emma with her eyes, and her gaze seemed almost to beg for reassurance. And Emma was always quick to gloss over any troubles she was having. Anything to clear that worry from her mom's face.

So she tried something new this time. She gave the half-smile she'd been practicing with her friends at school, trying to mimic Elaine's casual smirk. "Mrs. Montgomery," she said, "has the personality of a wet fart."

She could still remember Mike's bark of surprised laughter. He tried to cover it, and even Julia, who usually had no trouble telling

Emma if she didn't like someone, made Emma apologize for her language. But Mike's laughter was a bond between them. He never minded Emma's sass, even when Julia frowned at her off-colour remarks.

"Lobotomy," Emma said now. "Good thought." She stood, scooping up her plate and cutlery. "Thanks for supper," she said. "I'll have to have you both over to the apartment soon."

"Think about it," her mom, urged as Emma pulled on her shoes. "Some time away, then you can start university with a fresh outlook."

"Cocktails, maybe," Emma said. "Or maybe I can book the chef from the Chateau Lacombe to cook us dinner. You think he's booked up through Christmas?"

"Remember when we used to talk about seeing Bali and Thailand?" Julia pressed.

"Or I can make popcorn and we'll watch a movie."

"That's what I'd like," Mike said, giving Emma a one-arm hug, crushing her windpipe into his shoulder.

In the end, it was the job and not a meditation retreat that sent Emma to university part-time. She couldn't handle the thought of a lifetime of answering the same three questions over and over for a team of seven thousand employees whose entire purpose was to make frozen fish sticks that didn't taste too much like fish. So she applied to the University of Alberta, and the following September she was a part-time Bachelor of Arts student.

The fish stick company let her drop down to twenty hours a week, and she scheduled her first-year classes around her shifts. The company seemed to be under the impression that she was going to university in order to move up the corporate ranks, and she did nothing to disabuse them of that idea.

That first year, she did well in her two History courses. She found herself absorbed by the readings and the lectures. The classes inspired her in a way that none of her other courses managed to do, so the following year, she changed her major from Communications to History. She hoped that she might be able to work in a museum or archives with that degree. She imagined the soothing hush of a job like that, searching out documents and artifacts for people delving into the past, rather than constantly updating software for colleagues who demanded faster and faster internet from cheaper and cheaper systems, but she pushed aside any thoughts of real career planning. After all, it would take her six years to earn her degree part-time. Six years of excavating the past, of inhabiting the lives of people she could know but who would never know her. A lot could change in six years.

Not much did change, though. She plugged away at her degree. Kept resetting passwords and uninstalling malware at the fish stick company.

In her final year, Emma enrolled in Dr. Isabella Fuentes's seminar on the History of the Canadian West. It was a good class. Fantastic, really. Dr. Fuentes's own research focused on women who worked outside the home—mostly teachers and nurses, unsurprisingly—and she brought her own interests into the classroom. Emma was captivated by the women who worked for the Canadian Pacific Railway during the First World War, keeping the trains running across the country. But as often as she found herself immersed in the lectures and readings, she found herself distracted by her awareness of the other students in the room. Over the course of her university career, Emma had watched the age gap between herself and most of her classmates grow. Now, at almost thirty years old, Emma felt like the aging dolt in the room, and she imagined that her classmates looked at her askance, assuming she was too slow to keep up with their intellectual acrobatics. She armed her attitude in permanent self-defence. Smart-Ass Mode.

One afternoon, the discussion turned to digital archives. Another student, a pretty woman in her early twenties with blonde cornrows, commented that her generation was probably more adept at searching these databases than older researchers who had honed their own research skills on microprint machines.

Emma thought she felt her classmates' eyes shift to her pityingly. She felt pinned, pressed tight by their sudden attention. She snorted, forcing a grin. "Sure, but when the zombie apocalypse hits, where will you be?" she asked the blonde. "Try searching survival strategies on your iPad with no internet. I'll be at the library checking out all the paper books on edible weeds and making weapons, while zombies are snacking on your sorry entrails." The blonde tittered nervously as her rows of exposed scalp turned crimson.

After class, Dr. Fuentes had invited Emma to join her for coffee. Emma felt a nervous tightening in her core, imagining she was in for a dressing-down about respectful discussion etiquette.

Instead, Dr. Fuentes barely waited until Emma sat down with her coffee before asking her what grad schools she was applying to.

Emma tried to cover her surprise. "I haven't decided," she said. Which was kind of true. In fact, she hadn't even considered grad school, so there was really no decision to be made.

"Listen," Dr. Fuentes said. "I know you've probably heard that you shouldn't do two degrees at the same university, but that kind of advice is pretty outdated. I think you have a strong chance of being offered a spot here. And we only accept grad students we can fund."

"Fund?" Emma asked.

"Departmental funding isn't a lot, but it'll cover your tuition," Dr. Fuentes said. "And you can apply to become a Research Assistant. Have you started your SSHRC application yet?"

"No. Not—not yet." Emma vaguely remembered hearing her classmates talk about SSHRC scholarships. They were the most coveted and revered awards, apparently.

"Better get started. The university application deadline is less than a month away."

Emma nodded. She cleared her throat, trying to find a way to catch up to this conversation.

"Yes," Dr. Fuentes said, leaning back to give Emma an appraising look.

"Yes?"

"I'll supervise your thesis. Assuming, of course, you're proposing a topic in Twentieth-Century Canadian History."

Good god, there was no catching up now. "Yes," Emma said, wondering what exactly she was agreeing to. A Master's thesis?

How long would that take? What kind of job did a person get with a Master's in History? She fumbled with the cardboard sleeve on her coffee and realized Dr. Fuentes was looking at her expectantly. "Yes," she repeated. "I was thinking about Canadian History. And the First World War. And...women." She was, was she?

But Dr. Fuentes was nodding appreciatively. Well, shit. Apparently, Emma was about to embark on an intensive study of Canada and the Great War. And Women.

"We can work with that," Dr. Fuentes said. "Come and see me during my office hours so I can look over your SSHRC application."

"Sure," Emma said. "I haven't gotten very far yet...."

Dr. Fuentes waved her hand. "That's fine. When you have a draft of your proposal, come see me. But don't leave it too long."

As she walked to catch the transit train home, Emma kept expecting panic to settle into her limbs, her chest. After all, she'd just committed to a Master's degree that she'd neither planned for nor really considered, hadn't she?

Lately, whenever she thought about what would happen in spring, once she'd completed her Bachelor's degree, she had to push the feelings of dread and unease back into the corners of her mind. Her old nemesis, dread for the future, and here it was, lurking at the edges of her thoughts once again. The thought of going back to full-time hours at the fish stick company gave her a dull sense of hopelessness. But now that school was over, what was she going to do? She'd started university with the sense that it would lead to something else, something better. But so far, she didn't have a strong sense of what that something better might be.

She'd started job hunting as her graduation date loomed, combing the online postings. But no one, it seemed, was looking for History graduates. What had all this been for?

Of course, she wasn't sure that a Master of Arts in History would make her any more employable. But surely it would give her another couple of years to put things off and to get lost in the past. Especially if they would actually pay her to go to school. Would it cover her tuition *and* her rent, she wondered. Would she actually be able to give up her job at the fish stick company? Yes, Emma thought as she approached the train platform. She actually felt lighter. This was a good move.

And so, the next week, Emma found herself clinging to the corner of the table in Dr. Fuentes's house, an aging dolt in a room full of smart, sophisticated early-twentysomethings. At their age, she'd just started university, fumbling her way beyond the Five Paragraph Essay she'd learned in high school in her Writing for University course. They were all writing Master's and PhD theses. Independent researchers. Academics. And there she was, a dilettante not quite thirty and already past her intellectual prime. All week long, she had kept suddenly remembering about the party—at work between calls, as she walked between classes, as she drifted off to the sounds of murder shows on her TV at night—and every time, her guts gave a sort of lurch and clench.

She didn't want to go to that party. After all, what drew her to studying history was the remote access to people that it granted her. She had always found archival research both intimate and comforting. She loved being able to absorb people's lives through the things they wrote, through the items they used, the places they lived, the wars and the politics, the science, faith, and society that shaped their world. She loved getting to know someone deeply, personally, with the buffer of a hundred years or so to keep her from making an ass of herself around these people she came to love. The idea of making a career out of befriending the long dead was wonderful. The thought of going to parties with live people who also wanted to know the same long-dead people, who were perhaps better at it than Emma, less prone to misinterpreting or misunderstanding, that idea was crushing. She didn't want to go to that party but she'd gone anyway. And now, because she had, she was here in Halifax, about to spend a glorious afternoon combing through undigitized archives, looking for any mention of an infamous family who'd lived just outside the South Shore towns for over two hundred years.

The library at the University of Nova Scotia looks like a fortress. Its windows are recessed vertical slits in the stone walls. I expect the archives to be in a dim basement, but they aren't. The microfiche collection lines the walls in a bright, newly renovated study space on the main floor. Already, a few students have colonized the tables in the centre of the room with laptops and books and unsettlingly large travel mugs.

"I'm sorry these haven't been digitized," the archives librarian tells me as she sets up the microfiche. "Have you used one of these before?"

"Oh, I am practically anchored to these at home," I reply. I smile a wan smile that says we are kindred; we both know the joys and pains of hours staring into these lighted screens. She nods sympathetically and leaves me to my research.

I start with the Lunenburg newspapers, as far back as they go. I'm looking for any mention of the Gaugins—birth, death, marriage announcements. Arrests.

In 1932, Margaret Gaugin married Arthur Besanson of Lunenburg.

In 1946, Grace Gaugin married Joseph Dauphinee of Mahone Bay.

In 1947, Elizabeth Gaugin married George Boutilier of Chester.

There are more—women of the Gaugin family marrying men from the surrounding communities. I don't find any marriage announcements for the Gaugin men, though. Who are they marrying?

Sometimes, I also find obituaries.

Margaret Besanson, née Gaugin, September 26, 1947.

Maureen Corkum, née Gaugin, March 3, 1951.

Elizabeth Boutilier, née Gaugin, April 11, 1984.

I don't find the men's obituaries, and I don't find obituaries for women who die with the Gaugin name. Who is mourning them?

It's not the Gaugins who place these notices, I realize. The Gaugins announce nothing to the outside world. And while a family from outside may accept a Gaugin bride, it seems that the good families of the South Shore are not particularly eager to announce that their daughters have gone to Gaugin Lake, have become a part of the clan.

And then there are the arrests and police reports.

In 1938, Henry Gaugin was arrested for battery after a fight outside a Lunenburg restaurant. In 1941 Charles Gaugin was sought by police for the theft of farm equipment, but if he was caught and arrested, the paper never reported it. 1946, Henry Gaugin is again arrested for assault and battery. 1952, Marie Gaugin arrested for public intoxication in Halifax. 1959, George Gaugin arrested for receiving stolen goods. 1971, Martin Gaugin arrested for impaired driving following a motor vehicle collision on the St. Margarets Bay Road. 1974, Charles Gaugin (surely not the same one?) arrested for possession of a controlled substance. 1982, Shauna Gaugin arrested for possession of a controlled substance. 1983, Andrew Gaugin arrested for impaired driving in connection with the death of Michel Melanson. The following year, he is convicted of manslaughter. 1987, Donald Gaugin and Gary Gaugin are charged with possession of stolen property. 1989, Jennifer Gaugin is arrested for shoplifting in Mahone Bay. 1990, Shannon Gaugin is arrested for loitering and public intoxication in Dartmouth.

☙❧

EMMA COMBED THROUGH EARLY SOUTH SHORE NEWSPAPERS (the *Lunenburg Herald*, 1936–1972, and the *Shore*, 1944–2003), logging any mention of the Gaugins. She tried the Kentville, Wolfville, and Windsor papers next—after all, Gaugin Lake was almost in the middle of the province, not much farther from the Annapolis Valley communities to the north than the South Shore towns to the south. But there was next to nothing in the Valley newspapers. Just two arrests: Sylvia Gaugin, for criminal trespassing in Windsor in 1962, and Doug Gaugin, for theft in Kentville in 1976. The Gaugins, it seemed, were drawn south, away from Acadie.

She already had a log from the Halifax papers going back to 1874. She'd been able to research those from home; they'd been digitized a decade ago. There were fewer mentions in the city paper; the occasional marriage announcement, and a few crimes—assaults, thefts, and one woman, Louise Gaugin, arrested for prostitution in Halifax in 1922.

Emma printed off copies of the South Shore articles from the early 1990s. She wasn't ready to read those yet. Would they name minor children? Surely not....

By six that evening, she'd exhausted the library's archives. She felt good, tired from the long day bent over the microfiche viewer, but also energized now, her brain tingling from the effort of digging, the success of unearthing. This was what had drawn her to history in the first place, back in her first year of university. The pleasure of finding proofs, little details, that made people's lives from decades, centuries ago, real, immediate.

She'd felt something like that excited buzz when she'd sent off the letter of inquiry to Community Services. No, it had been more than that. It had felt like a culmination of sorts, the sense that everything, the good and the bad, had led her there, to that letter that she'd spent days crafting. The excitement, the certainty that it would be answered, that she'd come to Nova Scotia to find the kinds of answers that shone a light on everything.

Except, of course, the letter had been a dead end after all. Emma's heart sank again as she recalled the feeling of disappointment, so sharp that it took her by surprise, when the clerk from Community Services had told her that there would be no reply. The contact form had not been returned.

It's better this way, she'd told herself. Keep the research clean. Archival stuff. Site visits. Third-party interviews. Anything closer, more involved, would get too messy. This way, she could still keep an academic distance.

Since she was already in town, she decided she'd try an evening out. She'd hold on to the excitement of a successful day of research and shake off the memory of disappointment. She asked the archive librarian, Joss, which restaurants were good.

"You want a gastropub," Joss replied, scrolling through her phone. "Here." She thrust the screen at Emma. "This one only carries local microbrew."

Emma had been hoping for a charming restaurant in the historic district, but she didn't want to sound like too much of a tourist. The gastropub Joss recommended was in a neighbourhood in the city's North End that was clearly transitioning from seedy to trendy. It was in a quaint-looking orange row house, but the inside had been gutted and fitted with industrial-looking fixtures. All the furniture—tables, benches, bar—looked as though it had been made from recycled wooden shipping pallets. There were no chairs, only long benches. She sat at the empty end of a table near the exposed brick fireplace and ordered a porter and a smoked haddock chowder.

While she waited for her food to arrive, she eyed the room dubiously. The long benches and tables seemed to Emma to be a painfully obvious attempt to encourage patrons to mingle, to get together with friends and strangers for one big democratic good time. Of course, other patrons used their bags and the gaps in between each other to demarcate individual spaces. Small groups of people kept to themselves. What the long tables and benches did accomplish, however, was to emphasize the apartness of a woman sitting by herself. In a normal bar with small corner tables, Emma would not have felt so exposed, so obvious. She would have settled into a quiet seat with a good view of the room and watched, building little lives in her head for all the other patrons. Or she could have sat by the window and watched people and cars go by outside. She would have felt invisible.

She pulled her laptop and her printouts from her bag and spread them out across the end of the table. She still didn't feel quite ready to delve into these stories, but it was better than marking herself as a friendless diner, feeling the looks the other patrons cast her. So she took up the whole section at the end of the table, making her work occupy at least four place settings. There. Now she was a diligent thinker, and academic, a busy person. Not a pathetic, lonely one.

There were few photographs in the South Shore papers. No new images, anyway. The photos she did see—pictures of police cars and vans and ambulances parked in the debris-strewn yard of the main Gaugin house; photos of adult Gaugins glaring through the back windows of cop cars—were familiar, the same (or almost the same) as those she had found in her online research before she left Edmonton. She imagined the small gaggle of photographers and journalists crowded together in a cordoned-off area of the dirty yard, each taking versions of the same picture.

The stories themselves were less-detailed versions of the ones that appeared in the Halifax papers around the same period. Here and there, there were a few inaccuracies that marked a rural reporting style—misspelled names, an incorrect accounting of the charges against the adults.

The *Shore* reporter, however, seemed to be the kind who cherished literary rather than journalistic ambitions, judging from the abundance of adjectives in her articles. Marian Rushdie used a whole paragraph to describe the general poverty of the property—the aging and missing wood shakes on the side of the house, the rusted car parts littering the yard, the chickens and pigs that roamed the property unfettered. She described the Gaugin adults as "grim and unrepentant" and the children as "dirty-faced." Emma touched her own cheek reflexively. She took a deep breath and opened a blank document in her laptop.

The reporter writes about the children's tears, their dirty faces, as they're loaded up into the social workers' vehicles. I wonder—was it true? Were they really dirty that day, or every day? Perennially unwashed faces, or just the faces of children who'd been playing outside on a muddy day.

Emma saved and closed the document. She opened an internet browser and searched "Marian Rushdie."

Several results about a painter from Chester Basin filled the screen. It could be the same woman. Or it could be simply a common Nova Scotia name, like Dan MacDonald or Michelle Boudreau.

Emma clicked on an article linked to a Lunenburg funeral home announcing Marian Rushdie's death in 2007. Marian Rushdie, painter, teacher, and journalist. Graduated from Mount Saint Vincent University in Halifax. Wrote for the *Shore* from 1989 to the paper's closure in 2003. Paintings on display in galleries across Canada. Survived by her husband, Jack Rushdie of Chester Basin.

So this reporter had family still alive in 2007. Emma searched Jack's name. The first result was for an art show coming up at a gallery in Mahone Bay. A Jack Rushdie retrospective. Evidently, he still lived in Chester Basin. He, too, painted. And his website had an email address.

Emma drew in a slow breath. This was good. Marian Rushdie had more bylines than anyone else who had reported the Gaugin story. She had covered the raid on the compound and the trials. If she were still alive, Emma knew she'd have to interview her. The idea of talking to someone who might remember made the skin on the back of her hands prickle—excitement or unease, Emma couldn't tell. But if she could talk to the reporter's husband, see what he remembered about the whole thing...well, there was that.

Emma started an email to Jack Rushdie. Her fingers sat on the keys for a long moment. How could she ask to talk to him about his dead wife? She was a stranger to him. He might not even remember about the Gaugin story.

What *would* he remember? Emma felt the curiosity tugging in her chest. Marian Rushdie's articles had been sympathetic. And she'd covered the whole story until the prison sentences. Emma had the impression that she'd actually cared about the Gaugins—not just the kids, but the parents and grandparents and aunts and uncles and grown-up cousins. This one reporter had written about them as though they were people, real people, and a family.

She tapped out an email. She explained that she was a graduate student researching the Gaugins. But before she hit *send*, she went back. Her hands hovered over the keys as she decided how much she should tell him. She typed quickly, then stared at the line, the short, simple line at the end of the message. Then, quickly, she highlighted and deleted it. She sent the message, then shut her laptop. She took a long swallow of her porter, surveying the printed articles spread across the table in front of her.

THREE

JACK RUSHDIE WOKE WITH A GROAN AT 6 A.M. HIS ALARM CLOCK WAS deliberately positioned on the dresser at opposite end of his bedroom, too far away to smack into silence without getting out of bed, crossing the cold floor, and fully waking up. Jack had always hated mornings.

No, that was not strictly true. He shifted Rosamund away from his side and sat up, his bad shoulder creaking in protest. The cat, too, seemed to be moving stiffly as she resettled on the corner of the bed—Rosamund wasn't so young, herself. No, Jack had always hated waking up in the morning. But once he was out of bed, he rather enjoyed the fresh sunlight, the early day promise.

He stood for a long moment, looking out the bedroom window. It looked toward the Atlantic, but he couldn't see the water from the house. Instead, a ridge rose up from the back of the property. It was covered in spruce and fir, maple, and, here and there, little stands of birch. This time of year, what he loved about the view was the colour of the leaves. There was a freshness to that green in June, a hue that would soon darken, harden. But now, when the leaves were still young, they looked so tender, so eager. And in the fresh sunlight of the early day, they seemed to glow with their own light.

Rosamund bumped her face against the back of his hand, demanding a scratch. He patted her affectionately for a moment and then lifted her up, taking her down to the kitchen for her breakfast. She gave a tiny, eager mew as they entered the kitchen.

"Wish I had someone to wait on me," he murmured as he set her cat food out on the mat next to the door.

In his younger days, back when he first started teaching at the art college in Halifax, he had gradually shifted his days, waking at nine or ten, then working in his studio past midnight. He seldom taught before noon, so he was able to punch the snooze button on his alarm clock as many times as he pleased, especially since Marian was up before six and out the door by eight every day. The nagging buzz every ten minutes would not disturb her.

Gradually, however, Jack came to realize that getting out of bed was every bit as rough at ten as it was at six. But it was not until Marian started painting that he began to see the advantages of confronting the excruciating hardship of getting out of bed with the sunrise.

When Marian first borrowed Jack's watercolours and his smaller easel, he feigned a gentle indulgence, a deliberate and affectionate condescension at her artistic efforts, but really he was annoyed, even a little alarmed, at her interest. He was the artist in the family. He'd endured a Bachelor's education in Fine Arts, he'd risen to the challenge of working part-time as a server and a landscaper and a hardware store stock clerk in order to pay the bills as a starving artist, then once he had sold enough paintings, had enough gallery shows, had earned enough repute, he had translated his talent, his *skill*, into a part-time teaching job at the art college. *He* was the artist. What business did Marian have dabbling in his métier?

Of course, Marian was not fooled by his show of gentle joviality at her sudden interest in painting. She was near forty by then, and they'd already been married a decade. A decade of relatively solid partnership. And with no children, it was a decade of uninterrupted tête-à-tête. She knew him. She knew his moods. She knew when his hackles were up, even when he was sensible enough to recognize the pettiness of his own defensiveness and tried to disguise it as something more gentle.

Knowing that he was feeling territorial about his role as the family artist probably steeled her resolve to paint, just a little bit. But if Marian had a contrary streak, she had a bigger sense of compassion, even protectiveness, toward her husband. So she didn't venture into Jack's studio, a converted workspace above the garage. Instead, she tucked her easel into the corner of the dining room, a space they seldom used except as a sort of office. And she didn't paint in the evening, as Jack did. Instead, she got up before work every day and gave herself an hour. On the weekends, she painted from six until Jack got up, tucking away the easel when she heard him shuffling from the bed to the bathroom upstairs.

Jack had to admire her rigour. In fact, she was doing exactly what he counselled his students to do: paint every day. Approach painting as a discipline. Don't wait for inspiration. Work at it. He knew that few listened to his advice, waiting instead for those frenzied bursts of creativity, then locking themselves away with their work for hours and days on end until they were delirious and elated and utterly sure of their own brilliance. It was how Jack himself had painted when he was young.

But Marian was not young when she started painting, and she did not have long, uninterrupted hours or days to give over to art. She had a full-time job as a reporter and the sole advertising executive for the *Lunenburg Shore*. Her body would not permit her to go days with little sleep and less food. And her sense of the world did not let her believe that her art was going to change it forever. So she approached it eagerly but dutifully, painting every day, looking critically at her work and knowing it was not as good as her husband's or his colleagues' or even his students'. She unsentimentally painted over or threw away completed but unsatisfactory paintings, even though she had worked long and hard at them. She knew they were not good. But she suspected she could do better. And she'd spent enough time at galleries with her husband to know what *better* actually looked like.

And in time, she got better. One Saturday afternoon, she caught Jack staring at a landscape that she'd been working on, a painting of their own backyard. She narrowed her eyes, critically surveying his expression, before asking, "It's pretty decent, isn't it?"

He nodded slowly. It was. It wasn't brilliant, but it was good. Better yet, it was nothing at all like his own style. Her painting had a wistfulness, a kind of half-acknowledged sadness to it. His own work was often described as *bold, strident*, or *unflinching*. "It's getting there," he replied critically. "But don't be afraid to use more paint. It's how you get texture." He pointed to a shaded area on the right side of the canvas. "Here. Really give these shadows some depth. Make me *feel* this darkness."

She nodded seriously and picked up her paintbrush again, daubing dark greens and greys to the area he had pointed out.

She never asked him for advice, never asked his help, but when he did offer a suggestion, she considered it critically, turning it over in her mind like a fact she uncovered when writing an article for the local paper, deciding whether and how to work it into the story.

Once, she was growing visibly frustrated at not being able to capture an old shed surrounded by apple trees on a nearby property. "It's too familiar to you," he said. "Try painting it backwards. Or upside down." She'd frowned, then picked up the canvas and flipped it over. He opened his mouth to tell her that wasn't what he'd meant, but stopped himself. The creases between her brows were easing away. She jabbed her brush into the paint, working away at the troublesome painting.

It was the first one she sold. Within a few years, she had a couple of modest shows of her own, and she had begun to make a name for herself among local artists. Jack was still, of course, better-known, more successful. He was a little ashamed at his relief that she had neither eclipsed him nor had she embarrassed him by peddling substandard works with the name Rushdie on them. He knew it was small of him to feel that her success was just the right measure to keep their relationship balanced.

Still, even after he started offering the kind of mild but honest criticism of her work that told her he wasn't threatened by her painting but that he still took her seriously, she didn't ask to move her easel up to his studio. She kept painting in the dining room early in the morning before heading off to work at the newspaper office in Lunenburg. She kept up that industrious, faithful approach to her art until the week she died.

The morning after Marian was admitted to the hospital in Halifax, her alarm woke Jack at 5:45. He rose without hitting the snooze button. He showered and drove into the city to sit with her in the hospital. Every morning that week, he rose with her alarm. The day of her funeral, it woke him to get ready, to tidy the house for the visitors who would arrive for the wake that afternoon.

The day after she was buried, Jack lay in bed, listening to the screaming alarm, not bothering to shut it off. Finally, as he had done for the last nine days, he sat up in bed, turned off the alarm, and rose slowly. Only today, he had nowhere to go, nothing to prepare for. He wandered down to the kitchen, making himself a pot of coffee that he had no taste to drink.

Marian's easel was still sitting in the corner next to the dining room table. Her last painting—as complete, he supposed, as it would ever be—stood upon it. The ache in the base of his chest, just above his stomach, was too much. He couldn't sit there staring at her painting. But he couldn't put it away, either. So he went to his studio to paint.

From that day onward, he rose early every morning to paint. When he taught, he painted before class. But he soon regained his old habit of slapping lazily at the snooze button, so he moved Marian's alarm clock across the room to force himself out of bed at 6, just a quarter of an hour past the time that she herself had set all those years ago.

His morning routine had since evolved somewhat. He didn't head straight up to his studio. He first gave himself twenty minutes to go through his emails, sip his coffee, and eat a bowl of bran cereal.

This morning, among the spam, the messages from the university administration about submitting outlines for his fall courses and an email from a woman asking whether the prices listed on his website were firm, was a message from a sender whose name he didn't recognize: Emma G. Weaver.

I am a grad student from the University of Alberta. I'm researching the Gaugin family. I've read your late wife's articles, and I was hoping I could meet with you to ask what you remember about the events of September 1991.

Jack raised his eyebrows. The Gaugins, eh? That was an old story. What exactly was this woman studying? He lifted his coffee to his mouth, mechanically petting Rosamund, who had settled on his lap and was bumping her head affectionately against his knuckles.

Sure, he replied. *Can you come out to my place?* He added his address.

He gazed at the message on his laptop for a long time, then he picked up his phone and pulled up Heather Publicover's number. He scratched the cat's throat absently as he waited for Heather to pick up.

FOUR

IT TOOK A FEW MOMENTS FOR HEATHER PUBLICOVER TO REGISTER
her daughter's wails over the baby monitor. She'd been intent on finding
an error she knew was buried somewhere in her client's income sheets, and
Charlotte's howls had grown indignant before Heather could sufficiently
draw her attention away from the laptop and the stack of invoices laid
across the table. With a sigh, she saved her work and reached for her tea.
Not on the coaster next to her computer. Where had she left it this time?

Heather stood slowly, her limbs and her thoughts both reluctant
to break away from the desk and her work there, and made her way
down the hallway to her daughter's room.

Charlotte's face was snotty, and not just from crying. Justin had
brought home a bad head cold from school last week, and yesterday
Charlotte had woken up with a stuffed up nose. As soon as she saw her
mother, Charlotte erupted into a giant toothless smile, the built-up wail
warbling instantly to a chuckle. Charlotte was such a happy baby. Not
like poor Justin, whose acid reflux had made him miserable until he
was over a year old. He had bawled and sobbed his way through baby-
hood. The fear of having another Justin—all tears and no sleep—had
kept Heather and her husband, Rafe, from having another baby until
Justin was five. Thank god Charlotte had turned out sunny and not
nearly as inclined to vomit up all her meals as her brother had been.

Heather hoisted Charlotte up out of the crib, kissing her forehead. She reached for a Kleenex to wipe the snot from the baby's face before settling into the gliding chair. She flipped absently through her phone while Charlotte nursed, checking her emails and social media feeds. As she scrolled, the phone vibrated in her hand, displaying Jack Rushdie's contact photo. The image was a few years old, taken when he had joined Heather and Rafe for a barbecue when Justin was still a baby, but Jack had hardly changed at all. His hair had been wispy and grey then, his moustache bushy and his smile wide. He had perhaps a little less hair around his temples now, but you'd have to look carefully to notice.

"Hey, Jack," Heather answered.

"How are you, my girl?"

"Oh, not too bad. The kids have been sick. Colds."

Jack made a sympathetic noise. "I got a peculiar email," he said. "From a grad student. She's researching the Gaugins."

Heather didn't answer right away.

"Heather, girl? Did you hear me?"

"I heard."

"She wants to know about Marian's articles."

"Right," Heather said. "The articles." She considered asking Jack to tell this researcher to fuck off. He would, she knew. But then what? It wouldn't stop her doing her research, would it?

"I told her she could come out and ask me about them. Though I suppose I could email her back. Tell her she'd best not."

"Meet her if you want, Jack. Up to you." She took a deep breath. "Kids need looking after. I've got to go."

"You all right?"

Charlotte released Heather's nipple and smiled up at her. Heather caught her little hand and kissed it. "I'm fine, Jack. Thanks for telling me."

"You don't want to be here when she comes, do you?"

"Nope."

Jack hummed an acknowledgement and was quiet for a moment. Heather listened to his faraway breath over the phone as she stroked

Charlotte's soft, fine hair. "All right, then," he said at last. "Kiss those babies of yours."

"I will."

She hung up and lifted Charlotte up to her shoulder to burp her. She pressed her face into Charlotte's neck, feeling the comforting warmth and weight against her body, trying to block out any other thoughts. The baby let out a loud belch just as the alarm on Heather's phone jingled, startling both of them. Charlotte's face hovered at the edge of tears, but Heather forced a smile, coaxing the baby back into good humour. She carried the baby downstairs, cooing nonsense at her, noise to cover the swirling thoughts. As they walked down the driveway to meet Justin's school bus, Charlotte squealed happily at the trees. Heather nuzzled Charlotte's neck, breathing in her warm, sweet baby scent.

FIVE

SATURDAY. EMMA WAS GOING TO SEE JACK RUSHDIE ON SATURDAY. She felt buoyed by the plan—so much so that she found herself looking forward to the trek through the woods to look for the original cabin. She drove out to the lake, waving back at the cottagers walking along the road on her way in. Once again, she parked at the end of the gravel and walked along the quad trail, taking out her phone to follow the map to the area she'd flagged. She'd used newspaper articles from the 1946 arrest of Henry Gaugin—apparently, he'd tried to evade capture by escaping up to the original homestead. A couple of the 1991 articles also made references to the cabin north of the main compound, and a cleared area on the satellite map seemed a likely place to start looking. She trekked her way into the bush, swarmed by clouds of blackflies.

When the house loomed through the trees in front of her she continued north, past the outbuildings and clearings. A thick stand of balsam fir and white spruce made the way miserably slow going, but thankfully the second-growth evergreens soon gave way to mixed Acadian forest once again, making her progress toward the clearing much easier.

After twenty minutes of walking the forest broke, revealing a wide field of lambkill and teaberry. Emma made her way into the clearing slowly. The earth was spongy and wet, and wine-coloured pitcher plants with delicately veined green insides flowered in the depressions. They were carnivores, pitcher plants, like wolves or raptors, their bulbous leaves devouring insects foolish enough to get trapped inside. She wondered whether they were full of blackflies now. The season had certainly supplied the plants with a feast. She picked her way through, trying not to trample the alien-looking plants or sink up to her ankles in one of the mossy pools.

She had planned to start at the centre of the clearing and make her way outward in a spiral, searching for the remains of the cabin, but she had expected a meadow, not a bog grown over with thick shrubs. So she started at the west edge of the clearing and picked her way north as best she could, turning at the end and making her way back. She zigzagged roughly, her pant legs quickly becoming sodden and her neck smeared with blood from mosquito and blackfly bites. She had only the description of the cottage foundation from a news article to go on. There was nothing in the Google satellite images that even suggested the regularity of a cottage.

Finally, near the north edge of the clearing, she found what she was looking for. A single shrub was growing out of what looked like a low rocky hill, but when Emma got closer, she could see that the hill was actually a fallen chimney made from smooth, round granite stones. It had fallen backward, forming a long, narrow mound, but Emma cleared away the moss and leaves from the front of the structure where the hearth and the base of the chimney were still intact. She pulled out her camera and carefully captured the open mouth of the hearth, the long mound of the crumbled chimney, the roots of the shrub anchored among the stones.

She stood, trying to gauge where the back of the hearth might have been, and dug her fingers into the moss and soil, searching for the cabin's foundation. Each time her fingers met stone, she pulled away the soil and the living debris, looking for an adjacent stone, a line, a pattern. It took a while, but she finally found the foundation of the cabin. She bared each of the angular red-grey slate pieces, following the rocks until they turned abruptly south about six feet from the hearth, leading some ten feet or so before turning west to form the front of the cabin. Directly in front of the decayed hearth,

Emma found two broader stones, almost perfectly rectangular, one placed before the other. The threshold, she realized, photographing them carefully.

Finally, she had finished pulling away the green growth, exposing the unbroken foundation. She leaned back on her heels, savouring the heavy feeling in her limbs, the remnants of her long walk and steady work in the hot sun. It felt good, this tired feeling, the sense of having done something, of holding that accomplishment in her hot, languid body. She'd dug a shallow trench in the moss and loose soil to expose the stones, the freshly-disturbed earth looking starkly brown against all of the early summer greenery. On the east side, she hadn't been able to remove a small clump of lambkill and its roots straddled the slate. Emma drew in a breath and set herself back to work photographing it all meticulously, beginning with close-ups, then moving further back to capture images of the whole ghost frame of the lost cabin.

Emma put away her camera and pulled her lunch—a sandwich and an apple bought at a café near her hotel—out of her bag. She sat on the exposed hearth and wondered when the last time was someone had eaten a meal in this cabin. She thought about the women, whose lives were so different from her own. Of the sameness of their days, cooking and cleaning; of the children and the men, the chickens and pigs to feed and keep and slaughter, probably, and the deer and the pheasants hunted and butchered, cooked and salted and stored. It wasn't a life she'd choose, not a chance, but there was something warm and safe about the idea of it, of your whole world here, in this one small space, in the simple but utterly essential activities that you performed over and over again every day, every year. Get food. Prepare food. Keep the house and the clothes sound and warm. Protect them, care for them. Your family, your world.

From her research she had learned that the Gaugins appeared in the Grand Pré parish records from 1740 until 1755. The name's first appearance, in 1740, includes a curious smudge between "Louis" and "Gaugin" on the handwritten page. Something written then crossed out. Emma had stared hard at it on her screen, zoomed in. She was certain it had said "Gauguin," like the French painter. That would make more sense—it's the common spelling of the name, and there are no records of Gaugins (no *u*) outside of Nova Scotia. Emma wondered who wrote the first version, and why they had crossed it out and tried again. And in 1755, when most of the Acadians in the area were deported to Louisiana or France, The Gaugins themselves simply disappeared. Then the 1770 census for Lunenburg county records fifteen members of the Gaugin family:

The Paul Gaugin family included 1 man, 3 boys, 1 woman, and 2 girls.

The Thomas Gaugin family included 1 man, 2 boys, 2 women, and 3 girls.

All are listed as Acadian and Catholic.

The Gaugin name does not appear on any census records after 1770, but there were occasional mentions of deaths and marriages in the Lunenburg parish records through the nineteenth century. It seemed that some of the Gaugins married in St. John's Anglican Church in the early 1800s (1809, George Gaugin to Esther Sarty; 1811, although Joseph Gaugin to Judith Knickle; 1812, Anne Gaugin to Paul Conrad). Emma could find no further mention of a male Gaugin's marriage after 1811, though, like the newspapers, parish records show the occasional female Gaugin marrying into another South Shore family. It was easy to imagine why, and harder to turn her thoughts away once they'd crept into her head, as they did now, again.

The Halifax newspapers described the house where the Gaugins were living in 1991, the place Emma had photographed two days earlier, as a "nineteenth-century home." It was likely that the building where Emma was now eating her lunch, whose foundation stones she had spent nearly three hours unearthing, was built between 1755 and 1770 and abandoned sometime in the 1800s, though it was possible that this was not the first Gaugin home in this area. It was equally possible that one branch of the family had lived in this small cabin while another larger, perhaps more affluent branch built the new home. She looked carefully at the small space, smaller than her own studio apartment, and considered that this was probably not the only home, even in 1770. The remains of the chimney extended a scant fifteen feet beyond what would have been the back wall, not tall enough, surely, for a two-storey building. It was unlikely that this small space housed all fifteen members of the Paul Gaugin and Thomas Gaugin families, though who knew whether they had all retreated into this remote area by then. Was there the carcass of another cabin somewhere in this clearing, in the surrounding woods, perhaps even at the most recent Gaugin compound?

She stood slowly, trying to imagine herself in a cottage, immeasurably far (by the standards of the day) from the society of people outside her own family. She closed her eyes, but could picture nothing more than the lush, green, early summer clearing. Tried but failed to imagine family sounds, barnyard noises beyond—she'd done too well to turn her mind away from the grimmer possibilities of what these women's and girls' lives might have entailed. She could not bring their daily lives back to mind now; she was locked in the present, in the quiet solitude of this place, abandoned and surrendered to nature. She felt only the warm sun, the squelching of her damp feet, the burning insect bites on her scalp, her neck, her inner elbows. She breathed deeply as she did when she meditated, drawing her attention to her body, to the sensation of the sun warming her face, the burning fly bites. She pulled her consciousness down into her belly, to the place where her dread and panic became a physical entity, a painful, quaking, burning stone—but not now, not today. Normally, when she thought about *them* she could be sure to feel at least a tiny pebble of unease. But here, now, she felt only a sense of accomplishment at having uncovered the remains of their cottage.

Of course, when they lived here they may not yet have become *themselves*. Perhaps they were just an ordinary family farming and living and going to church whenever they could make the trip. Perhaps the local families did not yet have reason to fear them or revile them. What would the Gaugins who lived in this house at some point more than two hundred years ago think of the Gaugins who shuttered themselves from the world in the twentieth century, letting their children grow up ragged and neglected and worse? There were hints, rumours that they had been marrying their own cousins, nieces and nephews, brothers and sisters, but that couldn't possibly be true, could it? Emma remembered what small towns and tight communities could be like. Hints became rumours, rumours became facts. The Gaugins were as much legend as Bigfoot or Skadegamutc, Baba Yaga or Wendigo.

Emma wondered what the Gaugins themselves had thought of these stories. What would they think of *her*, coming back to this place to unearth them all, good and bad, frightening and ordinary? She couldn't imagine what Louis Gauguin would have to say, what Paul Gaugin and Thomas Gaugin and their families would have to say about this project, this investigation, this exploration of their lives. The search for the point when everything went wrong.

A soft sinking feeling came over her as she considered it—not dread, exactly, nothing like the start of a panic attack. More like a heavy sadness. She opened her eyes, taking in the wide clearing one last time before setting off, back towards the road and the car and her hotel. She would certainly have enough to do this afternoon, sorting her photos and recording her impressions of this place, the spot that she'd chosen as the point of origin in the story she was committed to telling—or, if not telling, at least knowing, of holding for herself.

As she made her way through the dense bush, toward her car and past the compound, she wondered about the distance between the two homes—the house in the clearing and the once-white farmhouse. Between the people who had fled the ships bound for Louisiana and those who had been rounded up, arrested, herded into prison or foster care. How great was the distance, anyway?

SIX

EMMA SPENT FRIDAY COMBING THROUGH OLD PARISH RECORDS IN Lunenburg and Mahone Bay. The 1770 census listed the Gaugins as Catholic, but the first Catholic church in the area was not built until 1827, two decades after the Gaugins began appearing in Anglican church records. She had found no record of the family in St. Patrick's church records, which were archived online, but she went to the parish office anyway to look through the physical records. A nervous-looking secretary, a woman who appeared no older than fifty but who sported one of those steely-looking hairstyles that had seemed so popular among old ladies when Emma was a child, hovered nervously as Emma handled the ancient yellowed documents with their spidery handwriting.

Next, she tried St. John's Anglican Church, an imposing white Gothic structure at the centre of Lunenburg. The last online trace of a male Gaugin's marriage in the area's parish records listed Joseph Gaugin's wedding to Judith Knickle in 1811.

Shortly after noon, Emma gave up hope of finding any further mentions of the Gaugins in the parish records. She had one last stop to make: the Lunenburg Genealogical Society. Its website said the archives were open to the public Thursday and Friday afternoons, all day Saturday, or by appointment. Emma had parked the rental in front of a cafe just up the street from the Anglican church. She popped in for a cheese sandwich and a coffee, eating her lunch as she drove up to the Genealogical Society, which was housed on the second floor of a historical building perched at the very top of the town.

The building was an old school, and it still held that peculiar smell that only schools can have, something like crayons and stale clothing and disinfectant. The stone stairs leading to the second floor were worn and troughed by centuries of students' feet.

The door to the Genealogical Society was propped open with a rounded granite stone. The walls were lined with beige filing cabinets and a large bookcase opposite the east-facing windows. There was a flimsy-looking laminated office desk near the door and a long, antique-looking table in the centre of the room. A woman with black curly hair held back by a printed scarf was busy looking through one of the filing cabinets. She hadn't noticed Emma, and Emma didn't want to startle her. She made a soft shuffling sound with her feet and the woman glanced up.

"Are you looking for Municipal Services?" the woman asked. "They're at the other end of the hall."

"No," Emma replied. "Genealogical Society."

"Oh." The woman closed the file cabinet drawer and strode over to the cheap-looking desk. "Hardly anyone ever comes here on purpose. They just want to register their kids in day camps."

"No kids, no day camps," Emma said. "Just want to look through the archives."

"Cool." The corners of the woman's eyes crinkled when she smiled. She was wearing jeans and a blouse printed with sparrows in flight. From across the room, Emma had figured her for a university student, maybe early twenties, but up close, tiny lines in her face hinted that she was over thirty, perhaps closer to forty. But she had a springy, athletic aspect that made her seem much younger. "Do you know what you're looking for?"

"I think so," Emma replied. "I'm looking for records of a family that lived in the area. I've checked the census records online, but I wanted to have a look at the original copies."

The woman tilted her head towards a filing cabinet in the corner. Emma followed her over to it. The drawers were labelled by county, dated 1671 to 1901. "Anything I can help you find?"

"I think I've got it," Emma replied.

The woman nodded, then stuck out her hand. "Sam," she said. "Volunteer archivist. Tell me if you need anything. I promise, I know every single page in this place."

"I believe you," Emma replied.

Sam smiled again, then strode back to the filing cabinet where Emma had first found her.

It didn't take Emma long to discover that there was nothing new in the census files. Every mention of the Gaugins, she'd already found online. Sam was now sitting on the floor, making notes on the contents of the bottom drawer of her cabinet. She was holding a mechanical pencil in her teeth as she carefully stored a dark-brown ledger in its folder. She glanced up as Emma snapped the Lunenburg County census drawer shut.

"No luck?" Sam asked.

"Not really," Emma replied. "I was hoping to find something that isn't already in the Nova Scotia online archives."

Sam wrinkled her nose sympathetically. "Sorry. I could have told you. I scanned and uploaded them all myself last year. Every page. Was there someone you were looking for? Ancestors? Family members?"

Emma fixed her gaze on the buckle of her laptop bag. "I'm just doing some historical research," she said. "On…the Gaugins."

Sam's face brightened. She jumped up, sending the pencil skittering under the massive table.

"Oh! Let me show you this!" She darted to the bookshelf and pulled out a huge volume, *A.F. Church & Co.* embossed on the spine, and dropped it on the table.

Emma nodded. "I found the Church maps online too," she said. A. F. Church had produced the earliest maps of each county in Nova Scotia. They'd been part of Emma's initial archival research, long before she'd booked her trip to Nova Scotia. All the Church maps were meticulously scanned in high resolution and shared on dozens of websites.

Sam shook her head. "Not this one." She opened the book carefully, flipping it open to the Lunenburg County map from 1883. She pointed at the dart-shaped lake north of New Ross, just off the Windsor Road.

Emma nodded, recognizing the familiar marking. "Right. Taylor Lake."

Sam held up a finger and carefully flipped the page. There, a second map had been slipped into the book between the bound pages. Its outer edges extended beyond the rest of the book, and they had grown tattered. Sam carefully pointed to the same spot on the second map. Emma peered down at the yellowing paper.

There, on that arrow-shaped body of water, a faint line in blue ink crossed out the words *Taylor Lake*. Above, in looping scrawl, *Gaugin Lake*. It was strange—strange and exciting—to see it written down like that, the letters indelibly naming the place. The ink had bled a little, but just above the letter *G*, there seemed to be a faint blue point. And above that, a more definite point with the words *Old Settlement*. The handwriting stood out against the even print of the other names on the map, but seeing the words on the paper made Emma feel as though the place itself had crossed a barrier. It had been a ghost, but now it had taken form, firm and alive.

Emma looked up at Sam, who was smiling proudly. "Where did this map come from?"

"I don't know. This collection was bound by the printer. It was donated by the estate of a history professor who worked at Acadia University. This extra map was in it when we received the volume." Sam gestured to the inked notation. "Have you been there?"

Emma nodded slowly. "Both places," she replied. "I was at the main settlement on Monday." The omission—that she had, in fact been at the new compound long before this week—made her chest tighten as though Sam might be able to see what she was not saying. She pretended to examine the map. "And I found the old settlement yesterday."

Sam's eyes widened. "You did? Are you sure?"

Emma nodded, her gaze still on the map. Her chest was easing a touch, and the shakiness that threatened to overtake her legs was receding. She drew a deep breath, imagined the residue of her panic sweeping out of her lungs as she exhaled. "I uncovered the foundation of the old house."

"*No!*" Sam grabbed Emma's arm, her eyes filling with the kind of excitement you see in people who get to meet their favourite rock star.

Emma couldn't help but smile. She reached into her bag and pulled out her camera. "Here," she said, pulling up her photos.

Sam scrolled through them, making small sounds of dismay and glee. She looked almost reluctant to hand the camera back.

"Want me to email you copies?"

"Really?"

Emma nodded and Sam leapt to the desk to grab a business card. She thrust it at Emma. *Samantha Crowell, archivist. Lunenburg Genealogical Society.* Emma tucked it into her pocket.

"You want to take some pictures of this map?" Sam asked.

"Can I?"

Sam nodded. She watched as Emma carefully photographed the faint, spidery notation, the legend, the leather binding of the book.

It was nice, Emma thought, being able to talk to someone else who got as excited about the prospect of discovering something deep in an archival mine as she did. She couldn't remember the last time she'd felt this much at ease around someone. She hadn't connected with her university colleagues like this, and definitely not with anyone at the fish stick company. Probably the last person Emma could think of who'd made her feel this way was Elaine.

Emma had met Elaine when she and her parents were visiting her aunt and uncle one day. Elaine Janvier's family lived in north Edmonton, just across the road from Mike's brother Shawn (*Uncle Shawn*) and his wife Jeanette (*Auntie Jean*). Emma had seen Elaine and her brothers playing outside before when they'd come to visit. The three dark-haired kids—two girls and a boy—had a hockey net they'd haul out into the quiet cul-de-sac. Emma was always deeply impressed at the girls' prowess with the hockey sticks, snapping the orange ball smartly into the net. They seemed to be a different order of girl than Emma had encountered before. Certainly different from Nadine, Uncle Shawn and Aunt Jean's daughter, whom the Weavers always referred to as Emma's "little cousin." Nadine did not like to play outside. She usually wanted Emma to play in the basement with her, enacting complicated love plots that involved both girls pretending they had boyfriends. Emma tried her best, but Nadine seemed constantly frustrated by Emma's dramatic deficiency. She could never imagine what the imaginary boyfriend might say to her, or what death-defying adventures they might go on together. "That's *boring*," Nadine would huff whenever Emma suggested they all go to an Italian restaurant on a date. (Emma had the vague impression that Italian restaurants were the fanciest type, reserved for beautiful and tempestuous couples, and it seemed as likely a setting as any for their romantic adventures.)

This one particular day when Emma was about twelve, the Weavers arrived at Shawn and Jeanette's house and Nadine didn't declare that she and Emma were going downstairs to play the way she usually did. Instead, she announced to the adults that they were going to play outside. Emma was relieved. She'd discovered that playing outside with other children was much easier than playing indoors. Indoor play required much more direct interaction, and was almost certain to lead to accusations that Emma wasn't playing the right way. Playing outdoors, on the other hand, was usually wider-ranging. Emma could often wander off on her own after a short while without being missed. So on that late summer day, she gratefully followed Nadine out into the front yard. Nadine strode across the neighbouring lawns to her best friend Lauren's house, just up the street. Lauren waved enthusiastically at Nadine. Emma hovered for a moment, wondering whether she was expected to follow. It was soon apparent, however, that Nadine and Lauren would not miss Emma's company. Emma gratefully sat down on the concrete front step to watch the Janvier children play street hockey.

Elaine was the biggest of the three. Emma couldn't really tell if she was the oldest—her brother might be older—but she was the biggest. The brother and the little sister were thin, their arms and legs poking out from the loose fabric of their shorts and T-shirts. The brother had that gangly look of a boy who's just had a growth spurt, and the little sister had the sweet, wispy look of the kids they put in commercials for laundry detergent. But Elaine's belly strained against the front of her T-shirt. Her cheeks were full and round, and her flesh dimpled at her knees and elbows. She was on her way beyond being what parents lovingly call a chubby kid.

But her size didn't stop Elaine running nimbly after the orange street-hockey ball, or gracefully skirting her brother and sister to flick the ball masterfully into the net. It didn't stop her from bouncing raucously in celebration as she scored a goal.

Emma wasn't sure why Elaine suddenly stopped her celebration and stared right at her, the ball clutched in her left hand, stick in her right. "You wanna play?" she called.

Emma shook her head quickly, alarmed at being noticed. Had she been smiling? She slid backwards, pressing her back against the ornamental brick that surrounded the front door. "I don't know how," she called back quickly.

"I can teach you," Elaine replied. She swatted at her brother, who was trying to retrieve the ball from her.

"No thanks."

Elaine shrugged. For a moment, Emma was both relieved and disappointed. A small part of her suddenly regretted not agreeing to the street-hockey lesson. But Elaine didn't go back to her game as Emma thought she would. Instead, she tossed the ball carelessly at her brother and sister, who immediately went on playing as Elaine made her way across the small front yard. She sat down on the step next to Emma. There were beads of sweat across her forehead and she was breathing heavily.

"You're the adopted kid," Elaine said matter-of-factly.

"Yes."

"What's your name?"

"Emma."

"I'm Elaine."

"Hi," Emma said shyly. She couldn't remember the last time another kid had introduced themselves to her, outside of school. She wondered for a moment whether she was supposed to shake hands, the way she'd seen Mike and Julia do when they met people, other adults. But Elaine didn't stick out her hand.

"Where do you go to school?" Elaine asked.

"Castle Downs Junior High."

Elaine nodded. "I'm in junior high too. Grade eight at Lymburn School."

"I'm in grade seven." Surely, Elaine would lose interest now. An eighth grader seldom wanted to be seen with a seventh grader.

But Elaine didn't seem to care. She just nodded, her eyes still on the street-hockey game. "How come you don't want to play?"

"You guys are good. I've never played before."

Elaine shrugged. "Everybody sucks when they first start."

Just then, Nadine and Lauren made their way back across the lawn. They paused as they came up to the house. Emma and Elaine were blocking the way to the front door. Emma's first impulse was to bolt up, but she felt Elaine's stillness beside her. Elaine wasn't going to move.

"My fat ass in your way?" she asked, her tone lazy, completely devoid of aggression.

Emma was shocked. Lots of the kids in her grade swore, but they all spat out the curses like they were venom, *fuck* and *cunt* and *ass* and *shit* blasted with a false bravado. Elaine said "ass" the same way you'd say "shoe" or "arm." Plus, she'd called herself "fat." That was a word that Emma never, ever heard used, except in mean whispers. Girls never called each other fat to their faces, only behind each other's backs. And girls certainly never called themselves fat—not that way, anyway. A girl might tell her friends she felt fat, but the unspoken, unassailable rule was that the other girls had to assure her that she *wasn't*. This was different, though. When Elaine said it, it wasn't an invitation or a need for reassurance. It was bare fact.

Lauren tittered, her eyes darting back and forth between Nadine and Elaine.

Nadine just frowned. "We're going inside to play," she said to Emma, studiously ignoring Elaine. "You coming?"

Again, Emma's impulse was to obey her younger cousin and follow her indoors to be chided by both girls for playing the boyfriend game wrong. But she felt unexpectedly braced by Elaine's calm stillness next to her. "No, thank you," she mumbled.

Nadine hovered for a moment, unsure. Elaine had not moved from the centre of the step, and it seemed clear that she would not. Finally, Nadine led Lauren toward Emma, who shifted as close to the wall as she could get as the two younger girls picked their way up the steps between Emma's skittish frame and Elaine's still bulk. They banged the screen door closed behind them.

"Your cousin's kind of bitchy," Elaine said, still matter-of-fact, without any discernible malice.

"Yeah," Emma agreed. "She is." She felt suddenly buoyed by the admission, but guilty, too, traitorous.

They sat watching Elaine's brother and sister play road hockey for a while, not saying much of anything. Then a shadow appeared inside the Janviers' screen door and their mother's voice rang out into the street. "Supper!"

Elaine stood. "Gotta go," she said, and strode off to help her brother pull the hockey net back into the yard as their sister collected the sticks and ball.

"Bye," Emma called to her retreating figure. She watched as all three kids disappeared into the house.

"So what kind of research are you doing?" Sam asked as Emma handed the book of maps carefully back to her.

"Historical auto—" Emma stopped herself. She shook her head, waving her hand dismissively. "Just some boring local history. It's kind of bullshit." She stuffed her camera back into her bag.

Sam blinked, smiled tightly. She closed the map carefully and set it back on the shelf. "Was there anything else you needed?" she asked. Her voice had lost its buoyancy. It was clipped, professional now.

"No." Damn. Emma had done it again.

Sam headed back to the filing cabinet she'd been working on. "Thank you. This was really great."

Sam nodded without looking up. Emma hovered for a moment. Finally, she turned and left, her sneakers squeaking slightly on the highly polished stone floors of the hallway.

She'd felt that belly-heaviness before. At Dr. Fuentes and Dr. Melnyk's house, the warm light and soft laughter had carried through the front window of their university-area home as Emma stood uncertainly on the front step. She had taken a deep breath, focused on dissolving the stone in her stomach. She took another deep breath and rang the doorbell.

Inside the living room, Emma picked a spot right between two groups of laughing, chatting students. That way either group might reasonably assume she was a satellite of the other. It would be harder to see that she was, in fact, by herself, wondering how long she would have to stay before she could thank her hosts for a wonderful evening and slip away. The group to her right laughed. Emma imagined someone had made a terribly witty joke about Hobsbawm or Schlesinger or some other impenetrably eminent historian whose books Emma had barely understood and would never be able to remember under pressure. She smiled vaguely.

Coming had been a mistake.

Dr. Fuentes's wife, Dr. Melnyk, who taught in the Anthropology department, was in the laughing group. She caught Emma's eye and returned the smile.

"How about you, Emma?" Dr. Melnyk asked.

Oh, god. How about her, what? Emma nodded vaguely, her smile stretching wider to cover her panic. She took a deliberately long sip of her sparkling water.

"How does your family feel about grad school?"

Emma's guts eased with relief. Was that all, then? "Oh. Yeah. They're good. Great. Super excited."

The guy standing next to her laughed. He looked like a young Lenny Kravitz, Emma thought. Nose ring and all. "You're lucky," he said wryly. "My parents wanted me to go to law school. Can you imagine?"

The group laughed again, and Emma felt the muscles in her face tighten into an absurdly wide smile. How had she got *this* wrong? At least she'd only said "excited." She had been about to say "proud."

"Ah, you know," Emma said, digging deep for that swagger, that indifferent pose, the throwaway tone of voice. "First in my family to go to university. They get all weird about it." She'd learned long ago that trying to hide in the crowd, letting her shyness and embarrassment take the reins, was blood in the water. Much better to toss out your insecurities like they're worthless than let them be dug out of you later. If someone discovered something about you on their own—something you wanted to keep to yourself—well, then they had it over you.

Not-Lenny-Kravitz made a noise in his throat, a sound that could be sympathetic but really touches off a round of Suffering Olympics. "*My* parents are both tenured," he said. "The expectations are unbelievable. I *wish* I were the first in my family." He tilted his head at her. "So do your parents *work*, or…?"

"Yeah, they work," Emma shot back. "They own a business."

Not-Lenny-Kravitz blushed.

Emma felt a surge of power. "Fuck," she said, "we're not Gaugins or whatever."

A girl from the group, pretty, no makeup, hair in braids, looked at Emma curiously. "What's a Gaugin?"

"Hillbilly family from back home. Nova Scotia," she added. "The Gaugins, most of them got arrested in 1991."

"Yes," Dr. Melnyk replied. "I think I remember that."

This was when Emma noticed that Dr. Fuentes had made her way over. That in fact, the two social groups at the party had formed one, and right now, it centred on her. Oh, shit.

"I'm afraid I don't remember hearing about it," Dr. Fuentes said.

She was trapped now. She'd wanted to shame Not-Lenny-Kravitz, to rebuke him for his assumptions about her parents, and she'd gone too far.

"The Gaugins are kind of a local legend," Emma replied, offering a practiced half-smirk. "The Nova Scotia bogeymen. It's this family that lived out in the woods in the middle of nowhere, since forever, couple hundred years, maybe. The story goes that whenever one of the Gaugins needed a wife or a husband, they'd go into town and kidnap a kid, raise them to be the perfect new family member, and everyone in the towns was too afraid of the Gaugins to try and get their kids back. There's also a story that the Gaugins were just incestuous, but who knows." She took a theatrical swig of her almost-empty glass of water. "Anyway, in the '80s, there was this other family in Nova Scotia that lived in a shack in the woods, and they got raided or arrested or whatever. Big news at the time. So in the early '90s, Social Services started looking into other families that were living off grid, seeing what else might be going on in those places, and they ended up raiding the Gaugin compound. Scooped up all the kids and sent them off to foster homes, sent a bunch of the adults to prison. Who knows what happened to the rest of them. Maybe they're still out there in the forest. Probably not stealing kids anymore, though."

"Hmm," said Dr. Melnyk. She and her wife exchanged a look.

"Is this interest academic?" Dr. Fuentes asked. "Have you done any historical or genealogical research into the family?"

"God, no." Where was this going?

"Has anyone written about the Gaugins?" asked Dr. Fuentes. "An extended study, I mean."

"Not that I know of."

"How committed are you to your thesis proposal?" Dr. Fuentes asked briskly.

"Well, I...the topic interests me, of course."

Dr. Melnyk nodded. "There's a lot of really exciting work being done at other universities into historical ethnography, but we haven't really come across an appropriate topic here."

"We'd co-supervise you, of course," Dr. Fuentes added. "I'd stay on to advise you on your historical research into the family."

Emma nodded. Fuckity fuck. "Mind if I think it over?" she asked.

"Of course," Dr. Fuentes replied. "We'll talk it over at our meeting on Monday."

Monday. Good. That was enough time to find an excuse. Or at least to figure out what historical ethnography was.

Except that when she turned it over in her mind all weekend, when she tried out excuses, they all felt flat.

I'm really interested in my original topic. Nope. That had been a means to an end, a perfectly plausible thesis to get her into the program and get her a job that wasn't in a fish stick factory.

I don't really want to do this.

But that was the thing. She did want to do it. She felt a deep, subterranean ache to know more about them, the Gaugins, to unearth the kind of knowledge that she'd never be able to just pick up without truly moving some earth. Sure, there was a good chance she'd find out something awful, the kind of thing that makes the back of your mind squirm in revolt, but even if that were the case, she wanted to know.

Of course, she might have to tell the professors the whole story, everything she already knew—and she'd never told anyone that. She would have to get it all out and agree to wade in neck-deep, to really research it and tell the whole story, not just the salacious bits the newspapers and local gossip had already covered. She would have to spend a whole year really writing about it, talking it over with her professors, digging into all of it, even the worst bits, the parts she'd only imagined. Could she confirm it if it were all true?

She might, or she might not.

She did want to know, though. And she couldn't exactly ask her parents about it, could she? She might as well see where this Master's thesis led. Of course, there was a difference between *knowing* and *telling*. She'd deal with that when the time came.

When she arrived at Dr. Fuentes's office Monday afternoon, Dr. Melnyk was waiting for her there, too. The two professors stumbled over each other's sentences, offering critical theories and research strategies for Emma's study of the infamous recluse clan. Emma had never heard the words "exciting" and "promising" used so often.

"A truly fascinating topic, don't you think?" Dr. Melnyk said at last. The two of them sat, blinking at her eagerly.

Emma felt pinned under their gaze. Rather than squirm and stutter, she twisted her mouth into its customary smirk. "Kind of fucked up, though, isn't it?"

Dr. Melnyk's half-smile grew fixed for a second before it dropped.

Dr. Fuentes merely raised her eyebrows a touch. "I'm sorry?"

Emma faltered. "Backwoods family—who knows what kind of messed up shit I'm going to uncover?"

"Well, it will be interesting to find out," Dr. Fuentes said, her expression now cool.

Emma muttered a goodbye and backed out of their office, shame flooding the blood just beneath her skin.

So here she was now, in an obscure records room on the South Shore of Nova Scotia stuffing her entire sneakered foot in her mouth, offending some perfectly nice woman who'd helped her with her research because she didn't know how to admit to the ache in her chest, the urge to know, to really know what had happened in this family over the decades, the centuries, without that stupid defensive swagger, that swagger that had backfired so badly it had blown her all the way out here.

☙❧

SAM LISTENED TO EMMA'S FOOTSTEPS AS THEY RETREATED DOWN the otherwise still hallway. She heard the door to the stairwell open and bang shut. She stood up and walked slowly around the table.

Sam had reserved a small section on the bookshelf nearest the desk for private journals, photo albums, family Bibles with decades of births, deaths, and marriages noted in the blank front pages, and other diverse personal documents that had made their way to the archives over the years. Her favourite section of the entire collection.

She pulled the small, black, fabric-bound book off the shelf and turned it slowly over in her hand. She'd been about to hand it over to this woman, this researcher. She might even have let her take it over the weekend.

Sam had been volunteering for the genealogical society since shortly after her youngest started school—almost seven years now. She'd pulled the records out of dusty bankers' boxes, sorted and catalogued each one, and in the last couple of years, she'd started scanning and uploading them to the Society's new website. She started with census records, land titles, copies of the parish records obtained by the churches—the public records first, the kinds of things most people asked for. She was saving these private records for last. She was a little reluctant to start uploading them, these records of private thoughts and private moments, to start putting them online where anyone might read them, judge them, form their own opinions of the people to whom they belonged. Sam wasn't sure that was fair, to turn them over to the world like that.

Last year, Sam had applied for a full-time paying job with the provincial archives. She'd made it as far as the interview. The hiring committee was impressed, they said, with the work Sam had done with the Genealogical Society. They were openly surprised with the depth of her knowledge of local history. The hour-long interview had sped by, a pleasant conversation between history enthusiasts. Sam had felt elated on the drive home, sure the job would be hers.

But then the committee called to thank her for applying, and to explain that while her enthusiasm for the subject matter was evident, she did not have the educational background they felt was necessary. They offered the position to a man from Ottawa with a Master's degree.

Just some boring local history, Emma had said. *Kind of bullshit.*

Sam lovingly placed the cloth-bound volume back on the shelf.

❧

OUTSIDE THE IMPOSING OLD SCHOOL, EMMA SETTLED INTO THE driver's seat of her rental. She could still see Sam's face fall, close off; she felt the waves of offence and resentment hit her again. What a stupid thing to say.

She sat for several minutes trying to draft a cheery, conciliatory email. She'd send the pictures of the old Gaugin settlement to Sam as soon as she got back to the hotel. Should she apologize? Should she brush it off? She deleted her draft and set her phone down with a sigh. She'd figure out what to say once she got to the hotel.

She turned the ignition and chastised herself again: "Em, you fucking moron."

SEVEN

JACK RUSHDIE WAS IN HIS STUDIO SATURDAY MORNING, WORKING ON A painting of the street outside the university, dabbing a deep greenish-grey onto the shadowy side of a brick building, working the colour and the shape into that sense of grim intimidation the place always gave him on a cold winter's day, when the alarm on his phone startled him: 9:30 A.M. The girl researching the Gaugins would be here in half an hour. He set down his paintbrush.

By ten, he'd cleaned most of the paint off his hands, brushed his hair back into a ponytail—thinner than ever, he noted ruefully—and made a pot of strong black tea. He heard the car crunch its way down the long gravel drive. He opened the front door to greet her.

Emma waved at him as she got out of the car. She had a blue and white patchwork bag slung over one shoulder and across her chest. She was wearing grey slacks and a white button-down top. Her dark hair was pulled back into a tidy ponytail. Her skin was fair, and her ears stuck out a little, giving her an elvish appearance. When she got close enough, he could see that she had light eyes—grey or blue or green, he couldn't tell. *Could be, could be,* he reflected as he raised his hand in greeting.

"Miss Emma?" he asked. "Sorry. Can't recall your last name."

"It's Weaver. But call me Emma."

"Miss Emma G. Weaver," he said thoughtfully. He stuck out his hand.

She shook it quickly, firmly. "Mr. Jack Rushdie." She shifted the weight of her bag and he stepped aside, gesturing for her to come in.

"Leave your shoes on," he said as he showed her to the dining room. He pushed Rosamund gently off the chair. She stalked out of the room, brushing her tail against Jack's leg as she passed. "You're not allergic, are you?"

She shook her head and pulled a laptop out of the patchwork bag. "Thanks for meeting with me," she said.

Jack nodded. "What is it that you're looking for? Information on the Gaugins?"

"Yes," she said briskly, her gaze on her laptop as it powered on. "I'm researching the history of the family up to the arrests of 1991."

"Why?"

She frowned a little, still not looking up at him. "I'm a graduate student at the University of Alberta. I'm doing research for my thesis."

"Yes, but why the Gaugins?" He looked carefully at her face, mapping the features with his painter's eye. What expression would he try to catch if he were to paint her?

She looked up, and for a moment she seemed at a loss for an answer. He watched her patiently. "I'm from here," she said at last. "My family moved away when I was little, but I remember the stories. The Gaugins."

Jack nodded, but didn't say anything. He gazed at her quietly, waiting for her to go on.

"They were kind of a ghost story. I don't know. I wanted to know where it all came from, I guess."

Jack poured two cups of tea and slid one across the table. She thanked him and added a small spoonful of sugar. "Weaver," he said thoughtfully. "There was a couple lived here a few years. From out west, I think. Owned a deli."

"Yes," she said, her voice clipped. "That's my parents. But I actually really wanted to talk to you about your wife's articles."

"I think I have copies somewhere," he said, rising from the table.

"Oh, no, I have them all," she said quickly. He sat down again. "I just wanted to know what you might remember about the arrests, the investigation, the trial. If she talked to you about it. Anything like that."

"I suppose she did." He picked up his tea and surveyed her again. "We had a good marriage. We shared the things we cared about."

Emma took her hands off the keyboard and flexed her fingers. "I wondered…" she began. "Can you tell me…." He smiled a little, waiting for her to finish her question. "What did she think about them? The Gaugins?"

"I imagine she thought a lot of things. I'll never know all of them. But she talked a lot about the kids." He watched Emma fidget with the button on her sleeve.

"What do you mean?"

"She felt bad for them. Everyone did, of course. Or they said they did. The police arrested the parents, social workers came and took their kids, and everyone around here was suddenly so angry, so concerned for the way these kids were raised. Folks talked a lot about abuse and neglect. Of course, we all knew before the police swooped in there that there were kids. If we stopped to think about any of it, we must have known the situation was bad for them. But no one said so until after the arrests." Jack felt a flush rise from his collarbone up his throat. He paused, willing his anger to settle. "But Marian, she never assumed that everything was fine for those kids after social services scooped them up. That's what she talked about—how lonely they must have been in their foster homes. How scared."

"Didn't she…" Emma's voice shook. She stopped to take a sip of tea. Her nostrils flared as she started again. "Didn't she think they were better off, the kids? After the police and the social workers took them."

Jack didn't answer at first. He thought of Marian, the way her gaze would bore through whatever was right in front of her when she was lost in thought. She never liked to share what was on her mind, not until she'd worked it through first. It's what had made her such a good writer, her ability to think through things so thoroughly. "I don't know if that's what she thought," he said at last. "I know she felt bad for the kids. Even if she did think they were better off, she knew it wasn't easy for them, being taken away from everything they knew."

Emma's eyes felt wet. She pretended to scratch her eyelid. "Did she leave…do you have any notes? From her articles?"

"No. No notes. But I know one of the children. Grown up now, of course."

Emma's eyes grew wide. Her hands froze on the keyboard. "The children?"

"The Gaugin children. That's not her name anymore, of course. But she lives nearby. I can find out if she wants to meet you. Do you want me to ask her?"

"Yes," Emma said quickly. "Yes, please. Can you have her email me?"

"If she wants to, yes."

"What's her name?" Emma asked. "What is it now?"

Jack shook his head. "No, I won't serve her up to you. Not unless she wants to talk to you."

"Yes, right, of course," she said. "Thank you."

"Do you need anything else, then? Anything from me?"

"No." Emma stood up quickly and snapped her laptop shut. She poked her hand at him. "Thank you. Thank you very much."

He followed her to the door. "There is another thing," he added thoughtfully. "Have you read the ghost stories?"

She paused. "The ghost stories?"

"*Ghosts of the South Shore*. Collection of folklore from the area."

"I think I've heard of it," she lied.

"Researcher from Halifax talked to folks from all over the area, collected the stories back in the '60s and '70s. The book is pretty famous, but not all the stories made it to the book. Researcher died a few years back, and a couple of years ago her unpublished research wound up on the internet."

"Okay." She tilted her head, waiting for more.

"'Ghosts of Taylor Lake,' look it up."

"Taylor Lake."

"Yes, child."

"The Gaugins."

"Yes."

She reached out and shook his hand once again. The gesture was softer this time, less rigid. "Thank you, Mr. Rushdie."

"Jack."

"Thank you, Jack."

After her rental car had disappeared through the trees at the end of the driveway, Jack took out his phone.

"Heather, girl," he said when she picked up. "Do you want to meet your sister?"

THE PATH HAS MANY PERILS

|

"Ghosts of Taylor Lake"
Unpublished account collected in New Ross, 1972
Archived by the Lunenburg Genealogical Society
(online collection)

The Gerald Boudreau family moved into a Windsor Road farmhouse on Taylor Lake in 1964. The house had previously been owned by Ginny and Dale Lavoie, and was sold to the Boudreaus when Dale Lavoie passed away. In addition to the house, the farm includes a barn, a chicken coop, and 16 acres of pasture. Gerald and his wife, Toni, live there with their three teenaged daughters, Debbie, Maureen, and Patricia.

The Boudreau family had often spoken of the 'barn ghost' in town, and they invited me to interview them at their home.

Gerald admitted that Ginny Lavoie had warned him before he purchased the farm that he would have to put up with the 'barn ghost,' but at the time, he didn't think much of her warning. Mrs. Lavoie was getting on in years, and he thought that she and her husband were having trouble keeping up the farm. He thought that raccoons or dogs were probably getting into the barn and causing trouble. He didn't mention the stories to his family before they moved in.

There is a small storeroom at the front of the barn, and the first fall they lived in the house, Toni used the storeroom to put up her canning. Just before

Thanksgiving, Toni sent the girls out to bring in some pickles and chow. The girls explained that the storeroom door was still locked when they got out to the barn, but when they got inside, they found that most of the pickles had been taken. They came back in the house to tell their mother, and Toni thought that the girls or the farmhands had been taking the pickles and not letting on. The storeroom was kept locked, and only the family and the farmhands would know to come get the key from the hook inside the kitchen door. After that, Toni stopped using the storeroom for food and kept all her preserves in the kitchen.

That first year, the family noticed that their chickens didn't produce many eggs. They watched for broody hens and added another window to the chicken coop to let more light in. Then one evening, the girls were up in their bedrooms. Maureen and Patricia shared a room that looked out onto the chicken coop, and through the new window in the coop they saw what looked like the shadow of a man. They were frightened and called their father. He went to get his shotgun to see whether someone was out there stealing chickens or eggs, but by the time he got out there was no one in the coop and the chickens were all sleeping. He started locking the door to the chicken coop after that day.

The Boudreau family had a dog, an old retriever named Shelby, back when they first moved into the farmhouse. Shelby was a family pet and was allowed to sleep in the kitchen at night. One night after the affair of the chicken coop, Gerald woke up because the dog was growling. Gerald and Toni slept in a room on the lower floor just off the kitchen, and Gerald got up to see what was wrong with the dog. He didn't turn on the light, but the first thing he saw was Shelby standing in the middle of the kitchen. She was growling and her hackles were up. He looked over to see what she was growling at, and there in the door a man was standing. Gerald shouted and the man just disappeared. Gerald turned on the light and he and Shelby ran out into the yard, but the man was nowhere. The dog stopped growling and went straight back to her bed in the kitchen and went to sleep.

Toni and her girls talk about their 'barn ghost,' but Gerald has different ideas. "It's a bush man," he explains. "The Gaugins used to live out on the other side of the lake. Some of the folks say they still do. Our 'barn ghost' is one of those Gaugins who'd rather some eggs or some nice pickles than raccoon meat, or whatever else they eat out there."

Barn ghost or bush man, the family has settled on a way to keep him out of their kitchen. They've taken the lock off the storeroom in the barn and keep food out there for their visitor. "We leave things we don't mind him taking," Toni says. "Tins of soup and vegetables, mostly. But not my good pickles. He can't have no more of those."

EIGHT

DRIVING HOME FROM JACK RUSHDIE'S, EMMA FELT AS THOUGH SHE WERE buzzing inside. Her legs felt jumpy, and she could feel an excited flush in her face. Was it her sister? It might not be. It might be a cousin, even, someone she didn't remember at all. But it could be her big sister. Had she kept her first name? Was she still Heather? Was that her?

This wasn't what she'd come looking for. It wasn't the discovery of a long-dead relative, but a living person, someone who was connected to her, who might even remember her. The excitement Emma felt about meeting another Gaugin child surprised her almost as much as Jack's revelation had.

Most of the people on the Gaugin compound were an indistinct mass in Emma's memory by now. Children—how many children? She remembered a baby, maybe more than one. She remembered helping to look after a baby, feeding it pureed carrots. She remembered an older boy—a brother or a cousin? She couldn't be sure. She remembered being angry with him. He'd taken something she wanted, and because he was bigger, she couldn't get it back. She remembered other kids, the feeling that she was always surrounded by children, but she couldn't be sure how many there were, really. Two, ten, twenty? The newspapers were vague on the topic—the articles only mention children taken into the custody of Community Services. They don't say how many children, or where they ended up. When she got back to the hotel, she sat on the bed with her laptop.

I don't remember how many kids there were, how many sisters, brothers, cousins, babies, bigger kids, but I remember Heather. My big sister, Heather. When I think back to the day we were all taken, I remember the backseat of a minivan. I remember Heather next to me, holding my hand tightly. I remember that I was crying, calling for my mom, but Heather sat next to me not moving, not making a sound.

Then Heather and I were placed in foster care together. That same afternoon, someone in that white minivan drove us to the Weavers' house in Lunenburg. I felt the van slow down in front of the big blue house, and I started crying. The social worker, who by now is only a pair of brown wool pants to me, walked us up the front steps and rang the doorbell. I was still crying, Heather was still silent.

Julia Weaver opened the door. She tried to hug me, but she looked all angles, thin legs, short blonde hair cut sharply around her face, and I turned and pressed my own face into the front of Heather's dress—it was light blue, printed with little pink and green flowers. I can't remember what I was wearing, but I remember the soft fabric of my sister's dress. We were walked upstairs to a clean, sparse bedroom with two single beds pushed against opposite walls. "We'll be right back," Julia Weaver promised, and then we were left in the room, and I cuddled up to my big sister until she slid off the bed and took a couple of uncertain steps toward the door.

"Come on," she said, holding her hand out to me.

I shook my head, afraid to venture into this strange house.

"Come on!" she said again, grabbing at my hand, pulling me toward the door, but I slipped out of her grasp, pressed myself back into the corner where the bed met the wall. She hesitated a moment then, and I willed her to come back to me, to sit with me, to put her arm around me and squeeze. But she didn't. She set her face and slipped out of the bedroom, leaving me alone.

From downstairs, I heard the Weavers say goodbye to the social worker, heard the front door open and close, but there were no sounds telling me where my sister had gone. Then there were heavy footsteps on the stairs, muffled by the thick pile carpeting, and Mike Weaver came up to the bedroom. I was still sitting on the bed, scared to move. I had to pee, but I didn't know where to go. "Come on downstairs," Mike said. "Do you like grilled cheese sandwiches? Your sister is already eating one." I didn't want a sandwich, but I stood up anyway. And when I stood, I couldn't hold it anymore. Pee ran down my leg. I sat back down on the bed, hoping the strange man wouldn't notice, but he saw. "Uh-oh," he said. He turned and called down the stairs. "Julia?"

I was so ashamed, I had started crying again by the time the woman got to the top of the stairs. "Shhh, no need to cry," the man said, standing awkwardly in the bedroom doorway. "She's had an accident," he explained to his wife.

"I hate it when that happens," Julia Weaver said, her voice too cheerful, and I didn't believe that it had actually ever happened to her. I wanted to explain that I was a big girl, I didn't normally have accidents either, but I was too scared to say anything—scared that if I said something wrong, did something wrong, they'd come back for me, take me away somewhere else. Take me away from Heather the way they'd taken me away from my mom and the rest of my family.

But in the end, that's not what happened.

Julia helped me into the bath, then gave me some clothes that were too big. It was jeans and a sweatshirt, I remember, and the jeans felt stiff, heavy. The sweatshirt had a picture of a kitten on the front—the picture was raised, kind of puffy, and it was stiff, too. I remember thinking that the clothes would stand up without me, they were so stiff, hold the shape of my body even if I wasn't in them. She took me downstairs to the kitchen, where Heather was sitting, still and quiet, an empty plate with crumbs and the traces of ketchup in front of her. I tried to eat a grilled cheese sandwich, but my stomach felt squishy. I was scared I'd throw up, and I couldn't bear the idea of having another accident in these people's big, clean, quiet house.

I don't remember Heather saying a single word that day—not to me, not to the Weavers. That night, the Weavers tucked us into our beds. As soon as they left, I slipped into Heather's bed. I tried to cuddle up against her. She put her arms around me, but not to sleep. She was alert, listening. She didn't sleep, and neither did I.

We heard the Weavers roaming around their house. We heard them in the kitchen, then their footsteps up the stairs. We heard them in the bathroom, first one, then the other. The toilet flushing, the sink running. The tap-tap of a toothbrush against the side of the sink. Finally, the soft clack of a bedroom door shutting.

Heather's body, already alert and tense, tightened further at the sound. For a long second, she lay perfectly still and rigid. The she sat up.

"Hurry up," she said, slipping out of bed. She grabbed her dress out of the white wicker laundry hamper in the closet.

"What are you doing?" I was so terrified I'd wake the Weavers, I could barely manage to whisper back to her.

"We're going home," she said, tossing the jeans and sweatshirt at me. I didn't touch them.

"I don't know how," I whispered back, "I don't know where to go."

"We'll figure it out." She was dressed now, and she stared at me. I didn't move. She grabbed for my wrist, but I pulled the blankets tight up under my chin.

"Come on, Em."

But I wouldn't move, couldn't move. What if we were caught? What would they do, where would they take us this time? Even if we did get away, something bad might happen. We could be hit by a car or attacked by wild animals or kidnapped. At least here at the Weavers', we were safe.

It was dark in the room, only the faint glow from the streetlight coming in around the frilled curtains, but I saw Heather's eyes harden then. She turned and left. I heard her feet, quick and light, down the stairs. I heard the front door open and close.

Then the Weavers' voices. Their door opening, their footsteps down the stairs. The front door opening and, a moment later, closing again.

Julia Weaver brought Heather back into our room. I pressed my face into the pillow, pretending to be asleep. She waited until Heather climbed back into bed—my bed, this time, empty since I'd left it—then whispered "Good night" and closed the door.

I wanted to climb into my bed with Heather, but this time Heather wouldn't let me. She pushed me back out of the little bed, turned her back to me.

"I'm sorry, Heather, please, I'm sorry," I whispered, but she wouldn't answer, wouldn't move. I got back into the empty bed, alone.

I tried not to let her hear me crying. I missed my mom. I missed our house with its familiar noises and smells and people. I wanted to go home. How long would they keep us here? I thought we must have been in trouble, and I kept trying to figure out what we'd done.

I must have fallen asleep. The next thing I remember is the sound of my sister screaming downstairs, and a horrible crashing sound. Heather's voice was a guttural ripping in the dark—an animal rage. A scream, then a crash. Another scream, then two more crashes. I lay still in the darkness, my legs quaking under the quilt. I wanted to run away, but I had no idea where to go. I heard the Weavers get up and run down the stairs. I heard their voices, low but alarmed, in between Heather's screams. I heard another crash, then more screams. Finally, I could only hear the Weavers' low voices. After a while, Julia Weaver led Heather back into the bedroom. Heather climbed back into bed, and the Weavers stood in the doorway for a long moment before finally pulling the bedroom door shut and leaving us in the soft orange light of the nightlight between the two beds.

"Heather, please don't," I whispered. "Please be good. Please." I remember thinking about it, what "being good" meant. It meant staying out of the way. It meant not being too noisy or interrupting the adults. It meant not leaving things lying around where they might get stepped on or tripped over, or left in a spot an adult needed for something else. It meant keeping our disagreements, our quarrels, to ourselves. It meant not breaking things that belonged to other people.

"Do you hear me, Heather?"

She didn't answer me.

The next morning when I came down from breakfast, I saw that the china cabinet in the dining room was empty. I thought Heather had smashed all the lovely crystal and porcelain dishes inside and I felt a deep burning shame, as though I had been the one to break all of those beautiful things. I learned later that Heather had only broken some of the dishes before Julia Weaver took away and hid what my sister hadn't yet destroyed.

I can't clearly remember the days and weeks that followed. It's odd, when I think about it, how much I remember from that first night and *how little I remember from the long string of days and nights that came before, and after. I remember Heather's rages, sudden, unpredictable, terrifying, and I remember her silences. I remember the Weavers' muted panic as they tried to calm Heather with lowered voices. Then I remember the day Heather's rage suddenly turned to me. We were out playing in the back yard. Heather had stalked through the gate towards the front of the house and I followed, not wanting to be left alone. I don't know what I did to make Heather angry—perhaps she was simply tired of me creeping after her always, everywhere, scared to be left alone anywhere in the big quiet house. I remember the unexpected jarring thump of both fists into my chest, I remember the burning feeling of the asphalt on my elbows as I fell into the street. I remember that was the first time I heard Julia Weaver scream.*

That day, the Weavers sent me to play alone in our bedroom. I remember the quaking in my guts, my legs, of wanting to burst out, to find Heather and stay with her. I remember the sound of a car outside, a knock on my door. Then the Weavers brought Heather up to our room. They told us to say goodbye, but Heather wouldn't say anything to me. She just stared through me. Then they took her back downstairs.

Julia stayed with me in my bedroom, the bedroom I had shared with Heather. She watched through the window as the social worker, the same woman as before with her helmet-like hair and wide hips, led Heather down the sidewalk. The social worker opened the sliding door of a white minivan and Heather climbed inside. I could see her sitting, rigid, on the seat, as the social worker pulled a seat belt across her and closed the door.

My crying turned into gulping hiccups. Julia Weaver wrapped both arms around me, pressing me to her middle. She was crying too.

❧

EMMA CLOSED HER LAPTOP AND SAT ON THE BED FOR A LONG MOMENT. She had read about childhood amnesia in her psychology class in her second year of university. She knew young children weren't supposed to be able to remember things that clearly once they'd grown up. She knew that even though the memory of those first days with the Weavers seemed impossibly clear, it was probably mostly a story she had constructed, that her parents had helped her to construct. But it didn't feel constructed. It felt real, and as raw in that moment as it had when she was four years old. Her mind darted to Dr. Melnyk and Dr. Fuentes. Surely this was more than they needed to know.

She had, of course, eventually worked up the courage to tell them about her connection to her research, to the Gaugin family.

They'd asked her to come to Dr. Fuentes's office to go over her application for travel funding. They had impressed upon her the prestigiousness of the grant, of how it would look on her transcript, but they never once mentioned the money itself. Without that grant, she'd have to pay her own way out to Halifax. It would mean asking her parents for money, and Emma didn't know if she could do that, if she could ask them to help her come out here and research her birth family.

"The thing is," Emma said, looking down at a patch of dark on Dr. Fuentes's desk, one of the few spots that was free from books and papers, "the thing is, I have a…personal reason for doing this research."

Dr. Fuentes looked on, calmly expectant, but Dr. Melnyk raised her eyebrows. It occurred to Emma suddenly that this might be a problem, that she might not be allowed to pursue research that was so personal. It might be some kind of academic conflict of interest. Her throat tightened and she took a slow breath before she went on.

"I'm actually adopted. My parents were Gaugins."

Dr. Melnyk made a small sound, the kind of gentle pitying sound you make when you see a dog or a cat in pain, but Dr. Fuentes leaned forward. "Interesting," she said. "So you'd be pursuing a project in historical auto-ethnography."

Emma made a quick mental calculation. She thought she remembered Dr. Fuentes talking about auto-ethnography in a seminar.

"A critical intersection between history, autobiography, and sociology," Dr. Fuentes said now.

Emma nodded quickly, as if she didn't need the reminder. She would have to write about her childhood, her memories, her feelings about her own research into her family history. This would not be the dispassionate research project she'd pitched to her supervisors. She'd owe them something of herself.

But she would get the chance to ask questions, to find out what kind of people she'd really come from. Who they were now. And she'd have this academic shield. A grad student performing historical auto-ethnography—that was the kind of research people, the kinds of people who knew something about the Gaugins, would have to take seriously. The social workers and journalists, certainly, but also ordinary people who had been there and remembered the events and who might be persuaded to talk to her if they could trust her...they would have to take her seriously, wouldn't they?

She took a deep breath. "I guess so."

Dr. Fuentes nodded vigorously. "Interesting. Very interesting."

Emma looked over at Dr. Melnyk, who by this time was smiling warmly. "You're almost certain to get funding now," she said. "No one else is doing this kind of project. It's very innovative. Very exciting."

"So exciting," Emma replied. She smiled, trying to tamp down the nervousness that was rising up inside her.

Emma lay back on the hotel bed, the soft pillows pressing in around her face, the feeling of them half-comforting, half-suffocating. She reached for her phone and dialled her mom.

"Emma! It's good to hear from you! How's Halifax?"

"Horrible," Emma replied. "Post-apocalyptic. No one warned me about the nuclear fallout."

"Funny," Julia said without laughing. "How is your research?"

"Great. I am an expert. On Gaugins."

"Have you found a yoga studio? Are you remembering to meditate?"

"Not really."

"You have to take care of yourself, Em."

"Says you."

"Says me."

There was a long silence. Emma didn't know how to ask about Heather. She wasn't sure what the question was. "Is Dad there?" she asked at last.

"Sure. He's here."

"I wanted to ask him something. Should I just call his cell?"

"No, no, hang on," Julia replied. There was a muffled scratching. "Emma! How are your studies?"

"Good, Dad. But I needed...I need you to tell me about my sister. About the time she spent in our house in Lunenburg."

"Ah." There was a pause, and more muffled scratching. Emma knew he was filling her mom in. "What do you need to know?" he asked at last.

"I'm not sure. Tell me...you couldn't keep her. Tell me about her."

Mike sighed. "Heather had more problems than we knew how to handle. We'd never fostered before. We'd read all the research, but we just weren't equipped for her rages. But we tried to help her, Em."

"I know."

"We didn't want to send her away, but when she pushed you into the street, we were afraid she'd seriously hurt you."

Emma felt her throat tightening. "Did you consider sending us both away so we could be together?" She hated asking, hated that he might think she was accusing him. She knew she could never ask her mom the same questions. Mike, though, would never let the hurt creep into his voice. Even if Emma did hurt him, he wouldn't show it.

"The social worker suggested it, but...." Mike sighed. Emma could picture him scratching at his hairline the way he did when he was choosing his words. "We couldn't keep you both safe. We didn't know what we could do for Heather, if we could even do anything for her, and we...we were scared for you, Em, with us or not."

"Did you know you wanted to keep me then?"

There was a pause. Mike hated lying. Even white lies. "No," he said at last. "Not yet." Julia would have said, "Yes, absolutely, we knew right away!" And she probably would have believed that was true.

"Thanks, Dad," Emma said, her voice sounding tight and weird as she tried not to cry.

"Emma, are you sure you can go through with this?" he asked. She could hear her mom murmur something in the background. "There's no shame in saying you want to study something different, you know."

"I know, Dad. I'm all right."

"Okay."

"And if I'm wrong, lobotomy's still an option."

"It always is. We love you."

"Love you, too."

ତ୦ତ

SHE HAD ASKED HER PARENTS, OF COURSE, ABOUT HER BIRTH FAMILY.
Mike and Julia had encouraged it, pretty much from the time the
adoption was finalized.

"If you ever have any questions, you can come to us," Julia would
urge. "You can ask anything."

But the way she said it, with that look on her face, so earnest,
with the worry not quite buried beneath the tenderness, always made
Emma change the subject. "Can we have lasagne for supper?" she'd
ask, or "Can Elaine sleep over this weekend?"

It was only after she'd met Elaine, when her new friend had
said to her, "You're the adopted kid," that Emma finally worked up
the courage to ask.

They were driving home from Uncle Shawn and Auntie Jean's.
Emma was in the back seat, looking at the backs of Mike and Julia's
heads. That's what made it easier.

"Everyone here knows I'm adopted," she said. She wanted to
make it a question, but she didn't know how without making it sound
like she was angry at her parents.

"Sure," Mike replied. She saw him glance at Julia. "Kind of hard
to pass you off for a newborn."

"Do they know who my family was before?" she asked. She
couldn't say *Gaugins*. She didn't want the sound of that name in the
car with them.

"Shawn and Jean know a little bit about where you came from,"
Mike replied.

"Like what?"

Julia turned around to look at Emma. Emma was sitting right

behind her, on the passenger side, so they couldn't really look at each other properly. Emma was glad. "Why all these questions, Em?"

"I don't know."

"It's okay to put all that behind you, you know," Julia said. She reached her hand back, awkwardly, to squeeze Emma's hand. "Bad things happen to everyone. But we can focus on the good."

"Okay," Emma said. *Bad things.* That's what they, the Gaugins, had been. When she tried to remember them, though, or when a little bubble of memories burst upon her unexpectedly—like the feeling of someone brushing her hair, or the warmth of a grownup's lap—they didn't feel bad. So what did that make her for wanting to know about them? She squeezed Julia's hand back, pressing the questions that had built up in her chest way back down.

ೋ

SATURDAY EVENING, A COLD RAIN PATTERED INTO HALIFAX. Emma spent the next two days travelling between cafés and pubs in Halifax with her laptop, editing photos, scouring the South Shore ghost stories on the Genealogical Society website, and nursing countless coffees and beers. She bought an expensive handmade wool sweater from a tourist shop on the waterfront; the soft, misty Nova Scotia rains crept into her bones and chilled her as though it were November and not June.

Late Monday afternoon, she was picking at a plate of fries and her account of her visit with Jack Rushdie when her cellphone vibrated on the table. Unknown Number. She picked it up cautiously, expecting a scam caller.

"I'm looking for Emma Weaver," a low female voice said.

"I'm Emma," she replied, her voice clipped. Telemarketer?

"My name is Heather Publicover. Jack Rushdie gave me your number."

Emma felt a hot gush of excitement rise from her chest to her cheeks. Heather. "Yes, thank you for calling," she said, her voice too loud for the sparse Monday-afternoon pub crowd. The couple at the next tabled turned to glare at her.

There was a pause. *Tell her tell her tell her!* Emma's head screamed, but she couldn't. She didn't know the words. This wasn't a hurt, angry seven-year-old girl on the phone. This was a woman, a stranger. "I'm researching the Gaugins," she said at last. "For my Master's thesis. Would you…can you talk to me?"

"Yes, I think so," Heather replied, her voice guarded. "It's for thesis research? You're not going to publish a book or something?"

"God, no," Emma said quickly. Then she reflected that she should have said *Maybe.* After all, isn't that what you were supposed to do with a thesis once it was finished—turn it into a book and publish it? No way. Emma still wasn't sure how much she'd need to edit her own memories, her own account of this trip, before she could turn it in to be read, analyzed, evaluated by her thesis committee. Send it to a publisher? For people to buy and read on the bus, to leave on their nightside tables, to lend to their friends? No way. No fucking way.

"Okay. Yeah, let's meet." In the background, a squawk. "Hang on," Heather said, her voice becoming muffled. "My baby."

"I can come to you," Emma said. "We can meet at your place, or a restaurant or something. Wherever you're comfortable."

The baby in the background was cooing now, making soft sounds that were almost words. "You mind coming out to my place? It'd be easier with the kids."

"I can do that," Emma said quickly. They agreed to meet the following afternoon. She got Heather's address in Chester and hung up the phone.

Kids. Emma had nieces or nephews. How many? Was Heather a good mom? Was the kids' dad around? Was there more than one? What kind of person had her sister turned out to be—was she someone Emma would like? What would she be able to tell her parents about Heather?

And what about Heather? Would she like Emma when she met her? Would she appreciate Emma's smart mouth, the brashness she could put on if she wanted? Would she like Emma better if she kept quiet, kept it together the way she usually did in her university classes and at work? What version of herself would please her sister more?

NINE

THANK GOD THE SOUND OF THE VACUUM PUT THE BABY TO SLEEP. Heather spent the afternoon chasing dust bunnies around the house with the hand-held vacuum cleaner, Charlotte sleeping soundly in the baby carrier strapped to Heather's chest. Cleaning the bathrooms was trickier—she didn't want to expose the baby to the fumes from the cleaning fluids, but Charlotte still refused stay alone in her playpen without howling. Justin had cried, too, when his parents set him down, but since he cried just as hard when they held him, it had been easier to lay him down to grab a sandwich or fold the laundry. Charlotte hardly ever cried when she was held, so it was hard to put her down and let her fuss.

Rafe got home shortly before five. He peeled his thick sandy-coloured coveralls off in the porch and dumped them into the bin in the hall closet where he kept his work gear. Heather kissed him and handed him the baby. Justin abandoned his cartoons in the living room, rushing in to hug his father's knee.

"Good day at school, kiddo?" Rafe asked.

Justin shrugged and tickled the baby's dangling foot. She squealed in delight and pressed her face into Rafe's neck.

"There's spaghetti and sauce on the stove," Heather said. "Can you feed the kids? I want to clean the bathrooms."

"Sure," Rafe said. He looked puzzled, but didn't ask.

The most disturbing thing about cleaning the bathrooms, Heather reflected as she scrubbed the toilet, was noticing afterward how clean they looked. How gross had they gotten without her really noticing? Before she had the kids, she used to hate using the washroom at friends' houses. Toothpaste-splattered sinks and crumpled hand towels always made her want to rush home and scrub her hands in her own immaculate bathroom. Of course, her standards were more relaxed these days.

Rafe looked at her curiously as she emerged from the main-floor powder room off the kitchen. "We having company I don't know about?"

"No," Heather snapped. She took a deep breath. The heat, the effort of housework, the hungry feeling always haunting her belly, all of it had made her cranky. She squeezed her husband's shoulder as she passed. Charlotte beamed up at her from his lap. Rafe had taken her out of her high chair, but she still had a fistful of mashed-up spaghetti. She was chewing on her other, empty fist. "Sort of," Heather amended. She helped herself to a heaping plate of supper. She always felt like she was starving while she was breastfeeding. "Someone…a student…." She felt like she'd run up against a block, a physical barrier that was preventing her from getting the words out. She cleared her throat and started again. "Jack put me in touch with some kind of student who's researching the Gaugins." Rafe raised an eyebrow. "It's—this student, she's actually my sister."

Rafe sat back in his chair. "Whoa."

Heather shot him a look and a quick head shake. She glanced pointedly at the kids.

"You have a sister, Mommy?" Justin asked. His mouth was rimmed with orange spaghetti sauce stains.

Heather forced a light note into her voice. "I do. But I haven't seen her since I was a little girl. Not much bigger than you."

Justin looked serious for a moment, then reached out to take his sister's hand. Charlotte immediately tried to stuff Justin's fingers in her mouth, squealing when he pulled his hand away. "She's slobbery," he said.

"She's teething," Rafe replied.

"What does she look like?" Justin asked.

"I don't know," Heather said. "I guess we'll find out tomorrow."

"Because you didn't get to see her." Justin frowned, considering.

"That's right."

"Because when you were little, you had to go away from your home."

"Yup."

Justin nodded and turned his attention back to a long noodle that he was trying to twirl on his fork. But Rafe was still looking at her intently. She gave him a little smile, reassuring, she hoped. She dug into her own supper even though, hungry as she was, she didn't much feel like eating.

That night, after they had the kids settled in bed, Heather collapsed against Rafe on the couch. "You sure about this visit tomorrow?" he asked as he started the TV series they'd been watching. It was about a bunch of strangers who suddenly develop the ability to hear each other's thoughts.

"Sure," Heather said. She wondered if she should go and make herself some popcorn.

"Do you want to get Jack to come over or something?"

Heather stood up, fussing with the couch cushions to give herself a moment to answer. She wanted to say, "No, I want *you* to stay at home with me," wanted to press her face into his chest, but she didn't know what would happen if she gave in like that, even for a moment now that the kids were in bed. If she let go now, she wasn't sure she'd be able to pick herself up again tomorrow when this girl, her sister, showed up.

While Heather fussed with the cushions, Rafe kept his gaze on her, that steady gaze that had first drawn her to him. She'd been working as an admin assistant for the electricians' union, answering phones and scheduling meetings, mostly. The guys—almost all the electricians had been guys back then—were gruff but not unkind. Most grumbled orders at her. *Bring up a pot of coffee*, or *Set a meeting with the contractors on the new box store going up in Bayers Lake.* They'd usually toss off their commands as they tromped past her desk, barely glancing at her. Which was fine with Heather, really. It was easier just to do her job and not have to bother with small talk and corporate politeness. It was ideal for her, really.

But Rafe hadn't been like that. He came in one day to pick up some paperwork left by the union steward. He stood quietly at her desk. Heather was at the printer, compiling some contracts to file, and she ignored him. The guys never waited for her. If they wanted something, they'd say so. But they did sometimes hover by her desk, waiting for a union rep or another electrician, sometimes just killing time and looking for a conversation with another tradesman.

It was a few minutes before Heather realized Rafe was looking at her. Not staring, just looking. She turned around. She noticed right away that his irises were so dark, she couldn't tell where his pupils ended and began. When she met his eyes, he didn't smile exactly but his face softened somehow.

Immediately, she felt a swell of annoyance. "You want something, or what?"

"If you're busy, I can wait." He did smile now, and she saw that one of his eyeteeth was a little crooked, angled forward. It was kind of sexy, she thought.

Immediately, she worried he'd notice her impression. She jerked her arms in the air in an impatient *Well?* gesture, fixing her face in a frown.

"Duncan left some papers for me to pick up. I'm Rafe."

She strode over to her desk and handed him the file wordlessly.

"Thank you," he said as he left. And he smiled again. Heather felt herself flush as she caught another look at that sexy, crooked smile. Not a grin. A *grin* would have put her off. It was a smile, gentle and warm.

The next time he came in he stood at her desk again, waiting quietly. She finished sending her email, then looked up at him without saying anything. *Well?*

"I'd like to take you out some time." He said it like that. Direct. But as he waited for a reply, those dark, dark eyes fixed on her, there was no expectation. Heather considered saying *No.* She didn't want to, but she was curious about how he'd react. Some guys pressed harder, wheedling for a yes. Some got defensive, insulting, even. Heather was certain he wouldn't do either of those things. How would he handle a *No*?

She didn't want to risk it, though, just to find out. "Yeah, okay," she said. And he smiled again. Heather wondered how long she'd have to wait before she could kiss that sexy mouth.

He kept his eyes on her as she finished with the pillows and settled herself back into the couch, her shoulder in the crook of his. "No, it'll be fine."

"Yeah?"

"Yup."

Rafe started the new episode. "Pause it a sec," Heather said, hoisting herself off the couch. "I need some popcorn."

TEN

MONDAY EVENING, EMMA SAT IN HER HOTEL ROOM RE-READING ALL the news articles on the raid on the Gaugin compound. She'd been down to the hotel gym that day, but that was the farthest she'd strayed from her room. She had been sorting through her interviews, photos, and news articles, and now she was trying to put together a list of questions for Heather, the kind of questions that any historical researcher might ask, but the questions she really wanted to ask crowded out the more academic sort.

What was the rest of your life like after they took you away from the Weavers? What do you remember from before? Why did you get yourself kicked out of the Weavers' place? Why couldn't you just be good and stay with me?

Even if she asked these questions, Emma didn't know if she could stand to hear the answers. Or record them.

After Heather was taken away from the Weavers, Emma used to ask her sister's empty bed these questions at night. *Why couldn't you just be good, Heather? Why couldn't you just be good and stay with me?*

The Weavers couldn't tell Emma where Heather had gone, or when Emma might see her again. "I don't know, sweetie," seemed to be the only answer they had to any of her questions—except one.

"Did she go home?"

"No. She didn't. There's no one there to take care of her."

"Why not? Where is my mommy?"

"I don't know, sweetie," Julia Weaver said. "I'm sorry." She reached out to hug Emma. Emma didn't want to be hugged by this woman, but she didn't want to pull away. She wanted to be good. She wanted to go to her sister, but she couldn't be sure that was where they'd send her. What if they just sent her to live with other strangers, people who were not as nice as the Weavers?

When Emma thinks back to those first years with the Weavers, she remembers *being good*. She remembers lying in her bed at night, worrying about whether or not she'd been good enough to stay.

She remembers one summer day when she started to feel sick to her stomach. She went to lie down on the couch. Mike was home from work at the deli he and Julia owned. "It's a nice day," he said. "You should be playing outside."

Even though her tummy hurt, she got up obediently. But before she made it to the sliding glass door in the kitchen, the door that led to the fenced-in backyard, she threw up on the clean sandy-brown carpet.

"Oh, damn," Mike muttered quietly as he made his way over to her.

Emma stared at the orange-brown puddle on the carpet in horror. Her arms and legs started shaking, her tears welled up and overflowed.

"Hey, it's okay," Mike said, rubbing her shoulder blade awkwardly. "Come on." He led her to a kitchen chair and gave her a glass of water. "Just take little sips," he said. He grabbed a roll of paper towel and went to clean up the vomit. Emma's shame swelled unbearably when she saw him gag twice as he cleaned up the mess.

Afterward, he sat across from her in the kitchen. "How are you feeling?" he asked gently.

"I'm okay," Emma whispered, even though her tummy still ached and her head was starting to feel hot and sore. She wondered whether Julia would make it home from the grocery store before someone came to take her away.

"Come on," he said, reaching out his hand. She took it and he led her back to the couch. He put the knitted blanket across her legs. She wasn't cold, but she didn't say so. He brought her a glass of ginger ale and a plate of soda crackers from the kitchen. "Just have a little bit," he said. "It'll make you feel better."

She nibbled the corner of a cracker and held the glass of fizzy pop in her hand. He put a movie into the VCR—*Star Wars*—and sat down in the easy chair to watch it with her.

All afternoon, she waited for someone to come and take her away. Her insides squirmed, but every time tears started to bubble up, she blinked them away, staring intently at the TV screen. That evening, she woke up to Mike lifting her up off the couch. He carried her into her bedroom, where Julia helped her get into her nightie. Julia left an empty ice cream bucket next to the bed. "In case you feel sick again," she said. Julia kissed her on the forehead and wished her good night.

Emma's head hurt and her stomach felt uncomfortably squishy, but she felt as though her chest was lifting up under the pride that she felt. She had managed to be very good today, after all.

The next fall, Mike and Julia started taking her to kindergarten every morning. The schoolyard was full of screaming, running children. Emma shrank away from them, from their noise, their unruliness. *Be good*, she reminded herself. *Be good*. The first day, she pressed herself against Julia's leg.

"It's okay," Mike said, misunderstanding. "They're nice kids. They'll let you play with them."

Sure enough, a girl with her hair in a messy braid ran up to her. "Want to play?" she asked, thrusting the plastic handle of a long jump-rope towards her.

Emma shook her head. "No, thank you," she replied politely. She did not cry when Mike and Julia left her in the noisy, chaotic schoolyard that day, even though she wanted to.

For the next two years, Emma was careful to always be good at school and at home. After a while, she lost the habit of waiting for someone to come and take her away. And when Julia reached her arms out for a hug, Emma squeezed her back, relishing the warm, safe pressure of her arms.

Then one day when Emma was seven, she came home to a white minivan in the driveway. Emma's legs started shaking as she let herself in the front door. Her mind flashed over her day at school, over the past days and weeks at home, wondering where she might have gone wrong. The C+ on the math test. Forgetting her plate in the living room when she'd made herself a peanut butter and jam sandwich. Getting jam on the arm of the couch. Losing one of the little silver earrings Mike and Julia had bought her for Christmas at the playground. Being good, she quickly learned, was more complicated at the Weavers' house. There were more things to pay attention to. But it was also sometimes harder to tell if she *was* being good. Emma sometimes found herself longing for the sudden sting of an open palm on her bottom or her face to let her know she'd crossed a line.

But here, with the Weavers, it was hard to interpret their gentle disappointment. There were certainly times when she could tell Mike or Julia were annoyed. The stiffness in Mike's body, the way his voice went flat when he said her name slowly, "Em-ma." Like when she'd left a piece of chocolate cake on a plate under her bed, saving it for later, and he'd found it, mouldy and covered with ants. Or Julia's way of flapping her hands up in the air and letting them drop. The first time she'd done that, Emma braced for a slap that never came. But those tells, they quickly became easy to spot. It was a quiet kind of disappointment, like when Emma did poorly on an assignment at school or when she'd lost the pretty butterfly-shaped earring. She couldn't tell whether they were angry, or just sad, but she tried her best to avoid doing anything that caused either reaction—the outright frustration or the gentle disappointment when they sat her down to talk to her, using that word, disappointed. Maybe those were some of the things she'd done, some of the wrongs, the marks against good behaviour.

Was it just one thing, or was it everything all together?

The social worker, with her close-cropped dark hair, was sitting at the dining room table. She was wearing a brown cardigan with little yellow and orange knitted flowers down the front. Mike and Julia were sitting on either side of her. A bunch of papers were spread out between them.

"Come on in, Emma," Mike said as she hovered in the entryway. Emma set her bag down next to her shoes and walked into the dining room, her insides hardening like cement.

"Emma, my name is Dorothy," the woman said. She had a deep voice. It sounded like singing. "Do you remember me?"

Emma nodded.

"Will you sit down? I want to ask you a question."

As Emma sat down at the table, Mike and Julia stood. Emma looked up at them, wanting them to stay, wanting to promise that whatever she'd done, she'd make up for it. She'd be *better*, she wanted to tell them. She'd tried, but she could try harder. She wanted to tell them how she always put her clothes in the hamper at night, how she did all of her homework every day. She cleared the table after dinner without being asked. She went to bed right at 8:30, even when she wasn't tired, because Mike had said that first week that bedtime was 8:30. She wanted to list it all off quickly, but that seemed like cheating somehow. Bragging, and bragging wasn't nice. It wasn't good. So she just sat, paralyzed, thinking of every good thing, and hoping Mike and Julia would remember some of them on their own.

"It's okay, Em," Julia said. She crouched down next to Emma's chair. Emma wanted to throw her arms around Julia's neck. She grabbed the seat of her chair instead. "We're just going to grab a snack." But she and Mike didn't go into the kitchen. They went to the basement instead.

"How are you, Emma?" Dorothy asked after they'd left.

"Fine."

"Good. Do you like living here?"

"Yes." Emma couldn't say more. Her throat was closing up. She couldn't stop the tears. They dripped off her chin and splattered on her T-shirt.

"Do you know what adoption means, Emma?"

Emma had a vague idea, but she couldn't answer, so she just shook her head.

"The Weavers would like to adopt you. It means that you would become their daughter. Would you like that?"

Emma's heart seemed to squeeze tight for a second, then gave a *thump* like a bubble bursting in a pot of oatmeal on the stove. *Become their daughter.* So she wasn't being sent away, then. "Yes," she managed to say. Of course, she reminded herself, she'd had parents before, and she'd been taken away. But today, today, she wouldn't be taken away from the Weavers.

She doesn't remember what else Dorothy asked her, but she does remember they talked a long time. She remembers the slow unfurling in her chest as the mental list of all the times she'd been good, and all the times she hadn't, ebbed away. The feeling of relief, the buoyancy of it. She remembers wanting Mike and Julia to come back, wanting to be with them, for them to be there in that moment, and it was just then that they came up from the basement with a bottle of pop, and they all talked together. Dorothy had a lot of questions for all of them. Mike and Julia sat on either side of Emma, each holding a hand, and she had to keep reminding herself not to squeeze too hard.

That year, Emma became Emma Weaver. Her middle name used to be Helen, but it became Gaugin instead, moving inwards. But it wasn't until the following summer that she stopped worrying about being taken away. That summer, the Weavers moved to Edmonton. Mike and Julia opened a restaurant just west of downtown with Mike's brother. Emma helped to pack up her clothes and toys and books. Men came and loaded the boxes with all their things into a big truck with a picture of mountains on its side, and the Weavers boarded an airplane for Edmonton. As the plane took off, Emma watched the runway and the trees and the roads and lakes of Nova Scotia shrink, then disappear through a veil of wispy white clouds, and she knew that they were leaving behind anyone who could come and take her away from the Weavers.

It wasn't until they landed in Edmonton, the plane bumping onto the tarmac, that Emma fully realized they'd left her sister and her first mother and all the rest of her Gaugin family behind, too. She'd known they weren't going to be there in Edmonton, of course, but it wasn't until the plane landed that she really thought about it. The realization sent a flood of relief through her, then faintly in its wake, a flush of guilt.

Now, so many years later, she was back. She was getting ready to meet her sister again.

Do you remember me? Did you love me? Did any of the Gaugins love me? She couldn't frame the other questions, the research questions she knew she was supposed to ask.

And what about Heather herself? What questions would she have for her, for Emma? What kinds of answers should she be ready to give? She didn't know, she didn't know. So she just kept re-reading the articles she already knew almost by heart.

"Raid on the Gaugin Compound"
The Lunenburg Shore. September 4th, 1991
Marian Rushdie, staff reporter

On the morning of September 3rd, seven adult members
of the Gaugin family were arrested at their home in
New Russell, while several children were taken into
the custody of Community Services.

RCMP officers executed a raid on the Gaugin com-
pound located north of Taylor Lake in the community
of New Russell. Kevin Gaugin, Maureen Gaugin, Gary
Gaugin, Mark Gaugin, Helen Gaugin, Daniel Gaugin,
and Shauna Gaugin face several charges, including
Child Neglect, Failing to Provide the Necessaries of
Life, Possession of Stolen Property, Assault, and Tax
Evasion. An undisclosed number of children living on
the compound were taken into the custody of Community
Services.

"The children were living in filthy conditions," a
social worker told *Shore* reporters. This social worker
has asked to remain anonymous, but told our reporter
that concern for the children prompted her to speak
out. "They're terrified. They've been neglected, and
a lot of them have hardly ever spent any time off the
compound. They need a lot of care."

This reporter was present at the raid on the
compound. Conditions for the children did appear to
be dire. The children were dirty-faced, many wearing

ill-fitting or damaged clothing. They were led, crying, into the waiting vans to be taken into care.
The main home seems ill-suited to accommodate a
large family, and especially a family with children.
It is in general disrepair with visible damage to
the wood shake siding, and conditions on the surrounding property seem hazardous. Vehicles and farm
machinery in various states of disrepair, as well
as unfettered farm animals, dominate the landscape.

If this scene affected the adults, they did not
let on, appearing grim and unrepentant as they faced
reporters. Some of the children have been placed
in foster homes, and others are currently in group
homes awaiting placement.

ELEVEN

THE BLAND VOICE FROM EMMA'S MAP APP TOLD HER SHE HAD REACHED her destination. Heather Publicover's house was on a pretty rural stretch just outside of Chester. Neat wooden houses sat back from the road on either side, and the ditches banked down steeply, giving Emma the sense that the road was actually a bridge.

The Publicovers lived in a blue Cape Cod–style house with dormer windows looking out onto the road. Tiny blue and tall pink flowers bloomed in beds along the front, and there was a small kids' playhouse between the house and the garage.

Emma sat in the car for a moment, trying to calm the nervous fluttering in her stomach. She put her phone and her keys into her laptop bag, checking that she'd remembered to pack her computer and charger. Finally, she got out and made her way up the front steps. She couldn't see a doorbell, so she knocked on the door.

☙❧

HEATHER WATCHED EMMA SIT IN THE CAR WITH HER HANDS ON THE steering wheel for a long moment before she gathered her things and came up to the house. She fought the urge to yank open the door before Emma knocked. She made herself count to three before she pulled the door open.

Emma flashed a tight smile as soon as the door opened. "Hello, I'm Emma Weaver. I'm the researcher from the University of Alberta."

Well, duh. Who else would you be? Heather thought. Instead, she stuck out her hand. "Heather Publicover." She showed Emma into the living room. Charlotte was in her playpen, chewing on her toy giraffe, and Justin was watching cartoons on her iPad with his little green headphones on. He didn't look up at the stranger who was settling onto the couch, pulling her laptop out of her shoulder bag.

"Cup of tea?" Heather asked.

"Um. Sure. Yes. Please." Emma smiled again, clearly nervous. Heather felt a pang of momentary pity. She watched her sister as she made the tea. Emma would be, what, thirty-two now. Heather noticed the faint lines under her eyes and at the corners of her mouth, but from a distance, Emma looked like a kid, almost. It was mainly her ponytail and her clothes, Heather realized. She was wearing a pair of black leggings with a dark-grey cat print and a long, loose-fitting lavender-coloured T-shirt over top. She had on a big, fluffy, light-grey cotton scarf. The front of her hair was pinned back, making her eyes look huge. Heather tried to remember what Emma had looked like as a child. All she could recall was the long, fine, dark-brown hair. Emma had always wanted it braided.

"Milk? Sugar?" Heather called into the living room. She tilted her head so she could see around the dining room wall.

Emma shook her head. "Thanks."

Heather carried two cups into the living room and sat down on the chair opposite her sister. She gripped the handle of her own teacup and waited.

Emma cleared her throat. "So. Um. Thank you for meeting with me. I wanted to ask you some questions about, um. The Gaugins. And what you remember from 1991, and from before that. My research—"

"What kind of research?" Heather interrupted. Charlotte squealed impatiently. Heather went to pick her up. She returned to her armchair with the baby, who sat in Heather's lap, chewing on her giraffe and staring at Emma.

"Um?" Emma glanced back and forth between Heather and

Charlotte as though she were not sure which of them had asked the question.

"What kind of research are you doing? I mean, what's the point? Why are you researching this?"

Emma blinked, then started talking very quickly. "Well. I'm a graduate student in the Department of Anthropology, but my thesis is an interdisciplinary research project. It's co-supervised by a professor in the History department. My methodology is rooted in historical auto-ethnography, and I'm on a research trip to do archival research, and to talk to people about their memories and impressions of the Gaugin raid."

As Emma talked, Heather felt the irritation build in her chest. "Well, that sounds right complicated," she replied, drawing out her vowels in an exaggerated South Shore accent. "Quite the education you've got."

Emma had the good grace to flush in embarrassment. She grabbed her tea and took a sip.

"You said 'historical auto-ethnography.' Is that anything like autobiography?"

Emma sputtered. "No, not really. It's…more a study of the people and the culture."

Heather set her cup on the coffee table. Her hands were shaking and she thumped it down harder than she intended, sloshing her tea. Justin looked up from his iPad, an after-school snack of milk and apple slices on the table in front of him. Heather brushed his hair behind his ear, and he returned his attention to the cartoon. "Oh, knock it off," Heather hissed, not wanting to raise her voice and startle the kids. "Do you think I don't know who you are? What kind of bullshit is this, showing up and pretending to be a researcher?"

Emma's eyes widened in alarm. "I—I am a researcher! I'm a grad student…."

"And?" Heather prodded, her voice hard.

"And…I'm—I used to be—a Gaugin."

Heather didn't say anything. She just kept staring at Emma, who was blinking fast.

"I'm your—I mean, you're my sister." Emma looked like a kid who desperately hoped the answer she'd just given the teacher was the right one.

Heather leaned back in her chair. She pressed her lips to the baby's fine, downy hair. "What on earth were you thinking?" she asked at last. "Did you honestly think no one would know?"

Emma shrugged. "I didn't expect to find you. I didn't think anyone else would remember me." She stopped. Her eyes widened. "Wait. Jack Rushdie?"

"Yup. He told me."

"Shit."

"Shit," Heather agreed. She looked at Emma with narrowed eyes. "But I would have had to be stupid not to figure it out anyway. You know that, right?"

Emma nodded, feeling the miserable shame creeping through her core. How dumb to think she could bluff her way through this visit. To think she could be the one to decide when and if she'd reveal herself, her real self, to Heather.

They sat in silence for a long moment. Emma looked at Justin, who was still absorbed in his cartoons, and at Charlotte, who was now chewing contentedly on her mother's thumb. "I'm sorry," she said at last.

Heather nodded. "Are you really writing your thesis on our family?" she asked.

"Yeah."

"Why?"

Emma froze for a second. She took a short breath and held it. "I just needed to know," she said at last. "But I didn't know how to find out until…." She gestured faintly at her laptop bag. "Until this."

"Okay," Heather said. "So what are you going to do with this research, then?"

"Nothing. Just…put it in my thesis. Get my Master's degree. That's all."

"Everything?"

Emma looked at her, right into her eyes, for the first time since she'd arrived. "I don't know."

There was a long silence. Heather appeared to be considering.

"I'm sorry," Emma said. "I'm really sorry. I should have told you who I am. I just didn't know how to say it. I didn't know what you'd be like, what you'd think about the whole thing."

"Just tell me one thing," Heather said. She started hard at her sister. "Do *you* want to know what it was like for *me*, what I remember? I mean, for yourself. Not for your degree or your professor or whatever. Do you give two shits about what happened to me?"

"Yes," Emma replied earnestly. Heather looked at her face. She seemed nervous, like she was scared to hear what Heather might have to say. But there was something else in her face, too. A longing. Heather could understand that feeling.

"Okay," Heather said at last.

"Can I record you?"

"No way," Heather said quickly.

"I promise no one else will listen to it," Emma said. She was looking at Heather again, those eyes clear and open. The same expression Heather remembered from when they were little.

"Fine," Heather said at last. "Whatever."

My name was Heather Gaugin. My parents' names were Gary and Helen Gaugin. My mom's maiden name was Campbell. Until I was seven, I lived on our family farm in New Russell. None of us called it the "Gaugin compound." That came from the newspapers in '91. It was just home to us.

We lived in the main house with my grandparents, Kevin and Maureen Gaugin, and my aunt Shauna Gaugin. There was my older brother, Kevin, my younger sisters, Emma and Jenny, and Shauna's daughters, Melanie and Kelly. There were also other buildings, and at different times, different members of our family lived out there. My uncles Mark and Danny lived in the loft above the barn, I think, and Shauna's son Jonathan lived up there, too. He was about sixteen, seventeen in '91. There was a big equipment shed, my uncle Mark used to live there with his wife, Arlene, and their son, Travis, but Arlene and Travis had left years before. Arlene was a Campbell, too. She and my mom were cousins. I think Arlene and Travis went back to live with her family in PEI. Anyway, no one lived in that building when I was little. We just used it to store farm equipment.

Us kids—Kevin (our grandparents called him Little Kevin since our poppy—our grandfather, I mean—was Kevin too), Melanie, and me—were officially homeschooled by my mom, but I don't remember any actual lessons or anything. I think my mom got the job of being our "teacher" because she was probably the most educated. She finished high school, and she'd done one year of university in Charlottetown when she met my dad. My sisters, Emma and Jennifer, and Shauna's girl, Kelly, were too little to start school, and Jonathan was old enough to leave school, to drop out or whatever, but we didn't talk about it like that. He was just old enough not to have to bother with any of it anymore.

My family had a few farm animals—we had cattle, some chickens, I think. There might have been more. I don't remember. There was a big vegetable garden, so I guess we probably grew a lot of our own food, but I remember that sometimes the adults would "go out to work" every now and then. Mostly in the summer. I think they'd take jobs as farm labourers up in the valley. That's how my dad and my uncle Mark met my mom and Arlene—working on the Campbell potato farm near Summerside, PEI. They came home that fall, and Mom and Arlene came back with them. I'm pretty sure "going out to work" meant some illegal stuff, too. Drugs and whatnot. I don't know. When I got older, after I left, I used to hear stories sometimes, about how livestock, farm equipment, other stuff used to go missing from farms around New Ross. Probably some of that was our family, but I think a lot of it was just convenient, you know? Something goes missing, Gaugins probably took it. Folks like to have someone to blame for when stuff goes bad.

Like I said, different family members lived with us, either in the house or in the outbuildings at different times. Sometimes someone would go out to work and just not come back. My Uncle Danny was living away for a long time, then he came back. I guess he had a kid while he was away. He used to talk about her sometimes. Desiree. He talked about sending her money, about going to get her and bring her home, but he never did. He didn't talk about Desiree's mother, whoever that was. I think he said Desiree lived in Halifax. It seemed like such a big, dangerous, exciting city when I was little, Halifax. My grandparents used to talk about my Aunt Gayle sometimes, too, but I never met her. I don't know where she went or when she left. I think she might have been my grandpa Kevin's sister, maybe. I'm not sure. I don't remember my dad or my aunt or uncles talking about her. Anyway.

I don't know why Social Services came when they did. I don't know why that's when they decided, "Okay, right now, we need to go out and save those kids." I guess there was that other family out near Wolfville a few years earlier, and things were really bad for those kids. They were in the news a lot, so that probably got the province all riled up, got them looking into all the old families like ours. But I mean, I don't think things had changed much for my family to trigger anything. It's not like anything had happened to make things any worse for us out there. My brother Kevin, my cousins Jonathan and Melanie were all older than me, and they didn't get much of an education. When anyone older than us thought we were doing something we shouldn't, we could get a swat on the backside. I used to get it for being smart-mouthed, or else for not doing what I was supposed to, looking out for you and the other little ones. I guess Shauna was rougher on her girls, but no one else was really smacking us kids around, you know? I don't know, maybe the boys were being hit. Maybe it was different for the girls. And nobody was messing with us. The uncles weren't perverted or whatever. So I don't know why someone decided that September 1991 was the time to come out and get all the kids and take them out of there. It probably wasn't even about the kids. Probably one of the adults went "out working" and stole the wrong thing from the wrong people, and the RCMP came out and Social Services just tagged along. Anyway.

We kids spent most of our time outside. Not a big surprise. It's not like we lived in a big house, and there were, what, ten people in a four-bedroom house. So we were outside, and I remember hearing a weird noise. We had a couple of old trucks and a farm tractor, but I don't think I'd ever seen a cop car or a fire truck or ambulance before. But that's what

I remember from that day—the sound of the police car's siren coming up the dirt road. I was fascinated by that flashing light. There were two white vans, and they loaded us kids up in them—me, my sister Emma, my cousin Melanie were together. My sister Jenny and Melanie's sister, Kelly, were babies. They went in another van. I don't know where they took the boys. Jonathan and Kevin. Maybe they got loaded in the back of cop cars, maybe they went with the babies, I don't know. I just remember sitting in the back of that van, staring at those flashing lights until two adults got into the front seats and drove us away. And that was that, I guess.

Heather stopped. Emma kept looking at her as though she expected to say more, but Heather just shifted the baby in her lap and took another swallow of tea. Emma stopped the recording on her laptop.

"Thank you," she said softly. She cleared her throat. "Have you ever been back out there? To the. Um. Compound?"

Heather shrugged. "I went out to have a look a couple times when I was a teenager. It was empty. Not much to see."

Emma turned her laptop around so the screen faced Heather. "I went out to take some pictures. Would you like to see them?"

Heather didn't answer, but she leaned forward, peering at the images of the ruined buildings, the overgrown yard. Charlotte reached for the screen. "You didn't take any pics of the inside of the house?"

Emma closed the computer, shaking her head. "Not yet. I'll need to go back out." She looked up suddenly. "Do you want to come with me?"

Heather was surprised. "When?"

Emma shrugged. "Whenever you want. I'm here until the end of next week."

Heather considered. Somehow, she didn't want Emma to tromp through the house by herself, taking photos of whatever she wanted. She felt oddly protective of the place. "How about Wednesday?"

"Sure," Emma agreed. She smiled suddenly, her first real smile since she'd arrived. Just like that, she looked familiar to Heather. Her little sister.

As Emma was leaving, she reached out to take Charlotte's little hand. Charlotte's fingers wrapped tightly around Emma's—her aunt's. "Goodbye," Emma said softly to Justin, who had taken off his headphones to watch the stranger leave.

"Bye," Justin replied politely. As soon as she was gone, he went back to his cartoons.

TWELVE

EMMA DROVE AWAY FROM THE PUBLICOVER HOUSE FILLED WITH GIDDY lightness. She'd done it. She'd seen her sister, talked to her. Heather was okay. She was living a nice life, by the looks of things. She had a house, a family, cute kids. And she didn't hate Emma for digging into their family history like this. Emma could see that Heather didn't *love* the idea of being researched, didn't quite trust Emma with their family story—with *their* story—but she didn't seem angry or hurt or betrayed at the idea of the research. That was something.

Emma wasn't exactly sure where she thought her sister would be by now, what she'd be like. She wondered whether she'd half-expected to find her back out at the Gaugin compound, isolated, wary as a wild animal, with a brood of dirty half-wild kids of her own…. She thought about that first trip out to the house on Taylor Lake. She'd been worried about so much that day, about how she'd feel when she saw the place, worried about what she'd find. But she realized that she hadn't worried about *who* she'd find, even though she knew that in the back of her mind, she'd come to Nova Scotia with the half-formed thought that the rest of the Gaugins had simply returned home, retreated back into the forest around Taylor Lake as soon as they were released from prison or foster care, or wherever else the authorities had dispersed them.

Well, perhaps some of them *had*, though they'd either left again a long time ago, or else they'd found a new home, deeper in the woods—somewhere they'd be less easy to find and round up. It occurred to Emma that she'd need to ask around, ask people like Jack Rushdie or Heather where the Gaugins were now. The thought flattened her elation instantly—actually asking where the rest of the family were, whether they were in prison or back in the woods, framing the words and putting them to Jack and Heather seemed impossible. And Emma realized that she hadn't asked her sister whether she was in touch with Kevin or Jenny, or any other family members, or what had happened to her after she was taken from the Weavers', or anything at all about her life. She should have asked. She should have asked to hold the baby—her niece!—or talk to the boy, her nephew. Shame flooded her, hot and oily under her skin.

The Publicovers lived on a road that let out on the west end of Chester. Emma had to drive through town to get back on the highway. The skin on the back of her hands and her chest was prickling uncomfortably as her emotion changed from excitement to shame. How had she not asked about her sister's life? Not for her research—for her sister. For herself. Emma didn't want to go back to the hotel to relive the conversation in solitude, to chide herself for every wrong question, every missed chance to really know her sister and her family. So she pulled off the main street, driving into the heart of the little seaside town. On her way to Heather's place, she'd seen a quaint-looking bakery with café tables inside. She'd noticed the long lineup at the counter, figured that meant it was a good place to eat. She found it again, and parked on the street out front. She was looking forward to the busy hum of a café, to being alone in a crowd, to being able to listen to the buzz of people without having to talk or expose herself to another situation where she could fumble, blunder, bumble her way through social niceties.

The day had started sunny, but it was clouding over now. It wasn't exactly raining, but there was a mistiness in the air she wasn't used to. Emma adjusted her light cotton scarf, pulling it right under her chin. As she walked toward the café, a woman, slight and with a bouncing step, emerged from the bank. Emma sidestepped, almost bumping into her. The woman looked up in surprise.

"Oh!" she said. "You." It was Sam, the archivist from the genealogical society.

Emma froze. The sight of Sam's open expression made Emma's own comment flood back to her ears: *Boring local history. Kind of bullshit.* In her mind, she saw Sam's expression falling, closing, hardening as she heard Emma's words. Again, shame flooded under Emma's skin. She opened her mouth to say *Hello* or *It's nice to see you* or some other reasonable greeting, and instead, only managed to stutter her own name: "Em-Emma."

Sam nodded, not unkindly. "I remember. Are you here doing more research?"

"No. Yes, but. Not." Emma stopped herself, took a breath. "I'm done for the day."

Sam tilted her head, looking carefully at Emma. "Are you okay?"

"Yes. Yup, all good," Emma replied. Her face burned painfully.

The corner of Sam's mouth twitched a little as though she wanted to smile, but she didn't. "Want to join me for a beer?"

"I was going to get coffee," Emma replied quickly, wishing she could just turn and run.

This time, Sam did smile. "We can get a coffee."

Emma nodded, and somehow, they were walking together toward the bakery. Sam waved to the cashier when they arrived and the girl waved back, familiar. *Small towns,* Emma thought. She felt a wave of envy rise in her chest. If the Weavers had stayed in Lunenburg, she might know the people she bought her coffee, her groceries, her gas from. She might be friendly with them. They might linger over the transaction and chit-chat about each other's lives. Or they might smile stiffly at her, then whisper to each other—*She's a Gaugin. No, really!*—as soon as her footsteps turned back towards the door.

Sam and Emma settled at a small table near the front window with their coffees and croissants. Emma wasn't hungry, but Sam had urged her to try one—"They're the best!" The bakery had a bit of a dingy small-town feeling: the tables were Formica-topped, the chairs were of the cheap chrome frame and stained upholstery variety, and the walls were papered with pink flowered wallpaper topped with a green-and-burgundy paper border. But the coffee was a good pour-over, as good as Emma had had in any Edmonton café, and the croissants were light and soft. The customers were an odd mix of trendy twentysomethings and dowdy women in their fifties and sixties. None of them seemed to notice the strangeness of the mix.

Sam stirred honey from a small jar on the table into her coffee, and Emma kept hearing herself drawl *boring local history*, kept seeing the hardening of Sam's expression at the end of their first meeting. "I was kind of an asshole," she blurted at last.

Sam looked up in surprise. "I'm sorry?"

"The last time," Emma blundered on. "I said local history was boring or something. I'm sorry. That wasn't what I meant."

"Oh?" Sam asked. "I don't remember." It was a lie, but a kind lie. Emma saw Sam's polite expression soften a touch as she said it.

"I didn't mean to be rude. I'm sorry."

"Nothing to be sorry for." Sam put down her spoon. "How's your research going?"

"Pretty well," Emma replied. She opened her mouth to say that she'd interviewed Heather, but stopped. Did Heather let on she was a Gaugin, or was that something she kept to herself? Maybe Sam knew Heather. Would she ask about Emma next time they ran into each other at the bank or the grocery store? And would Heather say, *Oh, the grad student? She's my sister. She's a Gaugin, too.*

"Any new historical leads?"

"No, not really. I've just been looking into the arrests and stuff in 1991."

Sam nodded thoughtfully. She tore off a small piece of croissant, sipped her coffee. "Have you looked into personal journals?" she said at last.

"Personal journals?"

Sam nodded. "We have the biggest archive of personal journals in the province. The earliest one is from 1782. I've been transcribing and scanning them to put them online, but I'm not even close to being finished yet. Still, there are a couple that mention the Gaugins."

"Really?" Emma felt a small bubble of excitement rise in her chest. Personal journals from the eighteenth and nineteenth centuries. This was the kind of material that was sure to impress Dr. Melnyk and Dr. Fuentes. No, it was more than that. Emma was excited about this research for her own sake. She felt suddenly hungry to delve into these sources, to read what the Gaugins' neighbours thought about them—privately, personally—without the editing and censoring of a public document. "Can I have a look?"

"Of course," Sam replied. "I can point out a couple that definitely mention the Gaugins. But you may have to wade through the rest to see if there's anything. Can you come by tomorrow morning? I'll be in, working on some other stuff until two or so."

"I didn't think you were open."

Sam flapped a hand in the air, waving off the question. "The opening hours are more of a suggestion."

"Sure. Hey, thank you."

"No problem." Sam rose, collecting her dishes and depositing them at the end of the bakery counter. The cashier smiled her thanks. "See you tomorrow?" Sam said to Emma.

"See you tomorrow."

After Sam had gone, Emma sat at the small table. *I should get out my computer*, she thought idly. Instead, she watched people walk past the café, and tried to pick out the tourists from the locals as the early summer sun slowly eased its light to the other side of the street. When she finally rose to drive back to her hotel, Emma felt warm and self-assured, as though she'd been sipping beer all afternoon, and not coffee.

THIRTEEN

JACK RUSHDIE SAT ON THE OLD BARSTOOL IN HIS STUDIO AND CONTEM-plated the painting he'd been working on. It had reached that exciting stage—it was turning out just a little different than how he'd planned it, like a teenager who was just discovering her own tastes and opinions and independence. Or at least, the way he imagined a teenager would be. Before she turned surly and disobedient and secretive. Of course, his experience with teenagers was pretty limited.

He remembered Heather as a teenager. She was exactly the opposite of the way he thinks most teenagers are. She seemed to feel that getting into trouble was a duty, an obligation. She had raised hell with a kind of resigned determination, but privately, she was a sweet kid. He'd run into her in Lunenburg or Mahone Bay, hanging out with rough older kids, and she'd always look down, quiet and ashamed—not of him, but of them.

He remembered once driving to pick her up at a classmate's house. She had brought weed to a slumber party, and the teenaged hostess had wound up drunk, stoned, and sick, throwing up on her mother's couch. It was just after midnight when the phone rang, waking Marian up. Jack was still awake, reading a Western novel in bed.

"Is this Heather's guardian?" a terse female voice demanded without saying *hello*.

Jack glanced at Marian, who was looking at him worriedly. "In a manner of speaking," he replied slowly.

"You need to come and pick her up. Now."

When he and Marian arrived, Heather was waiting on the front steps, looking hard and unconcerned. The hostess's parents barely opened the door to tell them in clipped tones what Heather had done. Jack could see the other girls peering out at them through the basement window. Heather didn't wait to hear the conclusion of the accusations—"She is not welcome in our home again," and a slammed front door. She strode down the sidewalk to Marian's car, her chin high, but as soon as she was in the back of the car, away from the stoned teenagers and stony parents, her cheeks flushed red. "I'm sorry," she whispered, her voice choked and tiny. She was perfectly sober. She'd been, what? Thirteen or fourteen. Instead of going back to her foster home, she spent the night on their couch. As she often did.

He'd been waiting for Heather to call him, to tell him about meeting Emma. He imagined Marian chiding him to be patient with her every time he picked up his phone. But she hadn't called or emailed yet. Finally, he sent a text: "Did you meet the girl?" He stared patiently at his phone.

It didn't take long for the reply to buzz in his hand: "Yup."

He frowned, his thumbs hovering over the touch screen. Finally, he typed "How'd it go?"

Right away: "Fine. Not much to report."

He sighed, setting his phone screen-down on his paint-stained worktable. "That girl," he murmured to the silent studio.

FOURTEEN

WHEN EMMA GOT TO THE ARCHIVES, THE PARKING LOT WAS EMPTY
and the windows were still dark, reflecting the bright morning sunlight
from outside. She drove back down to the main street to the little café
she and Sam had visited the day before. She paid for her coffee, then
turned back to the counter to order another for the archivist. It had been
nice of Sam to tell Emma about the journals. She tucked some extra
sugar packets into her jeans pocket and hoped Sam didn't take cream.

By the time she got back, the lights were on in the Genealogical
Society offices, and there were three other cars in the lot. Emma slung
her laptop bag onto her shoulder, careful not to spill the coffee in the
rental car.

"Good morning," she called as she came through the archive doors.

Sam's head appeared from behind a bookshelf. "Hey!" She waved
at the coffees. "One of those for me?"

Emma nodded. "I didn't know what you take, so…."

Sam curved her hands around the cup and breathed in its scent.
"Black's good. You are a lifesaver." She took a slow sip.

Emma shifted her weight from one foot to the other. "So, the
journals?"

"Right." Sam thrust her chin toward the shelf she'd been working
on when Emma arrived. "This is our private journal collection." She
gestured to the third row from the top. Just over half the shelf was

filled with journals—some cloth-bound, a couple leather-bound, and a couple of older coil-ring notebooks at the right end. "They're organized by date of first entry. These are the oldest." She gestured at the small leather-bound volumes on the left. "I've archived about up to here." She pointed to a marker about a third of the way across the shelf. "These three mention Gaugins. None of the rest do—at least to this point. After that, you'll have to go through them all on your own. And you'll have to look through them here. They can't leave the archives." She pointed at Emma's coffee. "And that—not near the journals."

Emma nodded. "Got it." She set her cup down on the corner of Sam's desk and settled down at the long table.

The journals that Sam had already gone through mentioned the Gaugins in only the most cursory way, but Sam had a near-photographic memory of their contents. "This one mentions the Gaugins about a third of the way through," she said, handing Emma the first volume, a small brown leather-bound book with a flap that tied shut. "Look on the left side, near the top of the page." The second journal, she said, had an entry in about June of the first year, near the first quarter of the book. The final journal, a pretty volume with an embossed blue fabric cover, had a mention right near the middle of the book.

Emma photographed these journals, recording the information about the Gaugins in her laptop as she went.

In 1802, Jeremiah Davidson recorded the sale of a three-year-old milk cow to Mr. Gaugin of Russell Settlement. He noted the transaction in his brown leather journal, which was mostly a narrative ledger of his farming. In 1822, Eleanor Schwartz of Lunenburg mentioned her cousin Henry Schwartz's wedding to Julia Gaugin. She was unhappy not to be allowed to go to the wedding in Halifax with her mother, who, Eleanor wrote, described the bride to her as a "small woman and handsome." She mentioned Julia's parents, who attended the wedding, but she wrote that her mother told her they "did not at all seem" *something*. Emma couldn't decipher the blotched, faded writing. She asked Sam, but Sam just shook her head.

"Some of these are pretty illegible," she said. "There are whole sections of the Schwartz journal I couldn't figure out at all. Water damage."

Jane Moore's blue 1847 journal also mentions a Gaugin wedding. The tone of this entry was strikingly different from Eleanor Schwartz's mention of Julia Gaugin's wedding a quarter century earlier. Jane's sister Mary "went off and shamed the family by marrying Peter Gaugin." Mary was apparently not Jane's favourite sister. "I never thought Mary could do much better anyhow," she wrote, "and I won't be sorry not to sit next to her in church anymore." Emma wondered what had happened in years between 1822 and 1847 to change the way the Gaugins were perceived in the community.

Emma snapped careful photos, wrote her notes in a table that organized the information by date, author, and town. Mike would be proud.

Sam had only catalogued the private journals up to 1855, so Emma would have to go through each later journal individually to look for more details about local families' interactions with the Gaugins. It was slow going. There were only a dozen or so more journals, but the writing was dense and looping, and hard to read. Some of the volumes had water damage, as Sam had warned her, and Emma had to squint to make out the words. And the contents of the volumes themselves were mostly tedious. Some were like Jeremiah Davidson's: a record of fishing catches, of farm plantings and harvests, of livestock and farm tools. The women's journals were usually dry accounts of marriages and deaths, births, church socials, and rural fairs. Occasionally, a younger woman's journal might include her feelings about her brothers and sisters, or about young men in the community—"Diana says that George Watkins is very handsome but Diana's brother William is much more handsome I think"—and sometimes a married woman's journal might hint at her true feelings about the neighbours—"I seen Martha Gregg in town and she looked quite well, she might of sent over a small thing for the wedding but she did not so theres an end to that"—but for the most part, the books were an account of the most mundane details of early rural life in Nova Scotia.

At noon, Sam nudged Emma's shoulder. Emma was reading about Samuel Conrad's fishing boat, which had to be painted once again. Her shoulders ached from leaning over the book, and her eyes felt dry and scratchy. "I'm going out for some lunch," Sam said. "Come with?"

Emma nodded and rose slowly, stretching her stiff back. "You don't mind?"

"It'll be nice to have someone to talk to. I usually eat alone."

They walked together to a diner off the main street. "You like burgers?" Sam asked. "They have the best ones here."

They settled in with their burgers and sweet potato fries at a table near the front door and watched tourists strolling up and down the street taking pictures of the brightly painted Victorian houses.

"It'll be really busy in a couple of weeks," Sam explained, "as soon as school lets out. Right now, it's all seniors."

"You have kids in school?" Emma asked.

Sam nodded. "Two. Sarah's fourteen and Henry's twelve. Sarah wants to help out at the archives this summer."

"That'll be nice," Emma replied.

Sam smiled. "We'll see how long it lasts." She finished her own fries and helped herself to one of Emma's. Emma found it oddly touching, this easy familiarity, as though they were old friends.

"So, do you know any Gaugins?" Emma asked carefully. She watched Sam's face, looking for signs of—what? Fear? Revulsion? Something Sam might not have given away at work, in her professional position as an archival historian helping a researcher find documents.

Sam shrugged. "I don't think so." She munched on another fry. "There's Heather Publicover, I guess. She was a Gaugin."

"You know Heather?"

"Sure. She's a bookkeeper. She does our taxes every year. She was one of the kids who lived out there. You've met her?"

Emma nodded carefully. "Yeah. Yeah, I got in touch." Sam took another of Emma's fries, and Emma felt ashamed suddenly to be keeping a secret from her. "The thing is, she's my sister." Emma leaned back in her seat and flashed her old faithful swaggering smile.

Sam looked up. Her face was surprised, yes, but not horrified, not repulsed. "Your sister?"

Emma nodded. "Yup." She took a bite of her burger, trying to maintain her veneer, protective and unflappable. "I was one of the kids too. I was really young, though, and the Weavers adopted me and we moved out west, and…." She shrugged.

"Huh." Sam stirred her lemonade thoughtfully. "Is that why you're researching the family?"

"Sort of. It *is* my thesis research," Emma said. "It was kind of my professor's idea, though."

Sam snorted. "Makes me kind of glad I didn't go to university. No offence."

Emma shook her head to say *None taken.*

"So you're from here, then. You grew up on the Gaugin compound."

"I guess. I don't really remember."

"Huh," Sam said again.

"Do you…" Emma began, then stopped. "What was it like, here?"

"What do you mean?"

"I mean, are there stories about the Gaugins? Like, now?" Emma cleared her throat, fumbling for words. "Like, do people talk about them still sometimes?"

"Sure," Sam said. "Sometimes."

Emma waited, but Sam didn't say more. Instead, she gathered up the empty wrappers onto their plastic tray and cleared the table. "Ready to head back?"

Emma nodded, following her.

As they started back up the hill towards the Genealogical Society, Sam turned to Emma. "There are a few more journals," she said, "but we don't have them. They belong to a family who's lived around here forever. But I could probably talk Brendan Inglis into letting you have a look."

"That would be great."

"Do you want me to tell him…."

Emma shook her head. "Can you just say I'm a researcher?"

"Sure."

As Sam unlocked the door to let them back into the Genealogical Society offices, she looked at Emma, her head tilted slightly. "Hang on," she said, and darted back into the stacks. She returned seconds later with a small black fabric-bound book. "Here," she said.

Something about the way Sam looked at it made Emma's heart flutter. She turned it over in her hands. There were traces of gold lettering on the spine and the front cover, but the words themselves had been lost long ago. Emma opened it carefully.

The first line was printed in heavy black ink: *Holy Bible*. Beneath it, hard-written, a name: *J. Gaugin*. A family Bible.

For a second, Emma felt deflated. She had expected, what? Answers? The key to the Gaugins, to who they'd been, and who they'd become? She turned the page over, already knowing what she'd see. A list of names and dates: births, marriages, deaths.

"The provincial archives keeps marriage records going back to 1763, but the registry of births and deaths only goes as far back as 1864," Sam explained, her face glowing with excitement. She jabbed her finger carefully at the page. "Look."

The first birth listed was Paul Gaugin, 1791. Born to James Gaugin and Alice Gaugin (née Bent). Their marriage is recorded as 1790. The Bible, it seemed, originally belonged to James Gaugin, but his death was recorded in a slightly narrower handwriting: August 17, 1834. Alice died a few years later in March of 1837. Emma scanned the lists, which ended in 1842. Some of the other names in the Bible looked familiar, but not all of them.

Emma felt a surge of guilt. Sam had clearly been excited to share this with her. And it was the kind of thing that would normally make Emma's mind hum. Only now, she had to tamp down the dull disappointment, the ghost of hope that this would have been something richer. She turned the pages carefully and noticed that James, or one of his descendants, had marked their favourite passages. She stopped to read one of the verses that was carefully and lightly underlined so that the ink wouldn't bleed through the page.

Ephesians 5:25. *Husbands, love your wives, even as Christ also loved the church, and gave himself for it.*

Had James loved Alice? Is that why he'd underlined that verse? Or did he need the reminder to love as a duty, a chore?

Emma looked at Sam, who was still beaming slightly at her.

"Thank you," she said. Sam nodded and winked, and Emma felt the weight of the guilt lift just a little.

She took the Bible to the table and carefully made notes, photographing the handwritten family records and the underlined passages, wondering whose favourites they were. Was it religious devotion, or a love of the words, the sentiments themselves? Was there a difference? The Weavers had never been religious, and Emma certainly couldn't remember going to church before she'd gone to live with them. She didn't know if there was a difference, or if it mattered.

It took about an hour to go through the Bible. The rest of the afternoon, Emma waded through about half of the remaining journals. Though some of them were hard to read—Edward Dauphinee's journal was water-stained, and the ink had all but washed away in the lower half of the pages—most of the handwriting gradually became less cramped and looping, the pages less yellowed, as she read her way into the twentieth century.

She found only two further mentions of the Gaugins. In August 1907, Sarah Jordan noted that George Gaugin was seen riding a horse that looked very much like Charles Matheson's mare, which had gone missing the previous spring. And in 1911, Donald Marchand overheard his eldest daughter, Elizabeth, tell her sister Flora that Henry Gaugin looked well. He promised to tan her hide if he caught her looking that way at one of the Gaugin boys again.

Emma still had a half-dozen or so journals to comb through when Sam snapped off the humming lights overhead. It was just a gesture, really. Clear June sunlight more than filled the space.

"Time to go, grad student," Sam said, brisk but not unfriendly. "I got places to be. But you can come back tomorrow."

Emma made a quick note in her laptop to remind herself where she was leaving off, then gathered her things. "Can't tomorrow," she said. "I have to go back to get more photos of the compound." *With Heather*, she reminded herself, fluttering somewhere between excitement and dread.

"Okey doke." Sam locked the door behind them and followed Emma down the hallway. "You know where to find our schedule."

"Yep. Thanks, Sam."

"Cheers, any time." And she smiled at Emma as they parted in the parking lot.

On the way home, Emma called her mom, knowing she wouldn't answer. Julia would be at yoga this time of day.

"Hey, Mom. Just wanted to let you know the research is going really well, and I'm fine. Love you. Hug Dad for me."

And she was fine, she reflected as she drove. No panic attacks, no anxiety she couldn't manage. But she knew she'd have a rough time convincing her mom it was true. She groaned at the thought of having one of those conversations with her mother—the kind where she had to insist over and over that really, she truly was okay. Julia worried. Who could blame her?

FIFTEEN

WHEN EMMA WAS IN GRADE ONE, BACK WHEN THE WEAVERS STILL LIVED in Lunenburg, back when Emma was still Emma Helen Gaugin, a boy in her class, Matt Jacobs, told her what his parents had told him about the Gaugins. Emma could never remember afterwards what brought on the revelation, but she remembers the look on his face—open and matter-of-fact, clean of any malice.

"My dad says your family are drunks and thieves," Matt said. "He says your house was filthy."

They were in the hallway outside her classroom, and she felt all of the air in the whole school suddenly crush her. It was the word *filthy* that clung to her, as though it itself were dirt caked on her skin. "My house isn't filthy," she said, barely able to manage a whisper.

Two girls had been standing on either side of her—Jennifer Crosby and Kristie Cuthbert. But they edged away from her, leaving her standing alone next to a bulletin board with pictures of different musical instruments tacked up on it.

"Not your new parents," Matt said. "The Gaugins. My dad said you couldn't stay at your house with them anymore because your house was too filthy, and your parents and the other grownups are drunks and thieves."

"It's not true," Emma whispered. But she felt uncertain. She couldn't really remember her parents' house. But she thought of the

Weavers, who went through a list of cleaning chores every week, and even gave Emma an allowance for helping with the vacuuming and the dusting. She couldn't remember her parents or her grandparents or her aunts or uncles having a list of cleaning to be done. Farm work, yes; she remembered the uncles and her father working in the barn. She remembered her mother and her aunt cooking meals in the kitchen. But she couldn't remember any cleaning.

Maybe it was true, then. Maybe her house had been filthy.

Then when the Weavers adopted her, when they changed her last name, she had felt so relieved, like the grime was covered over, painted fresh with a new name.

She can't remember any other comments about her family—her first family—but when she thinks of the time before she was a Weaver, she can hear the weight of the word *Gaugin* in other people's mouths—the disgust, the fear, the barely contained secret thrill. The filth of the word.

She was wary when she arrived in Edmonton. She listened for the word when adults came to the Weavers' house, or when they talked to her parents in the restaurant, when children talked to each other in the playground or the lunch hall at school, but she never heard that name. She watched her teachers' faces when they called her name on the first day of classes—*Emma Gaugin Weaver*—but her new middle name sounded light and clean here, no different from the way *Helen* or *Weaver* sounded in Nova Scotia.

One day, in art class, Emma had said something to the girls sharing her table. She doesn't remember what she said, but she remembers Priya Viswanathan's reply: "You say it wrong. It's not *youse*, it's just *you*."

Emma felt the words firm up in her mouth, like cement. Her insides went cold and her face went hot, and nothing she did could stop the tears from oozing down her face. She snuffled, not wanting to wipe her runny nose because if she wiped her face, the movement would draw attention to her and the other kids would see that she was crying. She kept cutting out leaf shapes from the construction paper in front of her.

Of course, they saw anyway. Priya jabbed her hand up into the air. "Ms. Bell," she called urgently, "Emma is crying!"

The teacher rushed over to their table and crouched down, her soft, loose flowered shirt brushing Emma's hot face, the tears making little dark marks between the printed flowers. "What's the matter, Emma?"

Emma shook her head and kept cutting, not wanting to let out any more odd funny words like *youse*. Because she could remember her mom yelling out the back door at Emma and her sister: "Youse kids stay out of the barn! Your uncles are working up in there." *Youse* was a Gaugin word. A dirty word like *shit* and *fuck*—words she remembered her brother and her uncles and her cousins using. Words that the Weavers never, ever used.

"Priya said she uses funny words," Dana offered when Emma remained silent, her eyes turning to Priya with the kind of subtle malevolence that only children can muster.

"I didn't! She just has an accent," Priya explained, her voice rising in pitch. "But I didn't make fun! My grandparents have an accent because they're from India. But Emma's accent is different."

"It's all right, Emma," Ms. Bell said, patting Emma's shoulder. "It's nothing to be ashamed of. I don't think Priya meant any harm."

"I didn't!" Priya said earnestly.

"Go to the bathroom and wash your face, Emma. There's no reason to cry."

Emma remembers the months, or even years, that followed as completely silent. She vowed not to talk at school until she could be sure that she was speaking properly, until she'd warded herself against any other Gaugin words. She remembers listening carefully to the teachers, her classmates, and to the Weavers, making sure she said the words exactly as they did. Of course, she couldn't have stopped talking altogether. If she'd gone completely silent, surely the teachers and guidance counsellors would have intervened. She must have spoken. But she doesn't remember it.

She does remember her first Christmas in Alberta. The Weavers had gathered at Mike's parents' big house in the river valley. *Your grandparents' house*, Julia and Mike called it. Emma still hadn't got used to thinking of them that way, though, of thinking of herself as one of the Weavers—not really and truly.

After Christmas dinner, Emma was sitting on the carpet with cousin Nadine, playing a board game that Nadine had gotten for Christmas. Emma was only vaguely aware of the adult conversation that buzzed around them when she was startled out of the game by Uncle Shawn's big, rolling laugh.

Emma's turn, and she counted out the spaces on the board aloud.

"Where'd your Nova Scotia accent go, Emma?" His smile was kind but still; Emma felt trapped, pinned by his attention, by everyone's attention now.

"I don't know," she managed, confused by the question.

"When you first got to Edmonton, you sounded like such a little Maritimer. Now, you wouldn't even know."

Julia smiled. "It's true. I never even noticed."

Then the festive adult conversation pinged away from her, landing on something else. Nadine reminded Emma it was her turn to play, but Emma's head was swimming. *Nova Scotia accent*. Was that what it was? It wasn't her family that had warped her language. It was just the way Nova Scotians talked. She felt a wave of relief wash over her. So her classmates, Priya, Ms. Bell, they didn't know. They didn't know who she'd been before she was Emma Weaver. They didn't know what the Gaugins were. They only knew she'd been Nova Scotian.

But now she wasn't. She was a Weaver, like her parents, and she sounded just like the rest of the Weavers. She'd managed to scrub away her past.

SIXTEEN

THE ALARM ON EMMA'S PHONE STARTLED HER AWAKE. SHE WAS surprised. Normally, she'd be awake before it went off, her body tense and waiting for the jingling sound of her phone, her mind already bouncing around all the things that could go wrong and scrambling for solutions to every scenario. But not this morning. This morning, Emma had been sound asleep. She'd been dreaming about cats—there were a bunch of cats outside, and there was a storm coming. She needed to get all the cats safe inside before the rain started. Her head still foggy from the dream, she rolled out of bed and shuffled to the tiny hotel bathroom.

As she got out of the shower, she checked her phone. No messages from Heather. She briefly worried that she should have called last night, confirmed their plans, made sure that Heather was still coming with her today. She typed a short message, pausing to change the greeting from *Good morning!* to *Hey.* to *Hi, Heather.*

Hi, Heather. We still on for today? I can pick you up at 9.

She stared at the phone for a moment, then turned away to find her clothes and pack her backpack. As she tucked away the bug spray, a bag of apples and granola bars, and a backup charger for her camera, her phone pinged back: *OK. See you then.*

Emma headed down to the lobby for breakfast. The bartender-waiter-desk clerk from her first evening in the hotel—Glen, she remembered—was refilling a vat of waffle batter.

"Good morning," he said.

She gave him a half-smile and a mumbled reply as she helped herself to toast and coffee. She was the only hotel guest eating her breakfast in the lobby. She set her food down at a little table near a window with a view of the parking lot.

Glen finished refilling the breakfast bar and retreated to the back room with his food cart. He re-emerged moments later and strolled over to Emma's table. He sat down opposite her with a warm smile.

"Emma, right? How's the research going?"

Emma swallowed her mouthful of toast, feeling off-balance by his friendly familiarity. "Good," she said, trying to remember what she'd told him about her work. "I'm going out to photograph the site again today."

"Nice. Have you been busy with the work, or did you get a chance to check out Halifax this weekend?"

"I've mostly been working, but I've been into the city a bit."

"Well, let me know if you'd like me to show you around this week. I'm working mostly days."

"Um. Thanks."

Glen smiled again and stood. "See you later."

"Yup."

He returned to the back room, and Emma munched on her toast, contemplating the exchange. He was cute, friendly. At home, she might consider accepting his invitation, but here, it just seemed like too much to plan, to think about. Though truthfully, even when she was at home, Emma was more likely to make excuses than to make plans. Leaving her apartment, getting dressed up, making conversation with strangers, it all seemed so exhausting so much of the time.

At 8:15, Emma's phone pinged to reminder her it was time to get on the road. She stacked up her breakfast dishes and headed out to the parking lot. Before she got started, she gathered up the empty coffee cup and a handful of receipts and empty granola bar wrappers from the front seat of the rental and dumped them into the garbage can by the hotel's front doors. She loaded her backpack into the back seat and headed back down the highway to Chester.

As Emma pulled into Heather's driveway, the front door of the house opened. Heather and Justin emerged. She gave the boy a quick kiss on the head and he stood on the front step, watching his mom get into Emma's rental. Emma gave him a tentative little wave. He didn't wave back, just looked at her, his dark eyes frankly curious, perhaps also a little suspicious.

"Morning," Heather greeted her as she got into the car.

"Morning. Did you have to get a babysitter so you could come out with me?"

"Nope. Rafe—my husband's day off."

"Oh." Emma turned the car around and pulled back out onto the dirt road, not sure whether she was supposed to ask about Rafe or not. What was her relationship to Heather, really? Was she supposed to treat her like a fellow researcher, another subject like Jack Rushdie or Sam? A sister? She searched for something to say. "Your kids are really cute," she managed at last.

"I like them," Heather replied.

"Your husband—Rafe? What does he do?"

"He's an electrician," Heather replied. "Works mainly in commercial and industrial."

"Oh."

"You're not married?" Heather asked, glancing at Emma's hands on the steering wheel. "Do you have someone?"

"No. Not right now."

Heather nodded.

"I was—there was a guy, Adrian. He started a PhD program in England last year. So."

"You guys decided not to do a long-distance thing."

"Yeah," Emma replied, though really, they had never discussed it. Adrian had been a teaching assistant for a Political Science class Emma had taken while she was getting her Bachelor's. They'd dated a year or so, and the whole while Adrian had been applying to PhD programs, none of them in Edmonton. The end of their relationship the previous August had seemed inevitable. He flew out early in the month, and the last week he'd stayed at her apartment. She gave him a ride to the airport, kissing him goodbye on the sidewalk. No tears, no promises. They still spoke online sometimes. Emma couldn't say that she really missed him. She'd liked being with him. He was good-looking and smart, and he had this appreciative way of looking at her that made her feel daring and edgy, but that was it. He made her feel like her show of daringness, her smart-ass facade, was convincing. It felt good in a way, but hollow, too. Now that he was gone, she sometimes wondered what Adrian would have made of her if he'd spent time with her when she was home, meticulously going over her notes and readings. If he'd seen her when she was trying to say and do things to keep that look of worry off her mother's face. What would he make of her then?

"That's hard," Heather said.

"Mm."

They didn't say anything else until they turned off at Taylor Lake.

"Do you ever come out here? Camping or swimming or whatever?" Emma asked, glancing at the neat, pretty cabins along the gravel road.

Heather shook her head. "Rafe's parents have a cottage on the Shubenacadie River. Northeast of here, near Stewiacke," she added, gesturing vaguely. "We go up there a few times a year."

Emma pulled the car off the end of the road, parking it on a flat, grassy spot. "Ready?"

Emma hoisted on her backpack, and Heather slung her small bag across her chest. She followed Emma onto the trail through the woods. They didn't talk as they walked, but Emma found the crunching sound of Heather's footsteps behind her comforting. She half-wished Heather had been able to join her on the first visit.

As they approached the clearing, Heather's steps slowed.

"We're almost there," Emma said.

"I know." Heather stopped. She grasped the strap of the bag where it was slung across her chest and stood, gazing at the thick growth that stood between them and the compound.

"You okay?" Emma asked.

"Fine." Heather let go of the strap, her hand falling to her side as she walked on.

As the two of them rounded a clump of caragana, the first outbuildings came into view. Emma glanced at Heather, trying to make out what this woman—her sister—was thinking. Heather waved her hand impatiently near her temple, batting away some flying insect or other, her expression flickering annoyance at the bugs. Nothing else. Emma slung her backpack off her shoulder to retrieve her camera.

"Ready?" she asked.

Heather nodded. Together, they made their way around the back of the house.

As Emma passed behind the kitchen door, her pants snagged on a tangle of thorns. Raspberry bushes. And further back, near the rambling line of caraganas, blackberry bushes arched and dove into the thicket of weeds and grasses. At the far end, furthest from the house, Emma thought she recognized blueberry bushes. She bent down and cleared away some long green stalks at her feet to reveal strawberry plants beneath, their tender stems trailing in among the leaves and dangling thumbnail-sized green fruits.

"I think I found the garden," Emma called. She hadn't noticed it before, and she stopped to snap a photo of the rambling, diving blackberry bushes whose white blossoms, she noticed, were just starting to open.

Heather, who was standing in a patch of sunlight, her hands slipped into her back pockets as she contemplated a broken upstairs window, glanced over. "That's ours," she said.

"Ours?"

Heather nodded and took a few slow steps towards the berry patch. "Yours and mine," she replied. Emma looked at her, uncomprehending. "We used to love berries. Blueberries were your favourite, and I liked blackberries. Mom used to call them Blackberry Snackberries. So Mom got Dad and one of the uncles, Danny I think, to clear this section so we could put in a berry patch. She let us help, though I don't imagine we actually got much done, we were so little. But we used to come out here all the time with our little shovels to weed, and with bowls from the kitchen to pick the berries when they were ripe."

Emma trailed her gaze across the tangle of bushes and weeds. "I don't remember," she said.

"You were pretty small."

"So were you."

Heather shrugged. She turned and pointed to a low, weedy area along the west side of the house. "That was the vegetable garden. Nanny and Poppy used to take care of it, until they got too old and Mom and Auntie took over."

Emma looked at the garden, trying to imagine herself, her younger self, digging and weeding and berry picking. None of it seemed familiar. Was Heather sure it was her? Maybe it had been their cousin, not Emma at all.

Heather put her hand on the kitchen door handle. "You ready?"

The door didn't want to open. It was wedged against the rough wood of the floor. Emma braced one foot against the doorframe and pushed her back against the door until it ground open a few inches further. She'd be able to squeeze through, she judged, but Heather's bigger frame wouldn't fit. She pushed again and the door slid open a few more inches before stopping solidly.

"Think we can make it?" Emma asked.

"You can," Heather replied drily.

Emily slipped through the doorway. Heather followed, her breasts squeezing through the narrow gap.

The inside of the house smelled thick, mossy, dusty. Emma stood for a moment, letting her eyes adjust to the dim. Next to her, Heather took a few tentative steps into the house.

"Careful," Heather said. "Some of these floorboards feel soft."

They were in the kitchen. There was still a square wooden table in the centre of the room and one chair that had fallen forward on a broken leg. Emma's gaze moved across to the countertop that ran the length of the wall under the window. The sink was filled with the dead leaves that littered the corners of the room, of the counter. There was a spot near the end of the counter where it looked like a fridge had once stood, and a yellowed stove that looked like it was from the '60s or '70s opposite. Emma wondered where the fridge had gone.

"Is there electricity here?" Emma asked, looking at the warped coils of the stove.

"There was. NS Power took the lines out years ago, after I was out of high school, I think." Heather opened a cupboard door above the counter. "Here, look at this."

Plates and mugs were still stacked neatly inside. Mismatched, the stacks uneven. The top plate was white, rimmed with a blue flower pattern. Emma snapped a picture. "Do you remember any of this?" she asked.

Heather nodded. "A bit. You?"

"No," Emma said. But that was not quite true. The light from the window splashing on the counter, the milled table legs, the blue flower pattern on the plate—it all felt familiar, like an echo somewhere in the back of her memory. She had a sense of herself standing in the corner, there, her back pressed against the wall, as adults' legs weaved and shifted around her.

Emma took a photo of the old oven, its door blackened and grimy.

In the corner of the kitchen, near the back door, there was a dirty plastic accordion door. Emma eased it open, expecting a closet. Instead, she found a toilet, mercifully empty and dried out, and a smashed pedestal sink. "Main bathroom's upstairs," Heather said.

They moved carefully through the kitchen doorway into the living room. Here, some of the floorboards had splintered and fallen inward. They didn't dare venture in any further. On the wall that separated the kitchen from the living room, the flower pattern of the wallpaper was still visible. An old couch, its cushions deeply troughed and its fabric grimy and tattered, was pulled halfway into the centre of the room. The window behind it was smashed, and the floor between the couch and the wall was strewn thickly with leaves and branches. The fabric was too water-stained and dirty to reveal its former colour, but Emma had a vague memory of a scratchy velvet-like fabric patterned with gold flowers. She could almost feel its rough upholstery on the skin of her cheek.

Emma snapped photos of the room. She was aware of her racing heart, the jumpiness in her limbs, but her guts didn't have that jumping, squishing feeling that signalled a full-blown panic attack was on its way.

"No way we can go upstairs," Heather said, pointing at the staircase. The bottom two steps were rotted through and the handrail had partially fallen outward, leaning crazily into the living room.

"Those the bedrooms?" Emma asked. She had a memory of bare feet going up those stairs, the stretchy jersey fabric of her pyjamas too short, her ankles and wrists sticking out.

Heather nodded. "Except Nanny and Poppy. They slept in there." She pointed at a half-closed door across the living room. Emma took a photo of the door, of the dark gap beyond it. As she lowered her camera, a gust of wind wrapped itself around the house. Dried leaves blew in swirls in front of the broken windows. The whole house seemed to heave and sigh, creaking disconcertingly.

"We should probably get out of here," Emma said.

"Yup," Heather agreed.

Emma edged through the doorway then held her hand out to Heather, who squeezed back through the narrow gap. As she emerged, another gust of wind shouldered the house heavily. Something inside fell with a crash.

Heather gave Emma a half-smile. "Probably not the safest thing we've ever done."

"Probably not," Emma agreed.

"So how much do you remember from this place?"

Emma shrugged. "Not much. More like impressions than real memories, you know?"

"Yup."

"It's weird, though. I remember so much from those first days with my—with the Weavers. But almost nothing from here, and it was the same time, the same day, even."

Heather nodded.

"How about you?" Emma asked. "Seems like you remember a lot from living here."

"More than you, I guess. But I was older." Heather tilted her head and smiled. "Also, we used to come out here and party when I was in high school."

"Why?"

Heather half-raised a shoulder. "Because we could. As soon as my friends got their licenses, we'd drive to the end of the road, hike in, camp out and drink all weekend." She jerked her chin in the direction of the front of the house. "The broken living room window? I did that. It was an accident...sort of."

Emma shook her head. "No way you would have got me back here when I was a kid."

"No?"

"Hell no. I can't believe you'd want to do that." Emma felt the shadow of a stomach quake, the ghost of how she would have felt if someone had suggested she camp out here in high school.

Heather blinked slowly, the gesture half-eyeroll, half-shrug. "When you grow up in a small town, you're always looking for places to go party," she said. "We'd tell our parents we were camping, then look for somewhere we didn't actually have to put up a tent. I was dating a guy in high school, Kyle, and he said we should come party out here. I could tell he thought I'd say no way, like he was daring me without saying so. I think he was freaked out when I said okay."

Emma swallowed, then forced her half-smirk to cover the emotion. "I wouldn't have," she said. "I'd have been more likely to come out here with a can of gasoline and a lighter, burn this whole fucking place to the ground."

Heather didn't smile. Her eyebrows jerked upward in a rather motherly show of disapproval. "Why do you do that?"

Emma faltered. She knew she'd miscalculated, but she wasn't really sure how to correct course now. She refreshed her smirk. "What?"

Heather shot her a withering look. "I'm supposed to think you were a real badass? Is that it?"

Emma turned, walked a few steps away from the house. There was a soft-looking mound of moss. She sat down, not looking at her sister. "Not really. No."

Heather sat down beside her. They were facing the east side of the house, where there were still vestiges of white paint. Emma stared at the flaking wooden walls. Whose job had it been to paint the house? She thought about the baby blue vinyl siding on the front of Uncle Shawn and Auntie Jean's house in Edmonton. Four houses on their street had the exact same siding. Two of the houses, in fact, looked exactly the same from the outside. Emma had noticed that there were only five different house designs on the block. They were all just copies of each other, with some minor differences—the colour of the siding, the front door, the type of fence that screened off the backyard. Elaine had lived in one of those houses, across from Uncle Shawn and Auntie Jean's next-door neighbours.

Elaine was Emma's best friend. Emma knew it was so because one afternoon when Emma and her parents were visiting Shawn and Jeanette, Elaine invited Emma to come read books in her room. As they passed Elaine's mother in the kitchen, Elaine had casually called over her shoulder, "Mom, this is my best friend, Emma." And Emma's chest had glowed with unexpected pleasure.

Elaine was the toughest girl Emma had ever known. There were some "tough girls" at Emma's school who liked to threaten to fight other girls, and who shoplifted and boasted about getting drunk on the weekend, who wore dark eye shadow and tight, high ponytails, but when Emma and Elaine became friends, those girls stopped making her feel nervous. Compared to Elaine's unflappable stillness, those girls seemed chattering, puffed-up. Emma knew they'd never threaten to fight Elaine if they caught her looking at them wrong.

But Elaine never looked at anyone wrong. That was the other thing Emma liked about her. Sure, she thought Nadine was a bitch, and she'd said so, but she didn't much seem interested in gossiping about other girls. And Emma suspected that other girls probably didn't gossip a lot about Elaine.

That's because Elaine left nothing to gossip about. If she caught someone staring at her, she'd ask whether they were looking at her fat ass. She was quick to call herself fat, disarming the word in that lazy way of hers. If someone were to ever call her fat, Emma knew what she'd do—she'd shrug and say, "Yeah? So what?"

She also farted in public. Loudly. Once, she farted in the living room, and her mother shook her head wearily and said, "Laine..." in a way that meant she'd asked Elaine not to fart like that many, many times before, and she didn't really expect Elaine to start listening now. Elaine had just glanced at her mom with her teasing half-smile, a smile that her mother returned, despite herself, it seemed.

And Elaine announced when she had her period. "On the rag," she'd tell Emma as she headed to the washroom. The girls in Emma's class never, ever let it be known that they were menstruating. Trips to the washroom had to be stealthy, the used pads and tampons slipped noiselessly into the school washroom's clanking metal garbage bins. But Elaine didn't care who knew. And who would make fun of her for it—for any of it? What would be the point?

For a long time, Emma simply admired Elaine's confidence, her ballsiness. Elaine didn't seem care what anyone thought about her. That was, until one weekend when Elaine was sleeping over at Emma's. They'd gone together to the mall to get smoothies. They were sitting in the food court sipping the thick purple drinks when some girls from Emma's school walked past. Usually, Emma dreaded seeing her classmates in public. They were fine in school—she could have lunch with them, hang out outside waiting for classes to start, even walk with them over to the sandwich place at lunchtime. But running into them outside of school hours made it painfully obvious to Emma that they were classmates, not friends.

But not today. Today, Emma was with her real friend who was so, so much cooler than they were. She even felt emboldened enough to give them a quiet "Hey" as they passed her table.

The girls stopped. There were three of them. Emma couldn't remember their names now. But they stopped to chat, and Emma introduced them to Elaine, and they spoke for a moment before the girls walked on to wherever it was they were going.

But as they walked away, one girl leaned her head in towards the other two. A giggle carried back to Emma's table. A giggle, and the word "fat." And then more giggles.

Emma flicked her eyes to Elaine, expecting her friend to call "So what?" or some other careless remark after them. But Elaine's eyes were fixed on the table in front of her. Her shoulders curved inwards. Elaine took a tiny sip of her smoothie before pushing the half-full cup away.

"Your friends are mean," she said quietly. Almost a whisper. Then she stood to dump her cup into the garbage.

Emma felt as though she'd swallowed a bag of sand. She stood up hastily. She didn't know what to say. She felt as though she'd betrayed her best friend somehow, as though she were responsible for this sudden sadness.

"They're not my friends," she said quietly at last. If Elaine heard her, she didn't acknowledge it. They walked back to Emma's house in silence. When they got there, Elaine said she wasn't feeling well. Emma called her mom to come pick her up, even though she'd planned to stay the night. The next weekend, Elaine said she had too much homework and couldn't hang out with Emma.

They still saw each other after that. Still spent nights and weekends at each other's houses. Emma still went over to see Elaine whenever her parents brought her to her aunt and uncle's place. But something had broken between them that day. After that, there was never the same feeling of closeness, of trust. Or maybe, Emma realized now, maybe she was just imagining it. Maybe Elaine still felt the same way about her as she always had. Maybe Emma just couldn't admire Elaine the same way after seeing her sadness, her surprising vulnerability. Until that day at the mall, Emma had thought her best friend was impenetrable.

Two years later, Elaine's family moved to Nisku, just outside of Edmonton. Their sleepovers became even less frequent. Their parents were not enthusiastic about driving the girls the extra distance.

Their friendship gradually dwindled to almost nothing by the time Emma finished high school. And whenever the Weavers went to visit Nadine and her family, Emma felt an odd, heavy feeling when she looked at the Janvier house, now occupied by some other family.

It was that moment of deflation, when Elaine's shoulders had curved in as though weighted by sadness, that Emma thought of now as she and her sister sat on the soft mound of mossy earth outside their childhood home. She wanted to tell Heather about it. She wanted to tell her sister that the way Emma had felt then, the faint sense of shame, that was what she felt right now. She wanted to take back her smartass remark.

Looking at Heather, though, Emma realized her sister had probably forgotten about it already. She was looking at the house, and there was a raw wistfulness on her face. Emma followed her gaze, taking in the peeling paint, the cracked windows. She'd hoped that coming here with Heather, she'd feel a sense of—what? Closure? That was dumb. After all, there was nothing really to close—she hardly remembered this place. Just scraps here and there. What had she expected—a surge of memories flooding back? A bundle of happy times she could cradle with her as she travelled back home to Edmonton?

Yes, she realized. That was exactly what she was hoping for. She looked at Heather, wishing she could find the question that would lead Heather to say just the thing that would bring the good memories, the memories of family, back.

But there wouldn't be just good memories, of course.

Heather caught Emma looking at her and frowned. "What?"

"Whose job was it to paint?" Emma blurted.

"What?"

Emma gestured to the flecks of white on the weathered boards. "Someone had to paint it. Whose job was it?"

Heather looked at the side of the house. "I think Jonathan and Kevin—Little Kevin—had to do it one summer. I remember them hauling these old wooden ladders out of the barn. Kevin couldn't have been more than nine or ten."

"Who asked them to?"

Heather shrugged. "Probably our granddad, we called him Poppy. He was always giving them the gears, the two boys. Giving them jobs to do around the place."

"What about us?" Emma asked. "Did we have jobs, too?"

Heather gave her a calculating look. "You want to know for you, or for school?"

"For me."

Heather looked back at the house. "You were mostly too little, but sometimes Mom or Nanny or one of the others would send you to go get something or else put something away. Me, I was mostly supposed to look out for you and the other little ones."

"Did you mind it? You were pretty little, too."

"Nah. I mean sometimes when you were fussy or whatever, but mostly we were always just together, you know?"

"Yeah," Emma said, wishing she really did know, wishing she could remember always being with Heather and their sister Jenny, with their cousins, their parents, with Nanny and Poppy and aunts and uncles. She hooked her mind back on the little details that came back then, smells and the textures, the patterns of the linoleum and the upholstery, pressing on the soft tugging feeling they gave her deep within herself. Trying to draw that feeling out, the gentleness of it, and the edge, too. But it was too deep now, and that's all it was, just a soft, faint tugging. The distance was too great.

She looked at Heather, wondering what she was thinking, what she was feeling. That wistful look was gone from her face now, but she didn't have that other look Emma had already seen several times. The closed look, the annoyance. She looked comfortable. At her ease.

Heather reached into her bag and pulled out a stainless-steel water bottle. She took a swig and passed the bottle wordlessly to Emma. Emma took a sip, glancing at this woman next to her, this woman who was both a stranger and the only person on the planet who was really a part of her family, her past, her blood.

SEVENTEEN

THERE WAS NOT MUCH LEFT TO PHOTOGRAPH ONCE EMMA AND HEATHER left the house. Emma had already taken pictures of the outside of the buildings, the overgrown yard and driveway. They couldn't venture into any of the other buildings. The barn, with its sagging roof, was too dangerous. They pried open the door wide enough that Emma could take some photos of the inside without stepping in. Boards had fallen inward from the roof and through the floor of the loft. They were speared diagonally into the soft earth inside, between the cattle stalls.

Heather pointed out the stairs along the opposite end of the barn. The back of the second storey was a hayloft, but at the front of the barn, she explained, was a two-bedroom apartment with a small living space. It had electricity, but no plumbing. Younger, unmarried male family members took their turns living in that bachelor space. On the day the police and Community Services vehicles had arrived at the farm, Uncle Mark and Uncle Danny had been living up there, and Heather and Emma's cousin Jonathan, tired of sharing a room in the house with his cousin Kevin, had just claimed the old couch in the tiny living room as his own.

"It kind of raised hell in the house, Jonathan moving up there," Heather explained as Emma took pictures of the stairs, the boards that jabbed through the loft, the empty cattle stalls. "The boys had had a room to themselves, and there were three of us girls in another room.

Wasn't fair for Kevin to keep a room all to himself, so you and I got moved into Kevin's room, and baby Kelly, she was about a year old then, she got moved out of her parents' room and into our old room with her big sister Melanie. Jenny was still small, so she stayed in Mom and Dad's room. But Kevin, he was pissed that he had to share his room with us girls. He wanted to move up to the loft too, but there was nowheres for him to sleep up there, so he got stuck with us. Wasn't for long, though."

Emma withdrew from the barn. Heather watched her as she gazed around the farm, her eyes alighting on each of the buildings in turn. Heather waited for her to say something, to ask questions, but she was quiet. Emma had said she wanted to know for herself. The university research, Emma was hinting, was more an excuse to ask than anything. Heather wasn't sure she believed it, though. She wanted to trust Emma, but how could she?

No, Heather realized, she didn't want to trust Emma. In fact, she'd been a little glad, that deep-down mean gladness, when she'd been able to call Emma out when she hadn't just said, "I'm your sister and I wanted to meet you." When she'd been able to catch that raw look on her face when she'd been caught out.

It was easier not to trust Emma. Easier, too, that Emma kept putting on that dumb smirk, playing at being hard. It meant Heather didn't have to take her seriously. *We're both tough, girl. I don't know why you think you need to prove it.*

They opened the door to the chicken coop and the toolshed, but there was not much to photograph inside. Heather kept up with her running explanation of the buildings, and Emma just nodded and took pictures.

Finally, the younger woman leaned against the shaded side of the house to scroll through her pictures. "I think I've got what I need," she said.

Heather nodded. She pulled a granola bar and her water bottle out of the bag for the hike back to the car. They didn't talk much as they picked their way back through the woods. Mercifully, the blackflies had subsided a little in the past few days, so their time in the woods was not as bad as it often was this time of year. Still, they passed through a cloud of the tiny insects in a low-lying hollow not too far from the car.

"I remember one time I went camping with Marian and Jack," Heather said. "It was early June, and the blackflies were so bad. They kept going after my eyebrows, and by the time we got back, it looked like I had two black eyes. Took a while to convince the social worker no one'd hit me."

Emma glanced back at her. "Marian and Jack Rushdie?"

Heather nodded.

"Did you live with them?"

"When I was older, out of foster care," she said. "But they were just there a lot when I was a kid. Spent a lot of time with them."

The rental car appeared in view. Emma rooted the keys out of a zippered pocket in her bag. As they settled in, Emma cranked up the air conditioning. They were both sweating from the walk back through the sun-dappled forest.

Heather watched Emma as she manoeuvred the car down the country lane. Emma kept chewing the inside of her lower lip. Her hands were held primly at 10 and 2 o'clock on the steering wheel.

"So, you need anything else?" Heather asked.

Emma shrugged. "I've got to make an appointment to look at a private journal," she said. "Maybe see if there's anything else in the Genealogical Society archives. Then find out if there are any other reporters or whatever from '91 who'll let me interview them. I'm in good shape to finish on time."

"I mean from me."

Emma glanced over. "Why? Is there…anything else?"

Heather sighed. She thought back to the foster homes. To the schools, the time she and her brother had briefly attended the same one. To the news that the Weavers had moved away. To her brother. Her mom. "You're the one supposed to be asking questions," she said at last.

They reached the intersection with the main road. Emma braked as a logging truck rumbled past before pulling out onto the worn asphalt.

To their right, Taylor Lake flashed by between the trees, the sun glinting off the still water. Here and there, cabins were visible along the shore. An orange canoe lay overturned on a dock. A yellow inflatable raft drifted near a rocky beach. Heather wondered about the people who had properties here. Where did they live the rest of the time? Halifax, probably. The Americans, the Ontarians, the Europeans, they all bought their vacation properties on saltwater coasts, never an interior lake. Maybe there were a few retirees living there year-round. What must it be like to have enough money to have two houses? Most of these places couldn't really be called cottages. When Heather thought of a cottage, she pictured something much more rustic, like her in-laws' place. No power, no plumbing. Something like the outbuildings on the farm....

"So, thanks," Emma said. "For coming out with me and everything." She made a soft sound in the back of her throat. A familiar sound, Heather realized. The kind of sound she'd made when she was little just before she started crying. Heather looked at her carefully. There was no sign of tears, but Emma looked uncertain. A little lost, even.

"You want to come have dinner at our place?"

Emma's eyebrows shot up. "Sure?"

"Yeah, why not. When are you free?"

Emma shrugged. "When am I not?"

☙

WHEN EMMA DROPPED HEATHER OFF, JUSTIN WAS GAZING THROUGH the living room window. He waved at his mom when she stepped out of the car. Emma caught his eye, two sheets of glass separating them. She raised her hand in greeting. His arm hovered mid-wave. He blinked, then opened and closed his fingers twice—shy, polite. He looked at her for a split second more, then broke away from the window and sprinted to the front door, where his mom was entering. Her sister. Her nephew.

Emma put the car in reverse, heading back toward the highway.

She would have to change her flights. She was supposed to return to Edmonton this weekend. There would be a rebooking fee. And she'd have to put a few more nights' hotel on her credit card, a few more meals. She'd need to stop eating at restaurants, grab more to-go sandwiches from the big supermarket near her hotel. The grant money was all spoken for. There wasn't a lot of room on her credit card.

But still—her sister had asked her to dinner. She had a chance to get to know her, her kids, her husband. To find out what her life had really been like.

She'd lost track of the line between what she needed to know to satisfy Dr. Melnyk and Dr. Fuentes, and what she wanted to know. For herself. What made the last twenty-five-odd years make sense.

As she was nearing the hotel her phone jingled, interrupting the upbeat pop song that Emma had caught herself singing along to. She jabbed the screen to answer.

"Emma? It's Sam." The background noise suggested that Sam, too, was calling from her car. "Listen, I got in touch with Brendan Inglis. He's going to bring the journals to the Genealogical Society. You can come look through them here."

"Sounds great! Tomorrow?"

"Yeah, we can do tomorrow afternoon. He's bringing them by in the morning."

"Great. Thanks, Sam."

"Cheers!"

Emma felt buoyed as she pulled into the hotel parking lot. Better yet, as she passed by the bar, Glen gave her a warm smile.

"You heading into Halifax tonight?"

Emma hesitated. "I wasn't going to…."

"You should."

"Yeah? Where?"

Glen leaned forward on his forearms. "Tell you what. Meet me down here at 7. We'll go in together, get a beer." He raised his eyebrows a touch. Hopeful, not expectant.

"Yeah, okay. Seven."

Up in her room, Emma took a long shower, running her hands

over her body to check for ticks. That was one thing she liked a lot about Edmonton—no ticks. She wondered if she should eat something. Were they going out for supper? Or just beer? If she went downstairs now for food, Glen would see her. If he thought they were eating together, he'd ask why she was eating now. So she sat on her bed, her hair wrapped up in a towel, and ate a fruit bar from the bottom of her backpack.

Her phone buzzed on the bed next to her. A text from her mom: *How are you doing?* Above it, a text from the day before: *Just checking in. Love you!* And a text from her dad: *Let us know how things are going.*

Emma sighed. She'd have to let them know she was extending her trip. But she'd also have to tell them why. *So I found my sister, Heather. You remember Heather, right?*

She knew she should call. If she didn't, they'd keep texting her. That, and the knot of worry in her belly would build all evening as she tried to picture their reaction.

Dad would be okay. He'd probably ask about money. But she couldn't handle Mom's fretting. So she tapped her father's picture in her phone contacts.

It took him four rings to answer. He was always setting his phone down and not remembering where. If he went into the kitchen for a glass of water, the phone would end up next to the sink. If he went to the washroom, it would be on the shelf above the toilet. If he was out in the garden, it'd be in the potting shed.

"Em!" he answered breathlessly.

"Hey, Dad."

"Your mother was hoping you'd call."

"Well, here I am."

Emma heard the fridge open and close. Dad's habit—checking for snacks, never actually eating anything. "So, you just wrapping up?"

"Not quite." Emma swallowed. "There's—I have a few more interviews to do next week. I'm gonna have to stay a few extra days."

"You have enough room on your credit card?"

"I'm fine."

"Good, good."

There was a pause. Emma waited for her dad to ask. Then, finally, she said, "I'm interviewing some locals who remember the '91 arrests. Could lead to some good material." She was trying to sound breezy, but to her own ears, it came out breathless, rushed, evasive. Her mom would never let her get away with such vagueness.

"Excellent."

"Give Mom a big hug for me, OK?"

"Will do. Call if you need money."

"I won't."

"Love you, Em."

"You too."

As she hung up, she felt looser. That was done, then. She'd rebook her plane ticket first thing in the morning. Now, she pulled the towel off her head and combed the tangles out of her hair. Put on a little makeup. Surveyed her travel wardrobe. Just jeans, leggings, and a pair of shorts. She picked out a pair of jeans that didn't have muddy cuffs, and a cotton blouse. Not exactly dressy, but it would be fine for a beer, wouldn't it? As long as it wasn't an actual dinner date.

Glen was still behind the bar when she arrived downstairs. She hovered a moment, not sure whether to wait for him in the bar. But when he saw her, he strode around the counter. "Be right back," he said, flashing her a smile before he disappeared through a door marked *Employees Only*. Emma perched on the arm of one of the dark grey couches that sat between the door and the desk. Glen emerged moments later, dressed in jeans and a button-down shirt. *Twinsies*, Emma thought, glancing down at her own outfit.

"Ready?" he asked, heading toward the door.

"Wait," she said, gesturing at her phone. "I need to get the address from you."

"Just drive in with me," he replied. "Catch a cab back."

Emma hesitated. If she was extending her stay, she didn't really have the money to pay for a taxi. Also, she didn't like the idea of relying on Glen to get her there. Afterward, she'd have to get back to the hotel. He'd probably offer to drive her back, and then she'd have to figure out whether it would just be a ride, or whether he'd expect to come up to her room. If things ended awkwardly, would Emma have to change hotels to avoid running into him every day? "I'd rather just drive," she said. She held her phone out to him, the map app open.

He took it and quickly entered an address just north of downtown Halifax. "You should be able to find street parking," he said.

"See you there."

The bar looked like the kinds of local pubs she saw on TV shows shot in Northern England. Emma parked her car just up the street, passing some brightly coloured row houses, an assortment of second-hand stores, a theatre, a beer store, a few run-down corner stores and fast-food joints. A handful of patrons a few years younger than Emma, university students probably, stood smoking and vaping outside. She hesitated a moment, wondering whether she should wait for Glen on the sidewalk. Then the door opened. Glen held it for her, smiling. "You made it," he said.

He led her to a table near the window. In the corner, a woman strummed a guitar and sang into a microphone, barely audible over the cheery rumble of voices.

"So?" he asked. "How's your visit to Halifax been?"

Emma forced a broad smirk. "Oh, I get it now. This isn't a date. You're still at work. Mandated tourist check-in. Well, fuck, do I ever feel stupid." Suddenly, she remembered Heather's disapproving frown. She felt foolish, rebuked.

But Glen smiled back. "You got me. I'm still on the clock."

A waitress arrived. Emma ordered the same beer she'd had last time she came downtown.

"You getting something to eat?" Glen asked.

There were days Emma wished that food came in pills. "What's good?"

"I like their pizzas. The Greek is good," he suggested.

Emma nodded.

"We'll split a medium," he told the waitress.

"Seriously, how's your research going?"

"Really well, actually." Emma thought about her trips to the

Gaugin compound, her interview with Jack Rushdie, her visits to the Genealogical Society. Objectively speaking, it was a research jackpot.

"So is this your job, researching?"

Emma ran her thumb across the front edge of the table. A light-coloured wooden square mounted on a black metal pedestal. It was the kind of table she associated with Legion bars, though she was not sure she had ever actually been to one. Actually, the whole place, minus the hip twenty- and thirtysomething patrons and the signs advertising local, organic microbrew, seemed like the kind of bar where you'd expect to see a bunch of white men in their seventies. She wondered whether the decor was intentionally ironic, or if some old dive bar just started attracting younger patrons by accident. She glanced up from the table. Glen was looking at her, his expression open, curious.

The waitress brought their beers just then. Emma took a sip of hers immediately, grateful for the extra seconds. She had to suppress the urge to lean her arm over the back of the chair, to announce that she was a Gaugin investigating her family to find out whether she really was the product of two centuries of incest. The look on Heather's face came back to her, though, the closing-off. *I'm supposed to think you were a real badass?*

"I'm a grad student. It's just research for school," she said at last, looking at him carefully. She noticed that a lot of people recoiled when she said she was a grad student, like they were imagining her weighing their education, their intelligence, and finding them lacking. *Don't worry, I'm a total fraud, I'm so not the kind of person who belongs in grad school!* she always wanted to say. She didn't, though.

But he just nodded, his eyes on her face. "You researching local history?"

"It's something like that," she said. "I'm researching a local family. It's a social anthropology thing. I'm basically trying to map out how they fit into the community, from a cultural and historical standpoint." *Also, a personal standpoint.*

"Interesting," Glen replied. "I took an anthropology course at university. I actually really liked it."

Emma smiled. "You *actually* really liked it?"

Glen shrugged, sheepish. "University wasn't for me. I didn't *actually* make it to most of my classes. Left after my first year."

"I didn't start university until I was twenty-three," Emma said.

"How come?"

Emma shrugged. "I didn't see the point before that."

"And now?"

Emma took another slow sip of her beer. What *was* the point? At first, she had simply wanted to avoid being the fish stick company IT girl her whole life. Of course, she'd imagined getting a stable, quiet job in research or archives someday, but she wasn't particularly confident there were a lot of jobs like that out there, even for someone with a Master's in History and Anthropology. She suddenly remembered Sam complaining of being passed over for a job in favour of a university graduate. Comforting thought. "I don't know," she said at last.

Their pizza came then. Glen hadn't been lying—it was good. As they ate, their conversation lagged. Emma didn't mind, though. The silence was comfortable.

Afterward, Glen suggested another drink. Emma shook her head. She worried about being pulled over on her way back to the hotel and blowing over the limit. Anyway, having more than one drink often meant middle-of-the-night anxiety attacks.

Glen walked her to her car.

"See you tomorrow?"

"I'm not working," Glen replied. "But call me if you want another mandated tourist check-in."

It was a nice night. There were no blackflies pursuing them here, in town. They stood for a moment on the sidewalk, quietly, not saying anything. Emma wasn't used to that. Her friends, Adrian's friends, liked to fill the silence. Glen was looking at her, but it wasn't an expectant look, not a demand or a question. He had nice eyes. Emma leaned in to kiss him. He set his hand gently on her lower back. It felt nice. "I might do that," she said as she got into the car.

THE WOODSMAN AND THE WOLF

EIGHTEEN

IT WAS A GOOD KISS, EMMA SUPPOSED. HIS LIPS WERE SOFT, NOT TOO wet or too tight or too urgent. The pressure of his hand on her back was warm, gentle, but firm enough to hint at the potential of a more ardent embrace. And he was attractive, it was true, in a kind of urban poet-looking way.

She remembered the first time she had kissed Adrian. They'd known each other a while. He was her TA, and she'd noticed him in the lectures, sitting in the front row. When she spoke to him in class, he'd look at her intently, always remembering her name. Then one afternoon, she was studying at a table at the campus pub and he'd wandered in. Joined her at her table. They drank cheap wine and talked well into the evening, and she'd gradually felt the attraction between them becoming more and more magnetic, so that when she finally kissed him, there was no question. They went straight back to her apartment, stopping to kiss every few steps. She wanted him so badly by that point that she almost came when he took off her shirt, trailed his mouth over her bra.

Of course, it wasn't always like that when they kissed. They were together a year, and soon enough there were perfunctory kisses, and even the urgency of their mouths pressed against each other never again had that same brightness, the same charge, as the evening they first slept together. But he'd been gone almost a year now, since last

August, and Emma hadn't kissed anyone else. She'd been attracted to other people, sure, but this was the first time she'd actually acted on it. This was her first first kiss in months. And it was fine, it was a good kiss, but frankly, after that long a wait, she realized now that she'd been hoping for something bigger, more magnetic.

She wasn't tired when she got back to the hotel so she turned on the TV, flicking impatiently through the channels until she found a movie she'd loved when she was in high school. She fell asleep to the familiar lines, waking up a few hours later to the same film playing over again. She flicked off the TV and fell back asleep.

☙

THE NEXT DAY, EMMA WENT DOWN FOR THE COMPLIMENTARY HOTEL breakfast, stuffing an apple and banana into her bag for later. She wasn't due at the Genealogical Society until noon, so she made her way down to the airless, low-ceilinged gym in the hotel basement. She pulled out a blue mat and did a few yoga poses, but her mind kept flicking to the upcoming dinner with Heather and her family, to the journal she was going to look at this afternoon, to the ways she'd assemble her research and her journal entries for Dr. Fuentes and Dr. Melnyk. It wasn't the manic channel-changing thought process that led up to a panic attack, though. She was simply excited—about her work, about spending more time with her sister, about the enthusiastic response she was certain she could expect from her supervisors. She couldn't remember the last time she had this much to look forward to.

The only thing that brought an anxious twisting sensation to her belly was her mom's inevitable reaction to her extending her trip, the contagious worries about money, about her own ability to cope with what she might uncover.

She also hadn't actually changed her travel arrangements yet. She always put this kind of thing off—planning, scheduling, organizing. Especially if it meant actually talking to someone on the phone. She knew she'd feel better as soon as it was done, but right now, she didn't feel ready to wade into that mess.

Fuck it. The gym was pointless, anyway. She couldn't focus on her poses. She stood up and wiped down the mat with disinfectant, wondering whether the person before her had bothered to do the same, then made her way back up to her room. She dialled the number for the airline ruthlessly, then waited through the '90s pop-grunge hold music.

Finally, she managed to talk to someone to rebook her flight. Wednesday was the cheapest, and wouldn't cost her any extra money aside from the rebooking fee. The extra three days should be enough, she hoped. As soon as she hung up the phone, she felt the heaviness lift from her chest. Like she knew it would. She stepped into the hot shower, her thoughts drifting back to the journal, to how she'd piece its contents together with her photos, her reflections, the historical, sociological, and ethnographical theories she'd assembled before her trip.

She got in the car and scrolled through her music until she found the Cranberries song that had been playing while she was on hold with the airline. She cranked the volume, rolled down her windows, and sang along as she weaved her way out towards the highway.

Sam had the journals waiting when she arrived. But Emma set them aside like a kind of after-dinner treat while she skimmed through the remaining archive-owned journals she hadn't been able to get to on her earlier visit. There wasn't much in them. A few perfunctory mentions, some aspersions cast about supposed criminal activities. The usual. With real pleasure, Emma turned to the Inglis journals. The unicorns, special because they'd been harder to find. Archival treasure. She tried to check her excitement, remembering the sinking disappointment she'd felt when Sam's last treasure had revealed nothing more than a few pages of bare biographical details. This was different, though. This was a journal, someone's private thoughts. And she already knew that some of those thoughts were about the Gaugins.

The first was a cloth-bound book. It must once have been black, but now the cover was faded to an uneven grey. Inside the front cover, in looping writing: *Minnie Inglis, 1891.* The journal began with an account of her wedding, though it seemed that she started the journal a few years after she got married. She made references to Richard, Albert, Laura, and Grace. Richard, Emma deduced, was Minnie's husband, and Albert, Laura, and Grace were her children. The family lived in Lunenburg, and Emma guessed that Richard Inglis was a fisherman, based on Minnie's occasional references to boats and cod.

The first mention of the Gaugins was halfway through the journal. It seemed that in June 1893, almost fifty years after Jane Moore had written so contemptuously of her sister's marriage to Peter Gaugin, and over seventy years after Eleanor Schwartz hadn't been allowed to attend her cousin's wedding to Julia Gaugin, Will Gaugin had come into Lunenburg looking for work, and there had been some kind of disagreement, though Emma wasn't sure whether Will Gaugin had actually been involved, or whether he had got the job he was looking for.

> Richard said Will Gaugin was in town today, hoping for some work. Said he wants to go to see, and Clarence" (there was a smudge where the last name should be. Did it start with a K?) "asked whether he'd even been to sea, and it seemed that the Gaugin fellow didn't care much for his tone and that business all ended in a kind of a dust-up right there on Montague Street.

That fall, it seemed that Rose Gaugin was in town selling "nice pie apples," and that Minnie bought some. And that was all in the first journal.

The second journal was also labelled Minnie Inglis, this one beginning in 1896 and spanning almost five years. The entries were shorter, and there were longer stretches of time between them. It seemed that Minnie and Richard had had another child in the interim, John. She still spoke of Albert and Grace, but there were no further mentions of Laura. Emma wondered whether Laura had gotten married and moved away, or whether she'd died. Or perhaps she'd gone off to become a teacher, or fallen into some disgrace. In any case, alongside the family events (buying new shoes for Richard, building a new henhouse, the birth of another child, Sarah), there were also town events (the opening of the new Academy and the Foundry) and even world events ("the terrible war in Africa"—the Boer War, Emma deduced). The entries often had a slightly more salacious tone when Minnie wrote of her neighbours. She called Deborah Morash's wedding "a rather shabby affair, quite hastily put up." She reported that Charles Zwicker and (here was another smudge—the first name could be Daniel, or maybe Donald) had had a "shocking disagreement" outside of the church. And she noted that Will Gaugin had been "skulking about again, and so folks must only blame themselves if they aren't watchful and the henhouses and storerooms are broke into at night." The final quarter of Minnie's second journal was blank, with only faint yellow water stains marking the pages.

The third journal, its cover a well-worn blue, belonged to Grace Inglis. It began in 1902. Grace mentions her father, her brothers, Albert and John, and her sister, Sarah. She writes of household tasks—the washing and mending, the hens and the beans in the garden, cooking and baking, but she never mentions her mother. It seemed likely that Minnie Inglis had died sometime between her last entry (late 1900) and 1902, and that Grace had taken over her mother's household duties.

Grace's journal was full of names. She had tea at Martha Smith's house, spoke to Martha and Paul Smith and their mother at church, saw Annie Young buying cloth for a new dress. Emma tried to guess how old Grace was. Fourteen, perhaps fifteen? A teenager. No longer in school, already responsible for her family. But still a kid, Emma realized, reading about Grace's friends, perhaps her former classmates.

It seemed that Will Gaugin had gotten a job at the shipyards, and that he brought his brother Walter in to work with him.

"Walter seems a fine young man, very respectable. He always touches his cap and says good day, and I seen him in church though his brother don't go."

Almost every week as Grace made her inventory of the people she spoke to at church, the new clothes the girls and women were wearing, she comments, almost—almost—in passing, that Walter Gaugin was there, too.

So. You have an admirer, Walter Gaugin.

Emma saw that Grace's journal, too, ended with a series of blank pages, and Walter Gaugin's name appeared throughout the journal. Emma took photos of each page before she read it through.

Journal of Grace Inglis, June–July, 1902

I seen Annie Young in town today and I invited her to have tea with me because I haven't much seen her since I left school, and I find myself thinking on her these days. When we was in school we was like sisters we was together so much and anyhow it's nice to see her again. While we was stopped to talk, Walter Gaugin come by on his way from the shipyards and he stopped to say good day. After, Annie said it's a shame we can't invite him to have tea with us, he's a respectable young man, and I said I thought so too. I'll make a nice rhubarb cake for our tea, and Papa will be pleased to have it for dinner, too.

✄

Annie Young came to tea today. I was happy all morning even though Papa was in a temper and Sarah wouldn't mind me, but the rhubarb cake came out quite pretty. But in the end, it was Annie what spoiled everything anyway. She didn't want to talk about nothing else but Walter Gaugin. She made me promise to keep a secret and she says that Walter is courting her. Imagine! Her mama will be properly shocked, and I must say I was shocked too. I never thought Annie was anything but a good girl and I never thought she'd of done something so shocking as to court a boy in secret. I wasn't sorry when Annie said her mama was waiting on her and she had to get home.

✄

Well here's one less person to cook and clean and wash and mend for. At supper tonight, Papa told Albert he'd settled for him to work in the shipyard in Halifax and Albert is to start in July. I asked where he'll live, will he set up a house of his own and Albert told me not to be so silly, there's plenty of rooming houses in Halifax. Only then John started blubbering and carrying on that he wanted to go to Halifax with Albert, and John got Sarah blubbering, and all the noise made Papa cross. I was doing my best to get Sarah settled and tell John to finish his supper and I seen that Albert was sitting there all still, not saying nothing and not even eating his dinner. He was just looking at his plate as if I'd cooked up a dinner of earthworms and snakes instead of a nice chicken pie. And Papa wasn't saying nothing either, he was just eating his pie and staring down into his plate and if it wasn't for the little ones kicking up a fuss, dinner would have been a terribly solemn affair for having such big news.

 confidence

Well I suppose Annie Young told her family that she's been courting Walter Gaugin because it seems they're to be married, Papa told me so just this evening. He saw Mr. Young at the blacksmith's. I suppose she's awfully happy now and I only hope her happiness lasts though I imagine it will be something to go and live at Gaugin Lake so far from her family. I suppose she'll be awfully lonely. Though they might stay in town and her husband stay on at the shipyard. I'm only surprised at Annie that she wouldn't come and tell me herself.

confidence

They read the banns in church for Annie Young and Walter Gaugin today so they'll be married next month. I saw Annie after church, she was standing with her family and Walter was with them. Most folks were stopping to wish them happiness and Annie looked right at me but she didn't smile, she just looked, and I knew I should of gone to wish them happiness, only John and Sarah needed minding, and Albert was gone off somewheres, and it was only me to get the children home. Only I was sorry the whole way that I didn't wish them happiness.

I'll send John and Sarah up tomorrow to invite Annie to tea again.

୧୦

I tried to make John and Sarah take a note to Annie Young to invite her to tea, but they wouldn't mind and I got cross. Albert came inside to find out what the fuss was about, and he told me to let the little ones be and go myself if I wanted to have Annie to tea. I asked him who would do the mending while I was out, and he told me not to bother him with silly questions. John wanted to follow Albert back out, but Albert told him to keep out of his way, and John started fussing and carrying on. Then Albert got cross with me and told me I needed to make the children mind, and I got cross with Albert and told him I'd be glad when he was in Halifax and I didn't have to do his mending as well as Papa's and the children's. Albert gave me a hard look and went back out, only he left me with John, who was still fussing and blubbering, and Sarah now too, she always cries when Papa and Albert get cross. And I told the children never mind, we'd all walk up to invite Annie Young to tea, and we did. Papa will be sore if I don't finish the mending tonight.

୧୦

Annie Young came to tea today. I didn't have time to make a nice cake, I hope she didn't mind. She asked if I would come to her wedding, and I told her of course I would. Her and Walter, he'll be her husband by then, imagine! Her and Walter will go to Taylor Lake (that's Gaugin Lake, of course, only Annie calls it Taylor Lake, the way it says on the maps they had at school) to visit his family after the wedding, and then they'll set up here in Lunenburg after all. I'm glad. It would be too bad not to see Annie any more, we've been awfully good friends since we were just little girls.

୧୦

Albert is gone off to Halifax. I thought Papa might of gone to get him settled, but it's just Albert gone. Papa saw him off at the house with the rest of us. There's one less mouth to cook for, and there's also one less pair of hands to help with the chores and looking after the little ones. Supper was a queer, quiet affair without him. John and Sarah fussed and cried when Albert left, and I even found myself a touch weepy, but not a one of us said a thing about him at suppertime.

꩜

Annie married Walter Gaugin today, I suppose she's Annie Gaugin now. She and her husband was talking to some rough-looking men at church and I suppose they must be his brothers or his uncles or such, though there weren't no introducing them. They've gone off to meet her family. I wished them happiness after the ceremony, and didn't Annie look happy, wed at just 16.

꩜

There was a bad windstorm last night. The children slept through it, but I could hear Papa up and walking about in his room, and I couldn't sleep neither. Makes me wonder how Albert is faring and whether he's warm and snug in his rooming house in Halifax, and whether the woman cooks him the things he likes to eat. I got to thinking about Annie, too, and what she might be doing. Could be the wind is keeping her awake out at Gaugin Lake. I could hear the waves hitting the shore mighty hard here in town, I wonder if the lake gets stirred up the same way as the ocean in a storm. Likely not.

꩜

I saw Mrs. Young today when I went out for some supplies, she says Walter and Annie (Mr. and Mrs. Gaugin, imagine!) will be back on Friday. I asked her and Annie to tea, she said she's too busy with her little ones, but she was sure Annie would come. I'll make some strawberry biscuits.

ɞ

Poor, poor Annie Gaugin. She says she's happy enough with her husband, but what a fright it was visiting his family. She don't say too much, she's such a good soul, but I could tell it was awful rough, and she did say there had been another wedding this summer, before hers I mean, though she couldn't tell where the couple had got married, it certainly wasn't Lunenburg. I can't imagine it was Mahone Bay, neither. It was Walter's cousins got married. Only at first when Annie got there, they said they were cousins, but at last before she went home, Annie started crying and confessed what she thinks, the bride and groom were actually brother and sister!! Imagine, in Nova Scotia, in a Christian country!! She says she thinks they have the same father, though no one come right out and said so. Poor, poor Annie, having to sleep under the same roof with them!! I'm sad for Annie, and I'm only grateful I never got caught up with that family. I don't know what I'll say next time I see her husband at church.

NINETEEN

"BROTHER AND SISTER." EMMA FELT HER HEART STOP AND STAGGER, beating up near her throat. She stared at the words on the page. They seemed to emit a sound, like a drum beat, hard and stark. They had a presence, real in the world in a way that words formed by voices were not. Writing on a page, preserved for over a century, long after the hand that had written them had weakened, died, decayed. The writing itself remained, indelible. Incontrovertible.

Brother and sister.

Who were they? They were never named. Did they have children? Did those children have children? Did they perhaps marry *their* brothers and sisters, have more children? Could those children have had children who perhaps had her father, her aunts and uncles? Brother and sister. Who were they? Who were they to *her*?

Emma suddenly felt acutely aware of her body. Her hands, first, then her feet. Then the bones of her arms, her legs, her head and face. Was her body like other people's bodies? Was it the right shape, the right density, the right makeup and order? When people looked at her, did they pause, wonder about the arrangement of her eyes, her nose, her forehead? Maybe the moment was so brief that she never noticed; perhaps they didn't notice it themselves, only reflecting in passing that something was not as it ought to be?

Emma tried to focus on the rest of the journal. There was more. Emma's eyes caught Annie and Walter Gaugin's names a handful of times before Grace's entries trailed off and finally stopped altogether. But Emma found she couldn't focus on the words, on the looping writing or the yellowed pages. Her attention was being drawn into her body, to the quaking in her thighs, the jumping of her muscles. The squirming tension shifted from just beneath her lungs downward. Emma stood. She wondered whether she should announce herself—*I'm going to the bathroom*—but she didn't trust her voice, didn't trust the look in Sam's eyes.

She fumbled a pill out of her purse as she stalked down the hall, her whole will focused on keeping her legs from running, not to the bathroom but down the stairs, out, and away.

She locked herself into the tiny, outdated washroom with its tiled walls and separate hot and cold faucets running into a discoloured porcelain sink. Her arms were shaking so badly she had trouble undoing her pants' button. She fought down the wail that was building up in her throat. She sat on the toilet, unable to keep her left heel from jumping up and down as her bowels emptied themselves.

Finally, she stood. The muscles in her thighs were still quaking, her chest still fluttering, but the urge to bolt or hide was subsiding. She still felt like calling out, weeping, but she no longer felt that she had to clamp her jaw shut to keep the cries down. She checked her watch. Nine minutes since she'd taken the anxiety med. In another six, it would have kicked in. She'd be normal. Her anxiety would be forced beneath the surface, no longer raw and visible and naked. She considered staying in the tiny washroom for six more minutes, but she couldn't bear the thought of Sam thinking she'd disappeared to take a shit. Which was, of course, exactly what she had done. Also, she didn't think there was another washroom on this floor. What if someone else was waiting, imagining what kind of bowel disorders could possibly keep Emma locked in here so long?

On top of everything else, the panic attacks were deeply, deeply humiliating.

At last, Emma washed her hands, rubbed some cold water over her eyes and forehead, and emerged cautiously. The hall was empty. The muscles in her limbs were still twitching. She slipped down the hall to the stairwell, into the parking lot outside. She couldn't just sit still yet, not out in the open near so many windows from which people might watch her, so she walked around the building once. As she neared the door again, she felt the familiar cottony sensation of the pill kicking in. The anxiety was still there, crackling deep in her tissues, but it was muffled now. She could be normal. No one would notice anything was wrong.

Sam was standing at the scanner when she returned. "Where'd you get off to?"

Emma forced a smirk. "Had to take a shit," she said. "Kidding! My eyes needed a rest. Quick walk outside."

Sam turned the page of the leather-bound book, hit a button. The scanner's cool light seeped around the pages. "Should've told me. I would have kept you company."

"I didn't want to interrupt you."

Emma sat down again, trying to read the last entries more carefully. But her mind kept jumping back. She tried to corral her thoughts. After all, she'd always known she might find something like this. That was just it, though. There was a difference between *suspecting* and *knowing*.

In grade one, just at the start of the school year, Emma had arrived one morning to find the health nurse waiting for her in the classroom. The nurse, wearing a set of pink hospital scrubs printed with grey and white kittens, had set up a tall chair at the back of the room, near the window.

Emma had been the first one into the classroom that morning. The previous year in kindergarten, she'd gotten into the habit of hovering near the door in the morning and at recess, so that she could line up right away when the bell rang. She didn't want to be one of the kids who the recess supervisor had to scold and usher away from the playground equipment. Perhaps that was why she was the first to be waved over to the health nurse's chair. But she thought she saw the nurse and her teacher murmuring to each other, gazing pointedly at her as she came in the door.

She climbed up onto the chair and the nurse parted her fine hair with the long tail of her comb. It felt nice, the plastic trailing gently along her scalp. Emma might have enjoyed it if she didn't feel so visible, sitting up above her classmates instead of at her desk in the second row.

The nurse stopped when she parted the hair behind Emma's ear. She made a little humming sound. "Hop off now," she said, "and wait for me out in the hall. You're not in trouble," she added quickly. Emma didn't know if she could believe her.

As Emma stepped out of the classroom, the nurse was spraying down the chair she'd just been sitting in with a bottle of strong-smelling cleaning solution.

Julia had to pick Emma up from school. She washed Emma's hair, then her own, with an oily-smelling shampoo. Then, as all their bedding tumbled in the washing machine, Julia sat Emma at the kitchen table, wrapped an old towel around her shoulders, and set to work picking the nits out of her hair. Julia tried to joke about it. She told Emma that three other kids in her class had lice, too. But Emma could feel the waves of revulsion coming off Julia. Every time she picked at one of the nits that had glued itself to her scalp, to little strands of hair, Emma felt Julia's fingers flicker in disgust.

"We're going to have to catch Mike when he gets home, too," Julia said, her voice charged with counterfeit good humour.

When she finished, Julia pulled the towel off Emma's shoulders and dumped it straight into the laundry sink, filling it with hot, bleachy water. "Go outside," she suggested. "Enjoy the rest of the day off school."

But Emma didn't want a day off school. She wanted to be back with the other kids, the ones who weren't infested, who hadn't brought insects home. The ones whose parents didn't have to wash their own hair in bug-killing shampoo. At the same time, she never wanted to go back, to face the kids who knew that she, first of all, had been sent home to avoid spreading the infestation to others.

Suddenly, as Emma remembered the shame, the disgust at her own hair and body that had housed the vermin, she regretted extending her trip. She couldn't bear the thought of staying in Halifax another half a week. Unearthing more evidence that her family was, had been, what she suspected all along. Seeing her sister and her family. Wondering if Heather knew. Suspected. Even cared. What would be worse, Emma wondered: if Emma told her, and Heather was as shocked as Emma herself was, if she looked at her own kids and wondered who their great-great-how-many-times-great grandparents were, what they were to each other? It could be she knew and just didn't care. Who would she be if something like that didn't bother her?

Finally, Emma closed the journal. She stacked it on top of the others.

"Hey, thanks for getting these," she said. "They're really great."

Sam smiled. "Find what you needed?"

Has Sam read them? Emma wondered suddenly. *Does she know?* Oh, god. She had to get out of here. "Yup. Thank Mr. Inglis for me?"

Sam nodded. "Take care."

"You too."

As she got in the car, Emma thought she remembered seeing a yoga studio not too far from her hotel in a residential neighbourhood on the way downtown. She pulled out her phone for a quick search. They had a drop-in class at five. She could probably make it—it was not quite a quarter to four now. Not that she wanted to go. She wanted to go back to her hotel, curl up under the covers, watch something stupid on TV. But she knew how that would end up. She'd find a mindless TV show. She'd feel relieved at first, distracted. Then her thoughts would wander. Before too long, she wouldn't be able to sit still anymore. As the pill wore off, she'd start pacing. Take out her phone. Open a dozen search windows as she decided whether to rebook her flight home for the following morning, call Heather and cancel dinner, drop out of school, email her mom and ask her to come stay with her for the rest of the trip, or delete all of her notes and pretend her laptop had been stolen. Chances were pretty good that the anxiety would get so bad tonight she'd spend the evening throwing up until her guts were empty and every dry retch was a raw strangling of her whole torso.

Yoga it was.

She sped a little on the highway on the way back. Not so much that she was likely to be pulled over, but enough that she'd have time to stop at the hotel and change her clothes. She got back to the business park in under an hour. Stopped her car next to the *No Parking* sign at the back of the building. Threw on her four-way flashers and dashed up the back stairwell to her room. She made it to the yoga studio just as the instructor was closing the doors.

She breathed her way through the beginner poses. Blocked out the giggling high school girls, the stiff, self-conscious middle-aged women, the earnest young man with the bun and moustache. Felt her muscles stretch and lengthen, her lungs fill, her mind settle. By the time the class was over, her limbs felt limber and still, her ribcage steady and full. She felt quiet. Quiet and hungry.

She wanted a beer and something greasy to eat, but she knew that after a panic attack, even a single drink would keep her from sleeping that night. And the grease would weigh too heavily in her guts. So she swung by the grocery store up the street. It had a big deli section. She bought herself a salad, some yogurt, fizzy water. Ate it at one of the euphemistically labelled "Café Tables" on the mezzanine above the front entrance. Next to her, two men who looked to be in their seventies drank coffee from the self-service machine. They told stories and cackled. Emma watched them, their easy friendship. The way they never glanced at the shoppers shuffling along in the store below or the cracked institutional tiles on the floor, the peeling paint on the metal tables and chairs. They could be at home, they could be in a park, they could be anywhere. They didn't care. What must it be like to be like that with someone, Emma wondered. As she cleared away her empty food containers the two men stayed on, laughing, falling into companionable silence, sipping from their Styrofoam coffee cups. She heard them burst into laughter once again as the automatic doors opened to expel her into the parking lot.

As Emma drove back to the hotel, her phone buzzed. An email. She always had the urge to check them right away. But she refused to let herself look at the screen while she drove. As soon as she'd parked the car, though, she pulled her phone out of her bag.

It was Heather. They were on for dinner the next day—Saturday. Jack Rushdie would be there, too.

Saturday. Emma had originally been scheduled to fly out on Sunday. She hadn't really needed to change her flights after all.

Of course, she could have told Heather that. She could have said, "Let's have dinner Saturday; I'm going home Sunday." But she hadn't. Why not? What was she hoping for? To have dinner with her sister and her family again on Sunday, perhaps. Maybe even Monday and Tuesday, as well. To stay over at their house, build LEGOs with Justin, cuddle Charlotte. Stay up all night talking to Heather, sharing secrets…. Three days to become part of her life, to become real sisters again. How was it that all of that had seemed possible just yesterday? And now these thoughts, these silly hopes, even the day she'd spent with Heather seemed tarnished, flimsy. Nothing had changed. Nothing real. Yet it had. Something had shifted. Subterranean, invisible, but immovable nonetheless.

Emma sighed. She felt so tired, so heavy. She crafted a cheery-sounding reply to her sister, then trudged up to her tidy, impersonal hotel room with the promise of a night of quiet anonymity.

TWENTY

HEATHER STARED AT HER LAPTOP SCREEN. "CAN YOU BE HERE BY 5? THE kids need to eat before 6 or they turn into little demons. Jack Rushdie is coming, too."

She'd thrown in that last line on impulse. Now she'd have to invite him. She knew he'd come. He never said no.

As Heather hit *Send*, Charlotte started squawking angrily. Heather had pulled Justin's old baby chair out of storage. She'd put Charlotte in it on the floor next to her, given her some pot lids to bang together. For a few precious moments, it had worked—the baby had sat happily making noise while Heather agonized over every word in the email. But now, it seemed, she had realized that her mom had set her down. And she was not having it.

With a sigh, Heather scooped her up and slipped her into the baby carrier she hadn't even bothered to untie from her chest. Charlotte beamed up at her, two tiny teeth just visible along her bottom gums. Patting the baby's bottom with one hand, Heather dialled Jack.

"Heather, girl," he greeted her.

"Hey, Jack. I need you to come for supper tomorrow."

"What's going on?"

"I invited Emma."

"Ah."

There was a silence. Heather pressed her lips against Charlotte's downy head, breathed in her warm, yeasty smell.

"I'll be there, my girl."

"Thanks, Jack."

My girl. It was a reflexive saying, a common phrase. Jack probably used it for other people too—perhaps cashiers he knew well at the grocery store, or his sister's daughters up in Truro. But Heather had only ever heard him use it for her. She imagined the sting she'd likely feel if she did hear him call someone else his girl. Which was silly, really.

Of course, there was a time Heather hadn't known Jack. Back before she'd been taken from her parents, from the farm, she'd had no idea he even existed. So she must have met him and Marian when she was seven. But she has no memory of a momentous first meeting. When she thinks of Jack, she thinks of him as someone she's always known. He and Marian were simply always there. First in the periphery of her life, then gradually moving inward. Then finally back out again, the way family members do when we grow up and make families of our own. The way her own family—the Gaugins, that is—would have, should have, perhaps.

When she thinks back to the part of her childhood that came after the arrests, after leaving the farm, she remembers seeing Marian. Always out in public at first. Grocery shopping with her foster parents. Marian would crouch down and look into Heather's face, her eyes clear, direct. None of that softening of the eyes and sugaring of the voice that adults do when they look at kids. "How you doing?" she'd ask. And Heather would want to answer truthfully. *I want to go home. I can't sleep in the bed alone. I want my mommy. I miss my brother and sisters and cousins.* She knew it would be okay to tell Marian. But she was always with a foster parent, sometimes a social worker, and she learned quickly that she couldn't tell the truth to them. They would just explain why the truth was wrong. *It's not safe for you in that house, your mommy can't take care of you, your brother and sisters are doing much better where they are.* So she said, "I'm okay." But she knew that Marian could hear what she wanted to say, knew the truth from looking in her eyes like that.

Later, when she was maybe ten or so, Heather can remember sitting at the kitchen counter in Marian and Jack's place. Marian making cinnamon toast for her. Jack giving her cups of strong, milky black tea, Marian scoffing that Heather was too young for caffeine. Heather loving her for thinking so, for caring enough to say so, but also wanting to prove her wrong and gulping down the slightly bitter brew and asking for another. By then, when Marian and Jack asked her how she was, when she came by their house after school instead of walking straight to her foster house, or when she wandered over when she was sent outside or to the park to play, when her foster family went out to dinner or an appointment and Heather told them she wanted to go to Jack and Marian's instead of staying home with a teenaged babysitter, she told them little truths—details about her day, her life, her foster parents, school. The old truths, the ones about missing her family, about finding it hard to sleep, about the loneliness of a bedroom all to herself—those had drifted off, fallen away. Life was just the little truths now, the daily excitements and frustrations and disappointments. Haley Langille not letting her jump double-dutch with the other girls at lunchtime. Her foster parents making Hamburger Helper for supper, even though the sauce made her gag. Learning to play the recorder in music class. And Jack and Marian always listening, asking questions, never giving her advice or telling her she'd done wrong or that she should think about things differently.

She can remember the way the light came into their living room late, late at night. The comforting softness of their couch under her, the heavy quilt over her body. The soft sounds of them sleeping, snoring, coughing, turning over in bed in the loft bedroom above her. Then later, the couch replaced with a pullout, the living room transformed into her bedroom after 9 P.M.

It was Jack and Marian that she told when Kevin appeared at her school suddenly. She was eight. She'd been in foster care just over a year. She started school again that fall, grade three, and on the first day, when the bell rang in the morning, the teachers all came outside to guide the students into orderly lineups to make their way in to their new classrooms. Heather stood in the grade three lineup, just behind Darren Harnish. And there, three rows over, in the grade six lineup, was her brother Kevin. Heather had looked at him a long moment, seeing, recognizing, but not quite registering him. He was taller, obviously, and his hair was cut shorter than she'd ever seen it. He was wearing a pair of dark grey sweatpants and a long-sleeved blue T-shirt. He had an oldish-looking backpack slung over his left shoulder, and he stood with a kind of a slouch under the weight of first-day school supplies. Heather stared hard at him, willing him to look up, look over at her. Then her line started moving forward. She followed Darren and the other third-graders into the school, her eyes on Kevin, and he disappeared, never glancing in her direction. She saw him again at lunchtime. He sat at the end of a table of sixth graders, but not with them. There was a border of empty space around him, marking him as alone. She took a step toward him but he glared at her, his eyes flat and forbidding. She turned and sat down at a table with the other girls in her class, her "friends," though they never spent time together outside of school.

Of course, Kevin shouldn't have been in their school. He should have been in junior high, grade seven. He would be thirteen in January. But it wasn't until they were taken away from the farm that Heather had ever heard about grades. She couldn't remember any kind of real schooling taking place at the farm, but maybe it did, maybe her cousins Jonathan and Melanie and her brother Kevin had started to learn math and spelling, science perhaps, and history. But she doesn't remember any of it. Or perhaps there was no learning, no studying, no reading and adding. Maybe that was why Kevin was here, instead of in junior high with the other kids his age.

After school, she saw him standing by the school buses. She sidled up to him. "Hi, Kevin."

He gave her a hard look. "I don't talk to grade one babies." He turned and slouched onto the bus, taking a seat as close to the back as he could. Though not the very back—those seats were coveted.

Only the coolest kids ever sat there. Kevin sat about a few rows ahead, alone, staring at the back of the seat in front of him.

"I'm in grade three!" Heather shouted. If he heard, he made no sign.

That day, Heather's foster parents dropped her off at Jack and Marian's as they headed off to some adult event or another. Jack made grilled cheese sandwiches as Marian folded laundry. Heather sat at the kitchen counter.

"You're quiet today, my girl," Jack said, flipping a sandwich on the grill.

"I guess."

"You're not going to tell us about school?"

Heather picked at a small chip in the surface of the countertop. She could see the end of her fingernail bending a bit as it caught on the edge, then released with a tiny *click*. "My brother's in my school now."

Marian looked up. "He is?"

Heather nodded.

"That must have been a surprise," Marian said, her eyes still on Heather's face. She had a T-shirt in one hand, but she wasn't folding it. Jack had his back to both of them, and he was pressing down on a sandwich with his spatula. But something about his shoulders, the tilt of his head, told Heather that he was really paying attention to her, and not to lunch at all.

"He didn't want to talk to me. He called me a grade one baby."

"Big kids can be like that sometimes," Marian said, carefully folding the T-shirt and laying it on the pile on the table.

Jack slipped the spatula under the sandwich and flipped it onto a waiting dinner plate. "Soup's on," he said.

"That's a sandwich, not soup."

"So it is, my girl."

Kevin stayed at her school almost till Halloween. Heather remembers him standing by himself, but always near a group of grade six kids on the playground, in the gym, in the lunch room. He seemed to always have the worn athletic backpack slung over one shoulder. He seemed to always be wearing sweatpants, which, Heather already knew, was social death. The cool kids wore jeans. Never sweats, except in gym class.

But then one day, Heather realized he was gone. Realized she hadn't seen him in a few days. *He probably got sent to a new foster home, transferred to a new school*, she thought. It happened. She wondered when she would see him again. *If* she would. She'd caught a glimpse of Emma once, climbing into the back of the Weavers' car at the grocery store in Chester. Her foster parents had taken her to visit some friends of theirs who lived there. Heather remembers giving a sort of half-yelp in the back seat. "Stop, it's Emma!" she'd wanted to call out. But she caught herself in time, realizing that they wouldn't stop. She'd asked her second foster family after the Weavers to take her to see Emma, and the third. They all told her it wasn't up to them. It was up to Community Services to arrange a visit. So she glued back the yelp into her throat, turned it into a cough.

Still, Heather had a pretty good idea she knew where Emma was—with the Weavers, in that same house. But Kevin, their baby sister Jennifer, their cousins Jonathan and Melanie and Kelly—she had no idea where they'd been taken.

Heather herself had been in three foster homes before she finally made her way to the Colfords'. The first was the Weavers', of course. Heather didn't remember much from there. She remembered Emma sniffling, crying. She remembered being so angry at her sister, wanting her to toughen up, to do something, to try to get home. She could tell Emma was miserable at those strangers' house. For a long time, she thought that if Emma had just tried, they would have gotten back home to Mom and Dad, Nanny and Poppy, to Kevin and Jenny, Jonathan, Melanie and Kelly, to all the aunts and uncles, the dogs and chickens and cattle. Emma had to stop being such a sucky baby. She remembers thinking the Weavers were keeping them there, in that stupid house with its stupid plates that were kept on shelves and that no one even ate from. If the Weavers would just let them go home, Emma would stop crying all the time. For a long time after she left the Weavers', Heather felt that anger bubble up in her whenever she thought about Emma. Sometimes, even now as an adult, if her mind drifted back to those early days with the Weavers, Heather caught a feeling of resentment simmering just below the surface. Now that she had kids of her own, now that she really knew how helpless, how easily crushed, a kid that small can be, what follows is a flush of shame, shame she'd felt that way about a frightened little girl.

After the Weavers was a young couple in Bridgewater. Heather couldn't remember much about them or their home. Then the couple in Mahone Bay. They had a teenaged daughter of their own. That was when Heather found herself in the same school as Kevin. Then finally, she was taken to the Colfords' home in Blockhouse, just outside Lunenburg.

The Colfords were old. That's what Heather remembers about them. They had a son, an engineer, who lived in Toronto. They were retired. Hope was already slightly bent, her shoulders stooped forward. She was always calling for her husband. "Teddy, where have you got to?" And he'd call back from the den, where he was watching TV, or the garage, where he was puttering with the car or the lawnmower, or the backyard, where he was weeding the vegetable garden. "I'm right here, Hope!" It was a constant call-and-response, Hope always wanting to know where in the house her husband was, always checking in, gauging his distance from her. She never called for Heather the same way.

The Colfords were kind, though. At first, they kept Heather in school in Mahone Bay. "So you won't go missing your friends," Teddy said. She'd been brought to them in February. She was nine, and in grade four. When she first arrived at their house, she was sure she wouldn't be staying long—the social worker would be back to take her to the next place. Or maybe finally, finally, they'd let her go home to her family.

But that June, after school let out for the summer, Teddy asked her, "Don't you want to go to school in Lunenburg next year? Take the bus with the other kids?" And Heather said *yes*, because she could see that's what Teddy and Hope wanted her to say, and also because she didn't really care. Her friends at school, they were just school friends. Sometimes they were friends who ate lunch together and hung together in the yard at lunch and recess. But sometimes, they weren't friends. Sometimes, the other girls would clump together, their backs to her, or shuffle away if she tried to join them. The times that Heather was left out of their circle of goodwill, they'd taunt her about being a Gaugin.

One time, Hayley Langille's pencil case had gone missing. It was purple, printed with My Little Ponies. At lunch one day, Hayley announced it had been stolen. Not lost. *Stolen*. She'd stared right at Heather and said, "We all know whose family steals around here." Heather had held her gaze until Haley led the other girls off. They'd iced Heather out for most of that week, until their teacher found the pencil case under the bench in the coat closet. She'd handed it back to Haley, and Haley had glared hard at Heather as she tucked it into her desk. Still, at lunch that day she and the other girls saved Heather a seat at their end of the table.

It didn't bother Heather much, this periodic freezing out, not really. Even though the comments about her family might have given her a quick flush of anger, she'd taught herself to tamp down her temper, to let it pass, rather than do something to make it worse. She knew that sooner or later she'd be back in and one of the other girls would be out, and they'd find some way to needle her, whoever she was. Except Haley Langille. Haley was the girl who all the other girls courted. She decided who was *in*, and who was *out*. And Heather had been *out* enough times that she wouldn't really miss Haley or any of the other girls. Why not try a new school, new friends? Because it didn't seem like she was going home any time soon, after all. But eventually, someday, she would. Wouldn't she?

She stayed with the Colfords for seven years. And they were good to her. When she misbehaved—when she refused to eat the pork hocks and sauerkraut that Hope made for supper, for example, and said her cooking was gross, or when the school sent her home for smacking Thomas Skinner in the face (he'd taken one of the new badminton rackets from her in gym class, from right out of her hand, and tried to leave her one of the crappy old ones with broken strings), or when she left the garage door open one night and someone stole the bike that Teddy bought her at a garage sale—Hope would call her husband. "Teddy, you get in here and speak to this girl or I don't know what!" And Teddy would stand in front of her, one hand on his hip, the other stabbing the air furiously. "I won't have any of that in this house, do you mind me?" And she wouldn't be allowed to watch TV or go to the park or biking (before her bike was stolen) for one week. But they never sent her off, never smacked her. Never called the social worker and said they couldn't handle her anymore. It took Heather a while to trust that they wouldn't.

They even had a birthday party of sorts for her, to mark the first anniversary of her coming to live with them. They bought a white cake from the grocery store. It had little blue and pink sugar flowers on it. Teddy carried it out to the table after supper, a sparkler blazing on top on it. And after he set it down, he gave her a sort of one-armed hug, roughly shaking her shoulder in his hand. Hope put both of her hands over Heather's and squeezed. A tendril of affection curled itself up cautiously in Heather's chest.

It's true that their care consisted mostly of what nowadays, Heather would call *benign neglect*. It was a term one of her clients had used once—a woman who owned a bakery in town. Heather had come to her house to work on her business's books and had commented on how beautiful the woman's gardens were, filled with lush, flowering bushes and ground cover.

"They thrive under my benign neglect," the woman had said, laughing, and Heather had thought of the Colfords. They had pretty much let Heather go her own way. Hope made them all supper in the evening, but Heather would eat her breakfast alone—a bowl of cereal or a couple pieces of toast. She'd pack her own lunches for school. In the evening, Heather could watch TV with them in the den, or not, as she chose. They didn't ask her whether she'd finished her homework. When she handed them her report cards, they'd glance through them and comment, "Good, good," whether she had mostly Bs or mostly Cs. They never bothered her about going out, as long as she was home by curfew (eight when she first arrived, nine when she turned twelve, then ten on weekends when she was thirteen). And Teddy always drove her to sleep over at friends' houses or to Marian and Jack's, and always came to pick her up in the morning.

But they were old when she first arrived to live with them, and getting older. By the time Heather reached high school, Hope had developed a new habit. She'd bustle into a room, her back ever more stooped, then she'd stop. Stand there blinking a moment, then call, "Teddy! What did I come in here for?" She sometimes burned supper, wandering out of the kitchen and forgetting she'd left the burner on. Heather mostly took over the cooking then. And Hope started to have trouble getting up out of chairs and out of bed in the morning. Plus, Heather noticed that she had started to smell like pee.

One day, when Heather was in grade eleven, she came home from school to find a strange car in the driveway—a shiny black sedan. Heather approached the front door cautiously. She slipped inside without a sound.

Jeffrey Colford was sitting at the dining room table with his parents. Teddy was shaking his head. "It's cruel, that's what," he said. "We'll just have to wait two more years, till she's done school."

"Mom can't wait that long," Jeffrey said.

Teddy looked at Hope, but she just shook her head. Then she saw Heather in the front hall and she said brightly, "There you are, girlie! I'll get supper on!" She put her hands on the table, struggling to her feet.

"I can make supper," Heather replied quickly, moving to the kitchen.

Hope shook her head. "I was going to make a nice roast, with Jeffrey home!"

"You don't have to do that, Mom," Jeffrey replied. "Why don't we order in? My treat." He looked to Heather for help.

"What about fish and chips?" Heather suggested, knowing it was Teddy's favourite, and therefore the take-out meal Hope was most likely to agree to.

They ordered the food, and Jeffrey asked Heather if she'd come with him to help pick it up. She agreed, and they set out in the pristine black car—a rental, Heather realized. As they wound through the streets of Lunenburg with their quaint gingerbread-looking houses, Jeffrey cleared his throat.

"How've my parents been?" he asked.

"Good," Heather replied reflexively.

"Oh yeah?" He glanced over at her then, his eyebrows raised.

Heather paused. She hardly knew Jeffrey. Every now and then, he'd come home to visit his parents for a few days. Heather usually made herself scarce during his trips home, staying with Jack and Marian or else at a friend's house. It felt weird, staying in the same house with a stranger—one who had a stronger claim to the home and to Teddy and Hope than she did. "Hope is getting old," she said at last.

"They both are," Jeffrey replied. He pulled into the driveway then. He turned off the ignition, but neither of them got out. Instead, they sat looking at the house. "Dad's not going to be able to shovel the walk this winter."

"I can do it," Heather said.

"There's a lot they can't keep up with."

Heather didn't answer.

"Listen, I know they've only been able to stay here in the house as long as they have because of you."

Heather shook her head. "That's not true."

"It is," Jeffrey replied. "And it's not fair to you. Stuck in a house like this, taking care of two old people, when you should be out doing kid stuff."

What kind of kid stuff did Jeffrey think she should be up to? What had he done when he was her age? There were photos of him in the house wearing hockey gear, at a piano recital. Did he think anyone was going to pay to sign her up for sports or music lessons? Did he think people were lining up to take care of her so she wouldn't have to keep making supper and doing laundry for Teddy and Hope?

She didn't trust herself to say anything without snapping at him, though, and that wouldn't do any good. She grabbed the Styrofoam boxes of food and carried them inside.

Jeffrey went home to Toronto the next day. He didn't say anything more about his parents, or about her. They nodded politely to each other at the front door before Hope and Teddy followed him out onto the front steps, kissing him and waving goodbye.

Later that fall, in November, Hope tripped over the edge of the carpet between the kitchen and dining room. Heather was at school when it happened. When she got home, the house was empty. It was unusual, but she didn't think much about it. Anyway, Teddy and Hope didn't have cellphones, so she couldn't exactly call and ask where they were. She pulled a package of ground beef out of the fridge and started making spaghetti sauce.

Teddy came home just as Heather was draining the pasta. He sat down at the dining room table.

"Our Hope's had a bit of a fall," he said. "Landed herself up in the hospital."

"She okay?" Heather asked, even though Hope was obviously not okay if she was in the hospital.

"Broke her hip. But she'll be mended and home soon, I reckon. She'll be all right, won't she."

Heather brought the pasta and sauce to the table. Teddy helped himself, then Heather did, too. But neither of them ate much.

Hope did not come home from the hospital. The next day, Jeffrey returned from Toronto. He stayed a week, and when Hope was released he arranged for his parents to be taken straight to an assisted living home in Chester. He waited until they'd moved into their little apartment with its walk-in shower and the rails on the separate beds before he contacted a real estate agent to put the house on the market.

"You'll come to visit us, eh, Heather girly," Teddy declared. Heather nodded.

The next day, the social worker met Heather at home after school. Jeffrey was in Chester, helping his parents get settled in. She was a woman Heather spoke to briefly once a month, older, with very short grey hair and red-framed eyeglasses. She was nice enough. Always distracted, always in a hurry. They all seemed to be that way.

"You're sixteen," the social worker explained, "so you have a decision. We can place you in another foster home, or in a group home. Or you can choose to end your participation in the foster program."

"Can I think about it?" Heather asked.

The social worker flicked her gaze around the living room. Already, the house seemed so still, so empty without Teddy and Hope. They hadn't taken much with them—their clothes, some photos, their favourite chairs from the den—but already, the place had a long-vacant feeling. Heather tried to tamp down the lonely ache that threatened to fill her up. "You'll have to make up your mind soon."

After the social worker left, Heather called Marian to come pick her up.

"Can I stay with you guys a while?" Heather asked as they drove.

"How long's a while?" Marian replied without taking her eyes off the road.

"I dunno."

"We'll talk about it."

They never did, though. Heather slept on their couch for a couple of days, then asked Jack and Marian to take her back to the Colfords' to pick up the rest of her stuff. When they got there, a *For Sale* sign had been pitched on the front lawn, and most of the furniture and things had been cleared out of the house.

That weekend, Jack and Marian brought home a pullout couch to replace their old sofa in the living room, and a small dresser for the corner by the fireplace.

ও০

HEATHER SET HER PHONE DOWN. SHE NUZZLED CHARLOTTE'S downy head once again, then stood and made her way into the kitchen. She opened the fridge door, peered inside. Closed it again. What was she going to cook for Emma? Was Emma a vegetarian, or a vegan? She looked like she might be a vegan. Shouldn't Emma tell her so if that was the case? It seemed pretty rude to just let Heather try to guess whether she was or not.

Bean chili. She'd make bean chili. Her recipe didn't call for any meat, and she'd just put the shredded cheese and sour cream on the table. If Emma didn't eat dairy, she could just skip those. Heather didn't know how to make the cornbread without eggs, though.

Well, too bad. If she doesn't eat eggs, no cornbread for her. She should tell me if she's a vegan so I can plan ahead.

Feeling suddenly grumpy about the prospect of cooking for her possibly vegan sister, Heather stalked to the cupboard and yanked it open to see if she had beans and tomato sauce. She'd have to start a new shopping list.

And what about dessert? What the hell did vegans eat for dessert, anyway?

Heather sighed. Picked up her phone again. Scrolled through the contacts. Dialled.

TWENTY-ONE

SATURDAY MORNING, EMMA DROVE UP TO GRAND PRÉ TO photograph landmarks from the Acadian Expulsion—Gaugin Ground Zero. She photographed the church and the museum, then went out to get some pictures of the marshlands and the dikes. She wondered whether the Gaugins had helped build these, whether they had helped to drain the waters for the marshlands to produce crops. When had they fled? Had they felt the tides turning in the war between the English and French? Had they known how badly things would turn out for the Acadians? Had they tried to warn their neighbours, or just disappeared in the night?

Emma took pictures of the coast and the marshes, the fields of young green wheat. It was all filler, really. Photos to pop into her thesis, picturesque fluff. But fluff was all she had the stomach for by now. Anyway, she'd pretty much finished all her serious research. She scrolled through the last photos she'd taken, pictures of vetch that had already begun to mound over a fence that ran along a pasture, its chains of purple flowers giving the boundary between the field and the roadside a soft, tender aspect, hiding the barbs in the wire, making the fence seem like an easy green hillock dotted with mauve. Looking at the images, she realized that over the course of the afternoon she'd been forming two parallel but incompatible fantasies of what the Gaugins had been like back then, back when they lived among other Acadians, up to the moment they fled.

The first had been forming at the edge of her thoughts today as she explored the picturesque tourist sites along the Evangeline Trail, as this section of Nova Scotia highway had been branded. She was imagining Gaugin men and women in their quaint late-eighteenth-century costumes, looking like contented peasants in a pastoral romance. She imagined warm hearth fires in tidy cottages, tender smiles between mothers and fathers at the end of a long day of labour. The hard work of standing alongside neighbours to build dikes and plough fields, to plant kitchen gardens and weave fabrics. She imagined their flight, a frightened slipping away as rumours spread of men rounded up, of women weeping and begging to see their husbands and sons only to be turned away by hard-faced red-coats. Regretful glances cast at neighbours' cottages, the homes of friends they could not save, could not take with them. This was the image that fit neatly with the early journals, the accounts of women who looked complacently at the prospect of having Gaugin in-laws.

But then there was the other idea, the one that had planted itself so firmly in her thoughts, rooted in the way she remembered people saying her name when she was a kid, *Gaugin*, rolling it out of their mouths as though it tasted bad, and cemented by Grace Inglis's horrible revelation. It was a version that smelled like pig shit and unwashed bodies, that rang of the sounds of too many people yelling over each other as they tried to wedge themselves in a hovel too small for so many bodies, both human and livestock. It was drinking and violence, resentments coddled deep in the soul, petty infractions on their neighbours, thefts and encroachments, harsh words and even blows, justified by real and imagined slights that were nurtured like seedlings deep in their hearts until they flowered into unbridgeable feuds. In this version, there was time to warn the neighbours, time to save other families, time to get the husbands and sons out, to keep families together, but hardened feelings made them leave their neighbours to their own fates, of thinking it served them right as these early Gaugins slithered away from Grand Pré and into the woods.

This was the easier version to believe. After all, how could the first idea, the version of the Gaugins harmonious and loving, how could they become the other—the family who hid in the deepest part of the Nova Scotia forest, who didn't bat an eye at a brother and sister marrying. This was the version that was humming in Emma's brain as she packed up, got ready to head back to her hotel. To wrap things up.

If she hadn't changed her flight, she'd be getting ready to head home, instead.

Why on earth had she changed her flight?

She got back to the hotel shortly after noon. Took the back stairway up from the parking lot to avoid passing by the front desk. She hadn't seen Glen since their date. She felt bad about not calling him.

Of course, he hadn't called her, either.

As she ate her lunch, she dutifully combed through her photos and notes, logging each one, backing them all up online. She managed to do it without really looking at the pictures or the research. She tried to read through her notes, but when she read her own words she was filled with shame. The part about taking a shit in the woods during her first trip out to the compound: what had she been thinking? She would have deleted it, but that would mean reading back through it, editing, actually thinking about what she'd written.

And anyway, she knew that was exactly the kind of "realness" that her supervisors wanted to see. They wanted her to record her reflections, her observations, yes. They wanted an account of how she responded to the archival research, to the interviews with her family, yes. But they also wanted "immediacy." Dr. Fuentes kept using that word. They wanted her to give them the moments of pure reaction, the visceral emotional response to the stimulus of her past. That, Dr. Fuentes had explained, was what would set her project apart from others in the field of historical auto-ethnography, new as that field was. And she and Dr. Melnyk wanted to co-supervise a project that stood out. She couldn't quite let go of the idea of their approval.

Finally, mid-afternoon, she shut down her laptop. Took a shower. Picked out a decent blouse, a pair of clean leggings, a soft scarf. Put on a little makeup, even blow-dried her hair. She looked nice. But not too fancy.

She'd have to bring something with her, she realized. You don't show up to dinner empty-handed. Her mother's lesson. Julia had even sent her on sleepovers as a kid with little gifts—boxes of cookies or old-fashioned-looking bottles of fancy soda. Should she bring a dessert? No, Heather probably already had the meal all planned out. Maybe a bottle of wine. But wine left the kids out. Flowers?

Who the hell brings their sister flowers?

In the end, she bought a bottle of wine. Rosé, because it seemed more seasonal somehow. An early summer wine. Then she stopped at a big box store and bought two little plush toys for Justin and Charlotte. A fox and an owl. They seemed cuter than stuffed bears. More memorable.

Then she set off toward Chester.

As she drove, she rehearsed what she'd say if Heather asked her about her research. "It was great. Found everything I was looking for. Couldn't have done it without you, sis. Thanks."

Of course, she couldn't tell Heather about the Grace Inglis journal. About the incest. Not yet, anyway. Emma wasn't great at social situations, but she knew incest wasn't an appropriate family dinner conversation.

Back when she and Adrian had been dating a few months, she had braced herself to suggest they meet each other's parents. The idea of sitting down to dinner with Adrian's parents, his mother the executive director of the provincial symphony and his father a financial planner, sent a fluttering of nervousness down her arms. But they were getting serious, weren't they? They spent most nights together. Their social lives were entwined.

Meaning, of course, that when they went out, it was with his friends.

"So what should I tell my parents to cook us for dinner?" That was how she asked him. They were on Emma's couch, watching a violent cable series. There was always some kind of battle going on. For some reason, the women fought topless.

He gave his barking little laugh. "Right," he said. "Can you even imagine?"

"You don't want to meet my parents? Or for me to meet yours?"

He rolled his eyes dramatically. "I'd rather drink lighter fluid." He reached for the remote control and edged the TV volume up.

There was a little sinking, just a tiny bit, in her core. But she adjusted. She twisted around to look him squarely in the face. "How else are we going to announce our honourable intentions?"

He gave another little bark-laugh, still staring at the screen.

"They'll want to know. Summer wedding or fall. Roses or hydrangea. Strawberry or pumpkin. Also, do you think you should impregnate me before the ceremony or after?"

"Fucking kill me now."

Emma mimed taking aim at his face with a rifle. Squeezing the trigger. He looked away from the TV long enough to feign having his head blown off.

She never did meet Adrian's parents. Or he, hers. Probably for the best. She really was bad at dinner conversation.

No, she wouldn't tell Heather. Not tonight.

But the idea of holding back, keeping the secret, made Emma feel guilty. It was Heather's family, too. What right did Emma have to keep it from her?

She reached Chester at 4:20. It was only ten minutes from the highway exit to the Publicovers'. Heather had said to be there by 5, but 4:30 seemed too early. Emma pulled off to the side of the road. She'd wait fifteen minutes, then go. She thought about calling her parents, but she just couldn't work up the energy. If she couldn't decide what to tell Heather about the Gaugins, how could she possibly figure out what to tell the Weavers?

Just then, Emma's phone buzzed to life, startling her. She snatched it, half-expecting it to be Heather phoning to tell her dinner was cancelled, go home now, nothing more to see here.

It wasn't Heather. Glen's name flashed across the screen. Emma's insides lurched. She swiped to send the call to voicemail. Sat back in her seat. Tried to meditate to push the memory of their kiss out of her head. She focused on the feeling of her breath filling her lungs. On the sensation of her legs and back pressing down onto the soft car seat, the oblong patch of warm sun that sliced through the window to warm her forearm.

It had been a pretty good kiss, though. And Glen wouldn't be calling if he didn't want to see her again.

Plus, it wasn't like there was a future here. It'd been a while since Emma had had sex. She hated the idea of a one-night-stand, but this wouldn't be that. They knew each other (a little). They'd been on one date already. And if it was any good, she maybe had time to see him once or twice again before she left.

She opened her eyes and checked her voicemail.

"Hey Emma. I know it's last minute, but I was wondering what you're up to tonight. I…ahhh. Anyway. Call me if you want to have plans. If you don't have plans, I mean. Right."

It was the stumbling, the self-consciousness that finally spoke in his favour. The disarming, endearing awkwardness. She decided not to call him—she didn't trust herself to put together a sentence any less awkward. But she started a text.

Hey Glen. Sorry I missed you. I have

She stopped. She couldn't say "dinner with my sister" because then she'd have to explain Heather. She didn't want to say "dinner plans" because that sounded too much like another date.

I have an interview to do tonight. Not sure when I'll be done. Tomorrow?

His reply pinged on her screen almost immediately. *Sounds good. Meet you at the hotel at 8?*

Sure, she replied. Checked the time after she sent the message. 4:27. Close enough. She turned the ignition and steered her car towards the Publicovers' house.

Justin answered the door. He was wearing a black-and-white checked shirt tucked into a pair of blue jeans and a little black vest. "Hello, Auntie," he said, tugging at the armpit of his vest. *Auntie.*

"Hey, Justin. You look very handsome."

He gave her a funny little smile, at once goofy and self-conscious, and shuffled into the kitchen. She followed.

Heather was buzzing around behind the kitchen counter. Two men sat at the wooden dining table. Emma recognized Jack Rushdie. His thin, curling, grey ponytail was the same as the last time she'd seen him. His tan trousers and flannel shirt looked to be much the same as what he'd worn when she interviewed him, but like Justin, Jack had a slightly starched look, as though he'd washed and ironed his clothing specially for dinner. He held baby Charlotte on his lap. She was chewing happily on a green plastic ring.

Across from Jack and Charlotte sat a broad-shouldered man with a shaved head and deep black eyes. His skin was relatively light in colour, lighter than most of the African Canadians she'd known, not all that much darker than Jack's weather-tanned face. Emma glanced involuntarily at Justin—she hadn't realized that her niece and nephew were biracial. Immediately, she was ashamed of herself for noticing, for her feeling of surprise.

He stood up and extended his hand. "Emma, right? I'm Rafe." His hands were big, warm. He smiled, a big, bright grin, but Emma thought she caught a guardedness in his eyes. Justin wrapped his arm around his father's leg and pressed his head into his side.

"I brought these," Emma said, fumbling through the cloth bag. She set the wine on the table and held out the plush toys. Justin's eyes fixed on the fox, but his arms tightened around his father's leg.

"What do you say, Justin?" Heather chimed from behind the counter.

"Thank you," the little boy mumbled obediently. He eased himself away from his father and reached for the fox. He held it in front of his face, staring deeply into its little plastic eyes.

"Will you give this one to your sister?" Emma asked, handing him the owl.

Justin nodded. He carried the toy around and passed it to Charlotte. She stared at it for a moment before seizing its wing in her little fist. She shook it and squealed.

"She's gonna put it in her mouth," Justin predicted, crinkling up his nose theatrically.

"That's okay," Emma said. Then she glanced at her sister, who was busily chopping vegetables for a salad. "Isn't it?"

"Won't be the worst thing she's put in her mouth," Heather replied.

"Today," Rafe added with a half-smile. "Guess we should open this," he added, picking up the wine. He pulled out the cork and poured glasses for the four adults.

"So how's the research going, then?" Jack asked.

"Great," Emma replied. "Heather's been awesome. We went out to the compound to take pictures, and she explained everything."

"So you don't remember the place?" Jack said, picking up the teething ring that Charlotte had thrown to the floor.

"Not really, no."

"And what are you gonna do with this research of yours?" Rafe asked.

"It'll go into my thesis," Emma replied. "For my Master's degree."

Rafe took a drink of his wine. "Then what?"

Emma shrugged. "Then nothing, probably. My supervisors will read it, and another couple of professors. They'll ask me questions about it, then hopefully they'll approve it and I'll get my degree."

"So you're not writing a book? To publish or whatever?"

"God, no." Emma shuddered. The thought made it feel as though her lungs were being compressed.

"Why are you doing this then?" Rafe asked. "Why not write your thesis on something else?" His eyes were on her. They were serious, still a little guarded perhaps, but soft somehow. His expression was open. He expected an answer, Emma could see, but he wasn't judging her. Not yet.

She paused. She thought back to the party, to the feeling that she'd been cornered into this topic. But that wasn't how she felt now. Her impulse was to say something smart, something rude or off-colour, but she felt Heather's gaze on her. *Don't you dare*, her sister seemed to be telling her. Anyway, Emma didn't think Rafe was the kind of person to be shocked into changing the conversation. "There are things I need to know," she said at last. "For me."

"Like what?"

Emma didn't answer right away. The idea of the Gaugins, the bogeymen she'd always imagined them to be, crowded her mind. The phrase *brother and sister* in the looping handwriting of that goddamned journal. Even if she wanted to find the words for all that, how could she, with not just Heather but her husband and her children sitting right there, and Jack, with his cautious, appraising look? "I want to know," she said at last, "how much I remember is true, and how much I just made up after I left."

Rafe nodded. He kept his gaze on her, and Emma felt as though she'd passed the test. She thought that perhaps some of that guardedness had fallen away.

"Give me a hand with this?" Heather asked.

Both Rafe and Emma obediently stepped toward the cooking area. She handed Rafe the big salad bowl and a couple of bottles of dressing, then she gave Emma a bowl of shredded cheese and a little tub of sour cream. They arranged them in the middle of the table as Heather carried over a big pot from the stove.

"Hope you like bean chili," Heather said.

"I don't think I've ever had it," Emma replied. "My mom makes it without beans. Just beef and bacon." *My mom.* Emma stopped, wondering whether she should explain, whether she should have said "Julia" instead. But no one seemed to have noticed. She let it drop.

Emma hovered for a moment as everyone found their seats, afraid to take someone's spot. Finally, she sat between Jack and Heather.

Justin sat across from her and watched her closely as she helped herself to a bowl of chili. "It's good with cheese," he advised.

"I'll try that," Emma replied.

Justin nodded and put a spoonful into his mouth.

"How much longer are you staying?" Heather asked. She fed a small spoonful of the chili to Charlotte, who sat in a high chair between Heather and Rafe.

"Wednesday," Emma replied. "I was supposed to go home tomorrow, but I changed my flight."

"What are you doing until then?"

"I don't know," Emma replied. "Sort through my research, probably. I don't really have anything else to look into. Unless you know of something, someone I should interview or whatever."

Heather didn't answer. She fed Charlotte another spoonful of dinner.

"So have you found what you were looking for?" Jack asked.

Emma paused. What *had* she been looking for? Just a couple of weeks ago, she thought she knew. She'd wanted archival treasure, the chance to dig into the lives of Gaugins at an academic distance. Remote access. But then she'd found Heather. She hadn't expected that, not after the letter. "I guess so," she said at last. "Did your wife ever look into stuff? Like the family history?"

Jack shook his head. "She covered the story for the paper, that was about it."

"My daddy builds big buildings," Justin said suddenly.

"Does he?" Emma asked, glancing at Rafe, who smiled.

"Big office towers and warehouses and factories," he said. "He puts the electricity in them."

"Wow."

After dinner, Rafe took Charlotte upstairs to get her ready for bed. "Half an hour, then it's your turn, bud," he said to Justin. Justin pretended not to hear.

Heather led Emma and Jack into the living room. Justin followed and busied himself with a box of LEGOs. Emma settled onto the couch with a cup of tea in her hands.

"Have you looked for any other family?" Jack asked. "Other than your sister?"

Heather shot Jack a sharp look, but he avoided her gaze. Instead he sat in the armchair, looking placidly at Emma.

"No," Emma replied. "Why, is there more family?"

"Of course there will be," Jack said. "Though it might be hard to find where most of them ended up."

"Do you know any of them?"

Jack leaned back in his chair. He smiled a bit and took a sip of his tea.

Emma looked over at Heather, who was glaring at Jack. Emma's heart started to pound in her chest. *Who?* she wondered. *Who, who, who?*

Heather cleared her throat. She shifted uneasily. "When I was a kid," she began. She spoke slowly, carefully. Choosing her words. "When I was a teenager, I mean. When you're sixteen, you get to decide, do I want to stay in foster care or not. And I was staying with this couple, they were really nice and all, but things happened and they couldn't keep me anymore. So I decided not to go into another foster home."

Jack nodded. "That's when she came to live with us. For a while."

"Right. I was staying with Jack and Marian. And they'd just got internet at home. We didn't have that at my foster home; they were kind of old-fashioned, my foster parents. So I started searching the online phone books. I found Mark Gaugin, our uncle, in Sydney, and Travis Gaugin, his son, in Saint John. But I didn't bother calling them. They were pretty much strangers. I didn't remember much about them. There were a couple of Arlene Campbells in PEI and Nova Scotia, but I don't know if any of them was our aunt, the one who married Mark. Mom's cousin. But then I also found two Helen Campbells in Dartmouth. And one Kevin Gaugin at the same number."

Emma felt her chest tighten, felt the flushing, racing feeling in her hands, her thighs. Her cheeks were hot, and she could feel her pulse throbbing on her skin.

"So I bought a bus ticket and headed out to Dartmouth."

Jack chuckled. "Worried the life out of Marian and me, disappearing like that."

Emma stared at her sister. So Heather had disappeared, after all. Had she gone back to the compound, the way she'd threatened that first night? Had she gone looking for Emma herself, or for their brother Kevin, their sister Jennifer? Had she gone to find their parents? Or had she simply run? "Disappeared?"

Heather lifted her eyes, met her sister's gaze. Her expression so mixed Emma couldn't tell what she was feeling.

THE BREAD CRUMB TRAIL

TWENTY-TWO

THE TRUTH WAS, HEATHER HAD BEEN THINKING OF SEARCHING online for her family for a while. But Teddy and Hope couldn't be persuaded to buy cellphones, much less home internet service. Heather did her homework on the ancient Dell hooked up to a dot-matrix printer in the Colfords' family room. She had often considered searching for her family on the computers at the school library, but the idea of firewalls and search histories deterred her. She imagined being dragged into the school guidance counsellor's office to explain to him, her social worker, and Teddy and Hope why she was trying to find her birth family. She knew she definitely wouldn't be allowed to go and live with them—after all, if her parents had been allowed to get their kids back, they would have by now. If they even wanted them back. But that didn't stop Heather needing to know where they were. She wanted a province, a city, maybe even an address. She wanted to be able to map them, to judge their distance from her. It had occurred to her that as adults, her parents might have been allowed access to more information than she got. Unless the social workers thought they were dangerous, or that they might try to take their kids back or something, there was a chance they knew exactly where she lived, who she lived with, what her life was like. And if that was true, if they knew about her, she wanted to know about them. It was only fair.

When she received the official letter from the Nova Scotia Department of Community Services telling her that she had been discharged from the foster care system, Heather started searching online phone books and directories. She started with the Gaugin name. Found listings for Mark, Travis. Nothing for Gary Gaugin, her father, or her mother, Helen Gaugin. Nothing for her Nanny— Maureen Gaugin. Could be that the Kevin Gaugin in Dartmouth was her Poppy. How old would he be now? She remembered him as old, old, old, but it's possible that the last time she'd seen him, he was only in his fifties. Or he could have been closer to eighty at the time. It was impossible to guess. He might not even be alive, still. So Kevin Gaugin in Dartmouth could be her brother.

There were no listings for Shauna Gaugin. Like Helen, she seemed to have vanished after 1991. Of course, Helen and her cousin Arlene could have gone back to their maiden name, Campbell, and shed the Gaugin connection entirely. But what about Shauna? She was born a Gaugin. Had she changed her name? Was she homeless, dead, in prison?

Were the other unlisted Gaugins in prison? Her dad, for example? Her grandparents? Aunts, uncles? Her cousin Jonathan? How many of them had actually gone to jail after the raid? How long had they been imprisoned? How would a person search for someone in prison, anyway? It's not like there was a list on the internet.

But then her search turned up Helen Campbell and Kevin Gaugin in Dartmouth. It might be her mom and Poppy, or it might be her mom and her brother. She wrote down the phone number on a page in her math notebook. Tore it out and stuck it in her pocket. Then she closed the browser window and shut down the computer.

For a day, she didn't call. Two days. Then on the third day, after the bus dropped her off at the Rushdies', Heather let herself into the quiet house. Jack was teaching in Halifax that afternoon, and Marian was still at the newspaper office.

Heather grabbed the phone from its cradle in the kitchen. She sat on the living room couch, her bed, with its view of the driveway through the front window. She took the scrap of paper out of her pocket, and she dialled.

One ring. Two.

"Hello?"

It was her. Helen Campbell. Helen Gaugin. Her mom.

"Hello?"

"Hi." It was all she could think to say. What now?

"Who is this?" Helen asked.

Heather hung up.

She looked at the slip of paper in her hand. There was an address in Dartmouth.

She had a little money saved—Christmas and birthday gifts from the Colfords, mostly, and bills Marian tucked into the pocket of Heather's jacket from time to time, "In case you need it." More than enough to get a bus ticket to Dartmouth. She could leave after school tomorrow.

That night, Heather packed as many clothes as she could into her school bag without stuffing it suspiciously full. A few pairs of socks and underwear, a couple of T-shirts. She'd have to make do with the jeans she was wearing. Some deodorant, a hairbrush. She could get by with this.

She glanced at the clock. Almost five. Marian would be home soon, though Jack wouldn't be back from Halifax until after ten.

She made her way into the kitchen and pulled a box of macaroni and a can of beans out of the cupboard. She got them started on the stove. Took out a bag of frozen peas. Sure, supper kind of sucked, but hot buttered peas were Marian's favourite. And she'd appreciate not having to cook.

Marian came in just as Heather was draining the noodles.

"Oh, that looks good," Marian said. She squeezed Heather's arm as she hung up her coat next to the kitchen door.

Kindnesses. When Marian said these things that weren't quite true, they were never really lies, but kindnesses. They had a deeper truth than the actual words themselves. Heather never minded hearing them.

When they finished eating, Heather moved to clean up the dishes but Marian shooed her away. "You must have homework. Go, get it finished."

Homework. It seemed silly, since Heather wouldn't be in school tomorrow to hand it in. Nonetheless, she spread out her books on the dining room table, opposite Marian's painting corner, and got to work solving math problems. She dragged it out until Marian settled in the living room with the TV on. She was watching a detective show. She always got lost in them, even though she scoffed at the improbable plots and dubious science. Heather settled on the couch next to her.

Marian moved her legs to give Heather more space. "Do you want to get ready for bed?" she asked.

"No, not yet," Heather replied, pulling the crocheted blanket over her legs.

Marian turned her attention back to the TV.

When Jack got home shortly before eleven, Marian and Heather were both asleep on the couch, the national news flashing across the TV screen.

"Bed time, my girls," he said softly, dropping a kiss onto Marian's forehead. He squeezed Heather's shoulder.

Marian blinked and stretched. She stood up slowly, her limbs still clumsy with sleep. Heather stood up too, and together the three of them unfolded the couch into Heather's bed.

"Night, you," Marian said.

"Night," Heather replied. She watched Jack and Marian climb the stairs to their loft bedroom, holding the moment in her mind. She might need it later.

༒

SHE WANTED TO WRITE THEM A NOTE, BUT JACK WOULD FIND IT before the bus left. He'd intercept her at the gas station that served as the town's Greyhound stop. She'd have to settle for calling them when she got there. Her coward heart wanted to email instead, but she wouldn't allow herself that sneakiness. She'd have to call them.

The bus stopped in downtown Dartmouth. Heather used a payphone to call the transit line. Her stomach squirmed uncomfortably at the idea of navigating the public transit system. She'd never taken a city bus before, had only a vague sense of how it worked from watching TV and movies. The voice on the phone told her where to catch a bus and where to get off, how much the fare would be. Heather walked across the street to the Tim Horton's. She bought a sweet, milky coffee to break her twenty-dollar bill.

Twenty minutes until her bus. She eyed a table in the corner. No. She'd have to call now. Get it over with. She took her coffee and dashed back across the street, toward the phone booth.

Jack answered on the second ring. "Something wrong, my girl?" he asked when he heard her voice.

"Nothing's wrong. Just wanted to let you know I won't be home tonight."

"Where you staying?"

"Dartmouth."

There was a pause. "What do you mean?" he asked at last.

"I want to go and see my mom."

"I see."

There was a silence. Outside the phone booth, a Greyhound bus chugged away from the station.

"You phone if you need us to come get you."

For one moment, just the briefest, most crushingly tight second, Heather wanted to ask him to come now, to come get her and take her back. She remembered his warm, strong hand on her shoulder as he'd wished her goodnight less than a day ago. But she didn't. She steeled herself and said, "I will."

"Be careful, Heather girl."

Heather hung up the phone. She walked slowly up the street toward the bus stop the man on the transit line had described. She found the stop and stood inside the glass shelter to try to deflect some of the noise from the busy street and the cold wind that blasted her. It was November, and the weather had been turning from mild fall to chilly winter. The back wall was smashed out, though, and the shelter wasn't much of one.

The bus pulled up a few moments later. Heather checked the electronic sign on the front. She got on and nervously dumped her change into the fare box next to the driver.

"Need a transfer?" he asked without looking at her.

Heather wasn't sure what a transfer was, but she didn't want to ask and sound like a yokel. "Yeah," she said. He ripped a slip of blue paper off the stack next to the fare box and handed it to her. She stuffed it into her pocket without looking at it.

"Can you tell me when we get to Guysborough Avenue?" she asked.

"Sit near the front," the driver replied.

Heather sat on the hard seat. She felt the scratchy velvet-like fabric rubbing against the back of her coat. She watched out the window as the bus lurched along, trying to catch the street signs they passed, not quite trusting the driver to remember. She watched as other passengers pulled the cords that ran along the tops of the windows, dinging a little bell to tell the driver to stop. She watched as old women with little wheeled bag trolleys got on and sat on the inward-facing seats at the front, as a group of teens maybe a little younger than her got on, laughing loudly and lounging across as many seats at the back of the bus as they could manage, watched as a tired-looking woman in a head-scarf got on, leading a dark-haired toddler by the hand. Heather felt as though she'd shrunk, disappeared. She felt anonymous, invisible, safe.

She'd been to Halifax before. A couple of times, Teddy and Hope had brought her in with them when they came for doctors' appointments or shopping trips. They always stayed in a hotel near Citadel Hill. Heather had always thought of it as a fancy hotel, but then, she had nothing to compare it to. Their room always had a small but shiny-clean bathtub, a big TV, and paintings of Nova Scotia on the walls. There'd be a bed for Teddy and Hope, and a few minutes after they arrived in their room, a staff member would knock on the door and wheel in a cot for her. In the mornings, they'd make their way to the little room off the lobby for free breakfast. Teddy and Hope liked the waffles you made yourself in the heavy round griddle, but Heather preferred the plastic case full of different kinds of breads and bagels.

Usually, they'd go to the Halifax shopping mall, or sometimes drive over the bridge to the mall in Dartmouth. Heather liked the big malls, even the areas in them that looked older and run-down. There were always groups of kids hanging out there, no matter what time of day. She had no desire to hang out with them, or even to spend time there with her own friends. She just liked the way they looked at her when she navigated the shops with Teddy and Hope, like the three of them were a family unit. Heather imagined they must have thought she was out shopping with her grandparents.

She liked eating in the food court with all its fast-food options. Teddy would hand her a ten-dollar bill, and she'd walk around, glancing at each of the counters, deciding what she wanted. Hope always wanted a burger and root beer from A&W, and so Teddy always ordered his meal from there, too. But Heather didn't have to. She could pick what she wanted to eat, bring her meal back on its plastic tray, and eat with her foster parents.

"Guysborough Ave," the driver called as he pulled up to a stop on a residential street.

Heather stood up quickly, before the bus was fully stopped, and lurched a little to keep her balance. She'd forgotten to keep watching the street signs. She slung her bag over her shoulder and stepped off the bus, nodding a thank you to the driver. He gave her a half-wave in reply as he reached for the lever to shut the doors.

She quickly realized she didn't know whether to go up the street or down. She turned down the avenue, rather than crossing the busy street to head in the other direction, but she soon discovered the numbers were going the wrong way. She turned around and followed the numbers across the main street toward the address.

It was an older house, its wood siding painted blue and peeling a bit. There was a wide, white-painted veranda across the front with mismatched lawn chairs at either end. Instead of a front yard, a narrow strip of shrubs bridged the veranda and the sidewalk. A gravel driveway ran along the side of the property toward what looked like an unpaved parking lot in back.

There were two doors on the veranda and four mailboxes next to the doors. The addresses for Helen Campbell and Kevin Gaugin were in C and D. The door on the right had those metal-plated letters stuck below the glass window. Heather opened the door and followed the narrow wooden staircase up to a small, dark landing. Doors C and D opened on either side.

Helen was in apartment C on the left. There was no doorbell. Heather drew in a breath and knocked.

Nothing.

Heather knocked again. No one answered, so she turned and knocked on D.

She heard a soft shuffling inside. The door opened, revealing a woman in her twenties. She was wearing pyjama pants and a sweat-shirt. She blinked blearily as though Heather had just woken her up.

"I'm looking for Kevin Gaugin?" Heather asked.

"Nah, he don't live here no more."

Heather hesitated, unsure how to ask whether it was her brother or her grandfather. "Okay. Do you know him?"

The woman shook her head. "I just rented the place when it came vacant."

"What about the woman in C?" Heather asked. "Helen Campbell?" What would she do if neither of them lived here anymore?

"Yeah, Helen's probably working," the woman replied. "She's a cashier over at the Sobeys."

"Oh. Okay." Heather hesitated, not sure what to do next.

The woman shrugged and closed the door. The landing was dark and still once again.

Heather made her way slowly back down the stairs. She could find the Sobeys and look for her mother there. No, Heather hated the idea of a public scene. So she could wait for her, or leave and come back later.

Where would she go, though? Another Tim Horton's, maybe. She'd seen one on almost every block along the bus route. What was it with Dartmouth and Tim Horton's?

She decided to wait for an hour. If Helen wasn't back then, she'd go and get a coffee, try again later. Heather sat on a fabric lawn chair on the veranda. The cool November air soon chilled the back of her legs and her butt where they pressed against the mesh of the chair. She wondered whether she should go to a coffee shop, anyway. It would be a cold hour, waiting outside. The day was bright and clear, and the sunlight sliced across the veranda onto her legs and torso, but it didn't warm her. The light in fall was so thin, she thought, and so white. She never noticed the colour of light the rest of the year, but autumn sunlight had that colourless, anemic quality. Even on mild days, the warmth seemed to be coming from the earth and the air and not the weak, retreating sun at all. She pulled her bag onto her lap and rested her chin on top of it, feeling the hard spine of her notebook inside. Heather hadn't been sure how to leave her schoolbooks behind that morning without raising Jack and Marian's suspicions.

She watched the cars that drove past the house. It was a relatively quiet street, only a vehicle every few minutes or so, and none pulled into the narrow driveway next to the house. A few people passed by on the sidewalk, some already wearing toques and scarves against the dropping temperature. A woman with shoulder-length hair showing under a grey hat walked along the sidewalk. Turned to come up the stairs onto the veranda.

Heather froze. The woman looked older than Marian, not as old as Hope. Heather was no good at guessing adults' ages. Maybe fifty? Deep lines ran from the corners of her nose to the corners of her mouth, and there was a softness to her jaw. She wasn't fat, but her hips were wide. She barely glanced at Heather as she reached for the door leading up to apartments C and D.

Heather stood up, holding her bag in front of her.

The woman stopped. Turned to face Heather. The outer corners of her eyes and her mouth pulled downwards, but that was her. Heather remembered those eyes, that face. It was her.

"Mom?" she asked. Her voice came out small. A peep.

Helen stared at her daughter. "Which one are you?" she asked. "I can't tell. Heather or Emma?"

"Mom, I'm Heather." Her voice sounded the way she felt—small, insubstantial. She stared hard at Helen, who looked immovable, as though nothing would ever catch her by surprise.

Helen nodded, keeping those flat, unsurprised eyes fixed on her second child. "Right. Emma'll be younger." She held open the door. Heather hesitated a moment, then followed her up the stairs. She waited on the top step while Helen fumbled for her keys.

Helen opened the door to the apartment. There was a narrow kitchen just off the front door. The counter was a cream-coloured Formica, and the cabinets were stained a warm wood colour, slightly battered, but clean. A bowl, a cup, and some cutlery sat in the drying rack on the counter next to the sink. A wall with a pass-through opening separated the kitchen from the narrow dining area, with its small laminated table and three mismatched chairs. Around the corner was the living room. It was bright—a big window opened onto the street side of the house. An easy chair and a futon folded into a couch were at angles to a small TV set on what looked like an old night-side table. There was a long shelf running the wall beneath the window, covered in plants. Heather recognized a spider plant and a jade, something with tiny red flowers, and a Christmas cactus like the one that sat in Marian and Jack's front window.

It was a small apartment, but still, Heather felt lost in it, adrift. And there was Helen, standing like a plinth in the centre of it. If Helen was at all affected by her daughter's appearance, she didn't show it.

"Can I use your bathroom?" Heather asked. She needed to shut herself away for a moment.

Helen pointed her to the door opposite the kitchen. There was another door off the living room. It was open, and Heather could see a neatly made bed with a flowered bedspread. She shut herself in the bathroom. She used the toilet—the coffee had made its way through her—then looked at herself in the mirror. Her own reflection was oddly comforting. Her hair was a bit lank, like it needed a wash, and her face looked oily. Spending more than a few minutes in the car always made her skin feel greasy, and the two bus trips had taken up a good chunk of her day already. She could see a couple of fresh pimples starting on her forehead. Still, it was a comfort to see her own face, as plain and pimply as it was. She didn't look the way she felt. Which was waifish and weak. Before she emerged, she ran some warm water and rubbed it on her face.

Heather emerged to find Helen in the kitchen.

"You hungry? Want some tea?"

"Glass of water?"

Helen took a glass out of the cupboard, filled it with water from the kitchen sink, and handed it to Heather. "Want a sandwich or something?"

"Sure. Thanks."

Helen pulled a loaf of bread, a package of ham, some cheese slices, and a bottle of mustard out of the fridge. She handed Heather a plate. "Should have everything you need here to whip one up."

"Good. Thanks." The plain offering awoke a faint hunger in Heather's stomach that she hadn't noticed before. She put together a sandwich and took a bite.

Helen leaned against the counter, watching her. "So you run away from your foster family or what?"

"Not exactly." Heather swallowed. "I'm not in foster care anymore. I'm sixteen. I opted out."

Helen frowned. "Where you living?"

Heather shrugged. How to explain Jack and Marian? "With some friends. In Chester Basin."

"They know you're here?"

"I called them from the bus station."

Still leaning against the counter, Helen looked down at the floor. Heather could see the roots of her hair. It was darker, with silver strands. The dyed yellow colour came in a few inches from her scalp, but near her face so much of Helen's hair was silver that you couldn't see where the roots stopped and where the dye began. "You thinking of staying?" Helen asked at last.

Heather swallowed her sandwich, a dull sense of disappointment settling in her chest. Heather wasn't sure how to answer. It wasn't exactly an invitation, was it? "I don't know," she said at last.

Helen drew in a long breath. "Well. Might as well sit where it's comfortable." Heather followed her into the living room. Helen sat on the futon so Heather took the armchair, balancing her plate and half-eaten sandwich on her knees.

They sat in silence for a long time. Heather could sense that Helen was waiting for her to start, to say something. A feeling of stubbornness rose up in Heather's chest. *I'm not going to be the first one to talk.*

Finally, Helen smiled, a flat dry sort of smile. Heather could see she was missing a front molar on top. "So this is a good talk. Anything else you want to get off your chest?"

"I could tell you where I've been?"

Helen nodded. "Sure."

So Heather told her about the foster homes, including the Weavers and the Colfords. She told her about the Rushdies, too. Made the story as simple as she could. She didn't want to sound like some great victim, but she didn't want to make it sound all Pollyanna, *Anne of Green Gables*, happy orphan story, either.

"But I lost track of Emma after the Weavers," she said. "I changed schools a few times, and at first I'd look for her and Kevin, but I never saw her."

"She was adopted," Helen said. Her voice was flat, matter-of-fact. "By the Weavers. Jenny was adopted, too."

"They took her away from you?" Heather asked. She felt as though she'd been slapped. Emma and Jennifer weren't even in the foster system anymore. They'd been adopted, given to other families. Heather felt as though something snapped in her chest, a long string that had been pulled tight, and was now loose and dangling.

"They took you all away from me," Helen replied. "But Emma and Jenny, they ended up in families that wanted them. Good families. So I gave them up."

"But you didn't give me up?"

"No." Helen leaned back against the futon. She looked out the window, resolutely, Heather thought. "I always thought there was a chance I could get you and Kevin back."

Heather suddenly remembered the other name in her pocket, Kevin Gaugin in apartment D. "And did you?" she asked. "Get Kevin back."

Helen nodded. "After a while. For a while."

"Was he in the other apartment? Across the hall?"

"Yeah, that was him."

"Where is he now?"

Helen turned and looked at her again. "Jail," she said. Her face seemed to have sagged since they'd entered the apartment. The skin seemed slacker, the eyes deeper. She looked old now, much older than Marian. Almost as old as Hope Colford.

"What happened?" Heather whispered. Her throat had tightened. She looked upward, blinking her eyes hard, trying not to cry. Remembering Kevin on the playground in his social-suicide sweatpants, staring sullenly at her and calling her a baby.

TWENTY-THREE

IT WASN'T THAT HELEN HADN'T EXPECTED HEATHER TO TURN UP. Heather, or Emma, or even Jenny. She had. She always did. It was just that she didn't know it would be today. How could she? She'd slogged home after an eight-hour shift on her feet at the grocery store cash register, and there was this hard-eyed kid sitting on her balcony in baggy jeans and an army-print jacket. Looking nothing like any of the sweet-faced little girls Helen remembered.

But here she was, on her doorstep, the way Helen always knew she would be. And she was ready, she really was. She'd practiced the story a hundred times. In the first years, it would include her begging her children to forgive her and promising to make everything okay. But as the years wore on, she felt less and less entitled to their forgiveness, less and less like begging for it. Or for anything. And by now, she knew better than to promise anything. So there was just the story then. The only problem was how to start it.

She hadn't planned to start with Kevin, with jail. He was awaiting trial on a Theft Over $5,000 charge. He'd stolen a car from a mall parking lot. Was probably planning to sell it for drug money. But he was pulled over and arrested. He'd be going to prison, that was certain, but who knew for how long.

That wasn't a good place to start. Nothing for it but to go back to the beginning. To the raids and the arrests. She kept it simple. Didn't talk about trying to get out of the back of the cop car, to get to her kids as they were being loaded into the social workers' vehicles. About seeing her reflection in the window and not recognizing it for a moment, it was so twisted and wild. She thought she was looking at her cousin's face, and her first thought was *Arlene, honey, you've got to calm down, you're going to do yourself a harm.* Of course, Arlene had been gone a good while by then. It was her own face Helen was looking at.

She did her best to cover the main points the way a newspaper would. She was charged with Failing to Provide the Necessaries of Life for her minor children. Remanded. Investigated for Theft Under $5,000 relating to some stolen farm equipment the cops found on the farm. Held for a couple of months then released, the charges dropped.

Heather nodded impatiently as she told this part. "Marian, the woman who's letting me stay with her, she's a reporter. She wrote all the charges up for the newspaper. In the end, Dad pled to Theft Under $5,000, got six months. Shauna got two years for Failing to Provide the Necessaries of Life and Assault. I guess Melanie and Kelly had some broken bones or something. The uncles had some other charges."

"Yeah," Helen replied. "Shauna used to knock those kids around something fierce. And the whole time, your Poppy would be yelling at her to go easy on them, they were just kids, and your Nanny would be yelling at both of them that kids have to have discipline, that they'd never listen if they weren't a little afraid of what'd happen if they didn't." She caught that hard stare of Heather's again. What kind of kid had eyes that hard? "I never gave you more than a smacked bottom," she added defensively.

"I know," Heather replied.

Neither of them said anything about the other charges. Mark and Danny, both charged with sexual assault and sexual interference a few months after the initial arrests. But those charges had nothing to do with Heather, thank god. She'd managed to shield her kids from all that—the assaults against herself and Arlene, the suggestion the two men had interfered with their niece Melanie, at least. Why bring it up?

"So you know the whole story then, or what?" Helen asked.

Heather shook her head. "Just about the charges and the trials. I don't know what happened to any of you after that."

Helen sighed. This part was harder to tell straight up. But there it was. It had to be told. The social workers who asked her if she wanted to go for visitation rights with her kids. No, Helen had decided. She didn't have anywhere to live. Nowhere that was fit to take kids. When she was released from remand, she stayed in a women's shelter. She'd been in touch with Arlene back in PEI, and she'd tried to convince Helen to come back too, but Helen was determined to stay in Nova Scotia and sort her life out, to find a way to get her kids back. At first, she thought about trying to get back to the farm, but she gave that idea up quickly. After all, how could she ever convince Community Services she could take care of the kids out there, especially without any of the men to do any kind of farm work or earning? No, it would be easier to build a life away from the farm. Away from the Gaugins, with their name all over the newspapers. In the remand centre, some of the most down-and-out women, awaiting trial for prostitution and drug charges, property theft and assault, had sneered at her. *Gaugin* was a byword for bad families, and she intended to give her kids a good family. The best she could manage on her own, anyway. But she didn't want to visit them while she was basically homeless. She'd get a job, get a place, get her shit together.

Except she didn't. She couldn't manage to find a job, nothing legal anyway. Spent a few nights in jail for this and that. Sometimes managed to rent a room from a friend who needed help covering the rent. Still no place a kid could ever call home. She thought less and less about getting her shit together, and what that might mean.

She kept in touch with the social workers, though. They kept pushing her to go for visitation, but she couldn't let her kids see her like this. She was doing a lot of drugs by then.

That's when the social workers told her that Emma and Jennifer were both living with foster families who'd expressed interest in adopting the girls. The woman couldn't guarantee the foster families would be allowed to adopt them, but the odds were good, she said, very good if Helen voluntarily placed the kids into permanent care. When they first brought it up, Helen refused to entertain the idea. They were *her kids*. Even if she didn't have her shit together yet, even if she couldn't bring them to live with her, they were her kids. She had that much, and she wasn't going to let it go. What kind of mother just let her kids go?

Then she wound up in the hospital. She'd been at a party, got into a disagreement over whether the time she was spending with a man there was a business transaction or a social visit. Ended up with a fractured cheekbone and a broken rib. Plus a shit tonne of bruises. When she was finally sober, after the party drugs and the stuff the doctors had given her wore off, she looked at herself in the mirror in her hospital room. The face she saw scared her. It was not the face of a mom. It wasn't even the face she saw reflected in the police car's window the day they drove her and her kids off in separate cars. It was the kind of face you'd avoid looking directly at when you passed it on the street. The kind of face that made you feel pity and fear at the same time.

So she signed the papers. Stood up in court and gave up her parental rights to Emma and Jennifer.

And decided if she didn't get her shit together now, she never would.

After she was released from the hospital, she got a job at a recycling depot, sorting bottles and cans for minimum wage. Got a bedroom in a rooming house. It was a bit of a dump, but none of the other tenants were selling sex or drugs, as far as she knew, so it was an improvement. She moved on from the recycling depot to a fast-food joint, first running the cash register, then eventually being promoted to shift manager. Which essentially meant trying to keep a half dozen teenaged staff members on track for eight hours at a time. But the wage was enough to let her move into a one-bedroom apartment in Dartmouth.

And that's when Kevin ended up in the group home in Truro. This particular group home, the social worker explained to Helen at their meeting, was where they sent foster kids who had severe behavioral problems. It was often the last stop on their way to a juvenile detention facility.

"How do I get him home?" Helen asked. She glanced around the coffee shop where they'd met, hoping her voice wasn't as loud as it sounded to her. She could feel her heart beating against her ribs. *Juvenile detention facility.* She kept remembering the long weeks in the remand centre. The claustrophobia. The knowledge that she no longer had control over any aspect of her life. That was not going to happen to her kids. She wouldn't let it.

The social worker, a woman Helen had met with half a dozen times or so over the last couple of years, stopped. Blinked. "Is that what you want?"

"Of course. You think I'd let him go to juvie?" Why else had this woman told her about the group home, about the path Kevin was on?

"Well…." The social worker looked at the black fabric surface of her bag as though her script might be written there. "I thought we could consider applying for visitations as an option, to bring some positive change into his life."

"Visitation while he's in a shitty group home for bad kids? How's that gonna help him?"

"This is a big step…."

"No shit." Jesus Christ, why wouldn't this woman put down her stupid bag?

"If you're sure…."

"You bet I'm sure."

"All right, we'll get the process going." The woman stood up to leave.

"How are my other kids?" Helen asked abruptly. If things had got this bad for Kevin before they decided to talk to her about it, what were things like for the girls?

"They're doing well. Heather is in a stable foster home. She's thriving."

"They don't want to adopt her?" Helen asked. Her heart pounded hard again. What if they did, now that she was finally, finally getting her shit together? They could be a great family who loved her and wanted to keep her. Could she let Heather go, too, like she had with Emma and Jenny?

"They're not in a position to adopt," the social worker replied. She shifted on her feet, as though she wasn't sure whether to sit back down or not.

"Okay," Helen said. She felt relieved. And guilty for feeling relieved. After all, she should *want* Heather to be with a family who wanted her.

The social worker nodded. She lifted one hand tentatively, a goodbye wave, as though she were asking for permission to go.

Helen raised her hand in reply. Goodbye. She knew better than to ask about the little girls. She'd given up her parental rights. She had no right to know about them anymore. But the social worker *had* said they were all fine, hadn't she?

So Kevin came to live with Helen. She gave him the bedroom, got rid of her double bed and bought him a single and a desk where he could do his homework. Got herself a futon to sleep on in the living room. The futon she still had, here, in this place.

And Kevin was a real shit at first. All snarky teenaged attitude, all defiance. Staying out till all hours, skipping school. Drinking, smoking weed. They got into a few good shouting matches that first year or so. The landlord was called, but not the cops, thank god. He got expelled from two schools.

Eventually, they came to a sort of truce. Found a set of house rules they could both live with—no drinking or smoking (at home, anyway), he went to school (most of the time), agreed to a curfew (on weeknights). Over time, things softened between them. They'd eat supper together most nights, in front of the TV. Helen would look over at him, this great big kid, almost a man, who was her son. Who was her little boy. Whom she'd brought to bed to sleep with her when he was a baby because he never stopped crying in his crib.

When he turned sixteen, he dropped out of school. Helen railed, argued, begged, but he was immovable. He got a job as a construction labourer, but it didn't last long. Soon, he was sleeping most of the day, getting up to watch TV, then heading out most of the night.

"If you're not going to school, you're gonna pay rent," Helen said flatly.

So he started paying rent. Spent more time out of the apartment. Wouldn't tell her anything about where he went or where the money came from.

Then one evening, Helen got a phone call at work. The teenaged cashier eyed her maliciously as she took her cell out of her pocket—she always made them leave their phones in the staff room. But since Kevin had come to live with her, she'd taken to keeping hers in the pocket of her uniform.

Kevin had been arrested outside a Halifax nightclub. Possession and trafficking of a controlled substance. He was remanded, eventually took a plea deal. Spent four months in a juvenile detention centre. In juvie. After all.

Helen was afraid he'd be hardened when he got out, a criminal to his core. But he was surprisingly contrite. When she brought him home, he stepped into his bedroom. She turned, wanting to give him the privacy he'd surely been denied in juvie. But instead, he folded her in a massive hug. She felt him sob against her shoulder.

He stopped selling drugs after that. Got another construction labourer job. He stopped selling, but he didn't stop using. He lost his job. Cleaned up his act for a bit. Got another job. Lost it, too. Again and again.

Then, almost a year ago, Helen got another phone call. Theft over $5,000. He'd stolen a car. And he wasn't going to juvie this time.

Helen wished she had given up her parental rights—to him, and to Heather, too. She prayed that wherever they were, Emma and Jenny were doing okay.

TWENTY-FOUR

HELEN NEVER ONCE LOOKED AT HER DAUGHTER AS SHE TOLD HER STORY. It meant that Heather could look at her, watch her face. It was odd how much her age seemed to change. One moment, she looked young, scarcely older than the way Heather remembered her, and the next, she seemed like an old, old woman.

There was a long silence when Helen stopped talking. She kept looking out the window for a long moment, then turned to face her daughter. Her expression was almost challenging, Heather thought. *Go ahead. Judge me. I'm ready.*

"So why didn't you apply for visitation for me?" Heather asked.

"I told you, I was trying—"

"I know, I know, trying to get your shit together. But then you did. And you got Kevin back. But you didn't even ask for visitation for me."

"Look, if I'd done a better job with Kevin, he wouldn't—"

"But you didn't *know* that," Heather snapped. "When you got him back, when you applied to get him back, the first little while he was with you, you didn't know it was going to turn out bad. So when you thought you could pull it off, why didn't you at least apply to *see* me?"

Helen shook her head. "It's better I didn't," she said stubbornly. "If I'd been in your life, you could have ended up in juvie too."

Heather stood up, exasperated. She walked over to the bedroom.

"Was this his room? Before he went to jail?"

"We had another place then, up in Highfield Park. Moved here when he got out of juvie. He rented the apartment across the hall when he was working in construction."

"When is he getting out?"

"He'll plead it out," Helen said. "Lawyer thinks maybe eighteen months. Could be worse."

There was a long silence. Heather looked around the apartment, trying to find clues that would tell her who her mother was, who her brother was, what their life was like.

What her life would be like if they'd been in it.

There wasn't much by way of decoration. There was a picture on the wall next to a TV. Helen and a young man, heavy-looking with dark hair and light skin. Kevin, Heather realized. They were outside. There were leafy green trees in the background. Summertime. They were both laughing—not smiling for the picture, but laughing. There was an empty pink glass vase on the table next to the TV. Heather could see water rings on the inside. And there were the plants beneath the window. Those lovely, healthy, bright green plants.

"So when are you heading back to Chester?"

"Chester Basin," Heather corrected automatically. Like it mattered. "I don't know."

There was a silence. The unasked invitation hung between both of them. A hot, bitter feeling rose up under Heather's skin.

"You can stay here the night if you need to," Helen said at last.

Heather's impulse was to refuse, to head back to the Greyhound station. But she didn't have enough money for a ticket. And she didn't want to make Jack get in his car and come right away to pick her up. He would, she knew, and at her core she wanted him to. Wanted him to rush in and scoop her up and take her away. But the thought of trying to explain to him and Marian why she'd travelled to Dartmouth in secret to meet her mom, then spent less than a day here before begging for a ride home, filled her with a deep sense of shame. "Thanks," she said. "Can I use your phone?"

Helen gestured to the cordless in the corner of the living room.

Heather picked it up and took it into the kitchen, her back to Helen. As though that actually gave her any privacy in the tiny apartment.

Marian picked up this time. "My girl, you can't *do* this to us," she said.

Heather's throat tightened. "I know. I'm sorry. Can you ask Jack if I can ride back with him tomorrow? After his class?"

"Of course you can," Marian replied. "But I can come get you right now, if you want."

And Heather knew that she would, and that if Heather told her she didn't want to talk about it, Marian wouldn't even ask her any questions. "No, I want to spend the night," she said. "I'll come back with Jack tomorrow evening."

"Okay," Marian said. "But you're safe? You're okay."

"Yup. I'm fine. I'll see you tomorrow."

In the living room, Helen had turned the TV on. She had the volume on low, but she turned it up when Heather returned to put the phone back on its cradle. "You wanna watch something?" she asked.

"I've actually got homework," Heather replied. She was suddenly, absurdly pleased to have her math books with her. She set up on the dining room table and pretended to focus as Helen sat on the futon, watching reality shows. When Heather's stomach rumbled hungrily a while later, she returned to the kitchen to make herself another ham sandwich. She ate it in the kitchen, one thin wall separating her from her mother, the sounds from the show Helen was watching keeping her company as she chewed.

At around nine, Helen said she had an early shift the next day. She helped Heather unfold the futon and handed her a blanket. Heather settled down into her bed—which had once been her mother's bed, she realized—with the TV on. The light gleamed in the crack under her mother's bedroom door until almost midnight.

The next morning, Helen and Heather both got ready quickly, almost wordlessly. They left the apartment together, walked down the narrow stairs. Hesitated for a moment on the worn veranda.

"I'm glad you found me," Helen said at last. Woodenly.

"Me too," Heather replied automatically. They stared at each other for a brief moment, then moved in for a quick, tight hug. As though someone was watching and might expect it.

Then Helen headed off down the sidewalk. Heather walked the other way, toward the ferry terminal. She'd find a way to kill time before she met Jack at the art college that evening.

As she walked, Heather realized Helen hadn't asked her where she was going or how she'd get back home.

એક

NOW, IN HER LIVING ROOM, HER SON SNUGGLED UP ON THE COUCH next to her, Jack staring at her with that exasperating, peculiar, amused look on his face, and her sister Emma sitting on the floor, Heather wondered whether Kevin ever tried to find her. Or their dad, or Nanny and Poppy. Whether he'd searched for their mom before landing in the group home. Whether Emma or even Jenny had ever googled the Gaugin name when they were kids. She was certain neither Emma nor Jenny had ever found their mother—Helen would have told her. They'd never contacted her at least. But that didn't mean they'd never looked.

She told the story the way Helen had told hers—as simply as possible. No embellishments. No recriminations, no self-pity. After all, as far as stories went, hers wasn't that bad. Lots of people suffered through worse.

She didn't tell her about the drive back to Chester. About pretending not to see when tears rolled down Jack's lean cheeks as he stared ahead down the highway. Of the crushingly tight hug Marian gave her on the back step, before Heather could even get into the house. Because when she thought too much about that part of the story, she couldn't keep down the shame and the guilt of having worried them so much, Jack and Marian, the only two people in the world who gave a shit about her back then. Couldn't stick to just the bare facts.

Emma didn't say anything when Heather stopped talking. There was a long silence. Then Rafe came down the stairs. He fixed his deep, warm gaze on his wife.

"Why don't the two of you go for a walk," he said, settling down next to Justin, who shifted over to snuggle up next to his dad. "The blackflies are almost done for the year, finally."

Emma rose quickly, and Heather realized that she was acting out of a kind of automatic obedience, not eagerness. She wondered briefly what would happen if she told her sister to sit down. Then stand up again. Then sit back down.

But she also knew that Emma wouldn't say much of anything with Jack and Rafe and Justin in the room. And Heather supposed she had the right to ask questions. Real questions, not that interview bullshit. She stood up, and Emma followed her to the front door.

The evening was cooling down. Birdsong poured from the woods all around them.

"What are those birds?" Emma asked, listening. "I know there's a chickadee, but I don't recognize the rest."

"Robins, mostly," Heather replied. "And mourning doves."

"We have robins in Edmonton," said Emma. "But not mourning doves. Is that the one that sounds like an owl?"

"Yeah, I guess." Heather bit back the impulse to explain the difference between an owl's song and a mourning dove's. It's the kind of thing she would have explained to Justin. Or Charlotte, eventually. Justin could imitate a mourning dove and an owl, a chickadee, a loon, and a crow. He loved spotting birds when they were outside. He liked to talk to them in their language. Heather remembered when he was tiny, before he was really even talking, how he'd call back to the crows and the gulls, chickadees and ducks, fire trucks and car horns and dogs, all in their own language. He wasn't yet able to form words, and here he was, fluent in all these other creatures' sounds. It was soon after that he began talking. Each word first a puzzle to Heather as she tried to decipher it, then a tiny miracle, that exchange between the two of them. *Mama. Dog. Water. Sun.* All miracles as he formed the words for them.

They walked down the road, heading toward the town. They stayed on the sunny side, away from the shade the forest cast along the gravel.

"Did you ever try to find Mom or Dad? Or any of us?" Heather asked.

"No," Emma replied. "Not before. Only when I started my thesis." She paused, frowning. As though she were trying to put together the right words, the right thought. "Our mother, though. She wasn't from here, she was in university. But then she married our dad and became a Gaugin."

"Why do you say it like that?"

"What?"

"*Gaugin*. Like it's some kind of insect or disease."

"I didn't think I did."

"You did."

"Sorry. I just don't understand why she'd do that. Go and live with them. Do you think it was like Stockholm Syndrome or whatever?"

Heather stopped. She stared at her sister. "Jesus Christ," she said, "we're not fucking monsters. She wasn't abducted, she got married. They were just a family. So they didn't want to live around other people. So they kind of sucked at raising kids. They were just people, Emma."

Emma stared at her for a moment, blinking. "I'm sorry," she said.

"What for?" Heather snapped.

"I'm not sure...."

Heather sighed. She didn't want to say what she had to say. She wanted to send Emma back to Edmonton so she could write her stupid thesis about the bogeymen of Nova Scotia. And how she had been one, but she escaped. She walked on in silence for a moment.

"Look at that," Emma said suddenly. She pointed to a tall shrub by the side of the road. "Is that a cardinal?"

Heather looked at the bright red bird. It hopped onto another branch. Stopped to peck at something among the leaves. "Yeah, I guess so."

"I didn't know there were cardinals here."

"Didn't used to be," Heather said. "People started seeing them in Halifax last winter. This is the first time I've seen one."

"Me too."

They stood watching the bird. It fluffed its feathers, pecked at the branch again. Then it tilted its beak upwards and trilled twice and flew away. Heather and Emma watched it disappear over the trees.

"When do you go back?" Heather asked.

"My flight's on Wednesday."

"You have plans for Monday?"

"No."

"Can I pick you up at your hotel around noon? There's someone you should meet."

"Who?"

"But not for research or whatever. Just for you to know her."

"Who?"

Heather kept her eyes fixed on the deepening blue sky, in the direction the cardinal had flown away. "Mom," she said.

TWENTY-FIVE

EMMA DRIFTED AWAKE. HER MIND TRIED TO MAKE SENSE OF THE position of the window and door relative to her bed. It wasn't her apartment in Edmonton, nor was it her hotel room. It wasn't until Glen shifted in bed next to her, sliding his arm over her hip, that Emma realized she was still in his bed.

It was warm in his fourth-floor bachelor apartment. The big picture window faced east, so the June sunlight was already heating up the space. His skin was just starting to feel slick against hers. It wasn't an unpleasant sensation.

The whole day before, Emma had tried to organize her research, start building a narrative for her thesis, but she kept losing the thread. Without realizing it, she'd get up and wander to the window. Or open a half dozen social media and clickbait browser windows. She'd force her attention back to the documents and photos, and only seconds later, it seemed, she'd catch herself doing something else again.

Her mind kept pinging between Glen, her mother and Heather, and Dr. Fuentes and Dr. Melnyk. She kept catching herself planning ways to cancel out on all of it—her date, meeting her mom, her thesis. Ways to just drop it all and disappear, to never have to see or talk to any of them again. Elaborate plots involving jobs overseas and name changes.

And her left foot wouldn't stop tapping against the leg of her chair.

Finally, she gave up. She'd seen signs for walking trails down the street from her hotel. She shut down her laptop and followed the road away from the big box stores. There was no sidewalk, so she had to walk on the gravel shoulder. It was rutted by weather and vehicle tires.

A gravel path veered off the road and into the woods. It climbed up a gentle slope. The forest was rocky with mossy granite thrusting up between the trees like teeth. A little stream darted back and forth along the trail, its banks green with ferns and moss, its bottom clean granite pebbles. Here and there, lady's slippers and partridgeberries bloomed. It was a pretty walk, but the busy highway sounds from just over the ridge almost drowned out the birdsong and the trickling of the creek.

Emma walked quickly. The tense feeling in her leg muscles was the same as when she was running late for an appointment—the urgent pushing-forward feeling. The trail climbed upward, and her muscles started to warm and slacken. The path curved and dipped around the other side of the slope, so she slowed her pace, managed to focus her gaze on the trees, on the ferns and flowers, on the birds that flitted in and out. By the time the path opened back onto the road, her mind felt steady.

Back at the hotel, she showered and dressed, touched her eyelids with shadow and blow-dried her hair. She looked good, she thought. And she was feeling better. Part of her still wanted to text Glen and cancel, to curl up under the hotel duvet and rent movies until she fell asleep. To hide in her room until her flight. But the exercise, the fresh air, the hot shower, and the polished reflection staring back at her from the mirror all pulled her out of herself and out of the room. It would be fun, she reminded herself. Glen was fun. She took the stairs down to meet him in the lobby.

Glen was just coming out from behind the bar. He took off his uniform vest and tucked it under his arm. She let him lead her out to the staff parking, into his car.

There was no quaint pub this time. He took her to a posh-looking restaurant on the waterfront. Insisted on paying for her meal. This was a date.

She'd never really dated Adrian, not like this. Sure, there had been dinners in restaurants, usually after a movie. Adrian liked talking about the film over dinner. He preferred "authentic" food. African, Asian, South American (but not—God forbid—Chinese or Mexican). More often than not, it was simply a tired diner with the usual diner fare and a couple of Thai or Ethiopian or Filipino dishes on the menu. For authenticity, she supposed. But these dinners were never planned, never really a vehicle to spend time alone together. They simply needed to eat, so one of them would suggest they eat out. Sometimes there were suppers at these types of places, or at pubs, with what he called their friends. Really, they were his friends. Grad students, mostly. A sharply critical group who seemed to dislike almost everything from politicians to television shows to fashion, but who nonetheless could cite individual episodes or clothing brands to support their criticisms. Emma would smile along, always a little afraid the conversation would somehow turn on her, that she would become the target of their barbed wit. Of course, she always kept a crude reflection, a curse-laden deflection at the ready. A blunt object to defend against their scalpel humour.

But Glen didn't criticize. He didn't make fun. He seemed to be the embodiment of the preschool adage "If you can't say something nice, don't say anything at all."

Emma had asked him about his job, about the difficulty of dealing with customers, the public. When she was in high school, she'd worked in retail for a while at a big mall that attracted a lot of tourists. The experience had been grinding.

"It's like they go on vacation just to traumatize the locals," Emma said as she bit into her smoked sea bass. It was heavenly.

Glen smiled. "People bring big expectations on a big trip," he said. "And that usually means some big disappointments they never expected."

"So people are never shitty to you in the hotel?" she asked.

"Sure. But I try to remember that whatever is bothering them, it's not about me."

Emma suddenly imagined Adrian and his friends discussing Glen, slicing into him with their snarky reflections on his kindness, his openness. She suddenly felt angry, as though they were there in the restaurant, making fun of him in that moment.

That was when she decided. Over dessert, Glen asked what time she had to be back at the hotel, and she had smiled and replied, "Sometime before noon, I guess."

· When they reached his apartment, he offered her a cup of tea. "I have rooibos if you don't want the caffeine," he said.

She kissed him. He responded slowly, but she pressed her body against him, against the length of him. And he pressed back, kissing her deeply, moving his hands along her hips, sliding her shirt off. Its fabric catching against their bodies, reluctant to part even for the moment it took to pull their clothes away.

Who knew that rooibos tea could be such an aphrodisiac?

In the morning, fully awake now, Emma lay quietly, gazing around the apartment. On the wall above the bed were two framed movie posters —nothing she'd recognized. Last night, she had asked him about them.

"They're mine," he replied.

"What do you mean?"

"I wrote and directed them. They're short films."

"You're a filmmaker?"

He nodded. "I'm making my first feature this fall. It's a micro-budget, but we have a really great actor signed on in the lead, and my DOP is incredible."

Emma didn't ask what a DOP was. Instead, she watched his face when he talked. His features were relaxed. His eyes fixed on hers with the same openness as over dinner, when he'd asked her about her thesis. He told her about his movie simply, no bravado, no embarrassment. Better yet, no false modesty. Emma wondered what it would feel like to just tell someone about her research, not stumble or deflect. Not make jokes or drop words like *fuck* and *cunt* just for the shock value.

Which was, of course, what she'd done when he asked over dinner.

"It's a fucking nightmare," she said. "Digging through two hundred years of archival diarrhoea."

He'd smiled a little, but didn't change the subject. Just looked at her as though he expected her to go on.

Of course, she could have told him then. She could have dropped the act (and in fact, she could almost picture Heather's hard gaze on her); she could have told him it was *her* family she was researching. Instead, she did what she always did. She doubled down. "I'll be glad when my supervisors sign off on this bullshit thesis so I can get my Master's degree—though what that'll be good for, I don't know. Wiping my ass, maybe."

God. Why had he let her come home with him?

He was waking now. He turned his head. Blinked twice and smiled. "Morning."

"Morning," she said. Tried to look at him and mouth the word upward to spare him her morning breath.

"I'm hungry," he said. "You?"

"Yeah."

He rolled over and swung his legs over the opposite side of the bed. Took his time finding his T-shirt and underwear as she rooted for hers on the opposite side. Waited to stand up until she'd pulled her clothes on. Gentlemanly, discreet.

"I've got cereal or toast. That okay?"

"Great."

"Or we can go out."

"Cereal is good."

In fact, he had an impressive collection of sugar cereals. An array of high-fructose corn syrups and artificial food colourings. Emma filled a bowl with Sugar Crisp. It had been Elaine's favourite when they were little. Emma's parents never bought sugar cereals, but Emma loved eating them with Elaine as they watched Saturday morning cartoons during their sleepover weekends.

And Glen had coffee, too. Thank goodness. Rooibos wouldn't cut it this morning.

Still, they wound up in bed again before Glen drove her back to the hotel. Glen had a way of exploring her body, of trailing his hands along her thighs, across her stomach, her breasts, between her legs, that made her feel completely lost, transported. Blissfully un-self-conscious.

"Tell me something," Glen said as he lay next to her. His head was on the pillow next to her and she could only see half his face, the other half lost in the soft bedding.

"What?" she asked.

"Anything," he replied.

She forced a laugh. What could she say? What could she tell him that wouldn't make him recoil or pity her or look at her like an object of curiosity. "I'm super boring," she replied.

"I don't think that's true."

She sat up and fumbled for her jeans. "I should get back," she said.

"Right," he replied. When she left, he showed her to the door, brushed her cheek with a light kiss.

Back at the hotel, she pulled her phone out of her purse. She should call Glen, make plans to see him again before she left. She caught herself smiling like crazy. God. She was fucking twitterpated. She typed a text message: *Can I see you again?* But as her thumbs hovered over her phone screen, she realized it'd have to be Tuesday. Because tomorrow she was going to meet her mom.

She felt the giddiness, the softness in her limbs, drain away. Literally. As though she'd flushed all that lightness and refilled herself with cold tension.

She was going to meet her mom tomorrow. Her birth mother. And she hadn't told her parents about it.

Her thoughts flicked back to Glen, to their goodbye at his door. Had he been a little cold? He hadn't kissed her on the mouth. Maybe he wasn't interested in seeing her again. Maybe it had just been a one-time thing for him. Maybe it hadn't been all that good for him. Maybe it had, but he just didn't like her, having to spend time with her, talk to her.

Emma sat down on her bed. Felt the jumping in her right leg as her heel bounced and her quad twitched. Willed herself not to reach for the bottle of Lorazepam in her purse.

TWENTY-SIX

EMMA COULD FEEL THE DAMPNESS SEEPING THROUGH HER JEANS AND onto the skin of her thighs. The rain had swept in overnight, hammering against her window. Gusts of wind smacked against the side of the hotel, and with each one Emma's body had flinched awake, disoriented and danger-alert.

The storm had swept back out by the time Emma got out of bed but the rain pattered on, gentle and relentless. She stood waiting in the hotel lobby. Glen had passed her on his way to the bar. She'd smiled at him, moved to talk to him, but he'd only given her a quick smile and strode on. And he hadn't replied to her text. *Maybe he's just busy,* she thought. Tried not to dwell on it. Knew she would, anyway. Then she saw the car pull up to the front door. She stepped automatically towards it, but hesitated, trying to see the driver clearly. That *was* Heather, wasn't it?

It was. Heather leaned down, looking into the hotel, looking for Emma. She caught Emma's gaze and made a *Come on, already!* gesture. Emma ran out toward the car.

A few steps. A dozen strides, maybe, between the door and the car. That was all it took for the rain to settle on her pant legs. She had on her raincoat, the hood up, but it stopped just below her hips.

What was it about denim and moisture? It was like wearing a sponge on her legs.

Heather took the back exit from the industrial park. A narrow road wound through a forested area before breaking suddenly into a residential neighbourhood. The houses crowded the road almost haphazardly. A few of them had front lawns, a few clung to the very edge of the pavement. The road curved its way in toward the heart of the city, and side streets wound up and away at irregular intervals. The houses themselves were smallish, neat and unremarkable. The ground was uneven, and here and there large boulders appeared, jutting some of the properties upward above the street. Finally, the road opened out onto a traffic circle. A finger of salt water dotted with small boats jabbed toward the rim of the roundabout. On either side, the little houses from the neighbourhood above made way for bigger properties, wider lawns, more impressive buildings. All along the road, the trees and shrubs seemed vividly, impossibly green in the soaking weather.

"You're quiet," Heather said.

"I guess." Emma glanced at her sister. "So are you."

Heather didn't answer right away. "Why'd you look so surprised when I said you should meet Mom? Didn't you think you'd find us when you started looking into the family?"

"No," Emma replied.

Heather sniffed, a disapproving sound. Emma considered telling her about her search, about the letter. But she couldn't bring herself to tell all of that now. There was too much to think about now that they were heading out to meet the person she'd expected would never want to be found. At least not by her.

She'd started off looking for Gaugins, and her own research—mainly Google and social media searches—hadn't yielded anything more than the old news articles she already knew. But when she first started looking, that was the only name she had to go on. At first.

Her mother had not started out a Gaugin. She had married a Gaugin. How far had she travelled to become herself? Emma's father had been born a Gaugin. As had she.

But it was her mother's name that had stood out to her in the court documents she had obtained from the provincial Department of

Community Services. Months ago, she had meticulously completed and submitted an Adoption Disclosure application to obtain the official Child Protective Services records—the documents that officially made her first the ward, then later the daughter of Mike and Julia Weaver. Her file had arrived by mail, photocopies of smudged and faded forms that explained, in clunky clinical language, the transfer of her person from the Gaugin compound into foster care, then finally, officially and permanently, into the Weaver family. The forms with ink scrawls in their curt boxes. The document typed in Courier font with the underlined heading Social History. Its sub-headings also underlined. Identifying Information. Reason for Report. Reason for Social Work or Agency Involvement. Statement of Problem. Family Background (Birth Family). It told her nothing she hadn't already gleaned from newspaper articles, from her parents (adoptive), from her own fragmented memories.

Several adult members of the Gaugin family, inclusive of Emma Gaugin's parents, are to be taken into police custody on suspicion of theft and trafficking of controlled substances. Investigating RCMP officers have reported the presence of minor children in the household and indications are that they may have suffered abuse and neglect.

The child's custodial parents as well as other adult relatives living on the family farm have been removed into police custody, and there currently are no adult family members to care for the minor children living on the farm. There is concern about the children's living conditions, following the visit to the farm. There are indications of neglect. The children may not have adequate food. Living conditions on the farm appear

*to be very cramped and possibly unsanitary.
Some of the other children show bruising
that may be indicative of physical abuse.
Older children do not seem to be getting a
formal education, and children don't seem
to be adequately supervised. Emma has not
yet communicated verbally with social workers or foster parents, though she seems to
communicate with her sister Heather Gaugin,
who has been placed in the same foster home.
Both children show signs of emotional trauma.*

*Other minor siblings are Kevin Gaugin and
Jennifer Gaugin. There was no foster home
availability for all four children together.*

Emotional trauma. What signs had she shown, Emma wondered.
What were the tells? Did she still have them?

And there, in the court documents that paved the way for her
to become a Weaver, that pretended to wipe the Gaugin from her,
was one telling line. *Only one custodial parent attended the Permanent
Care Hearing. Helen Gaugin consented to have her minor child Emma
Gaugin placed into permanent care and custody.* Consented to not being
her mother any longer.

When she'd called the Department of Community Services in
Halifax to ask how to get hold of her file, the woman on the phone
asked if Emma wanted to request contact with her biological parents.

Emma couldn't answer right away. She hadn't expected the question. She had thought maybe that Community Services would send
her some information, forms and reports, maybe. What exactly did
"contact" mean? It could mean she could talk to them on the phone,
ask them questions from far away. Or else it could mean she'd see
them, meet them. Would they want to hug her when she saw them,
she wondered. Would she want to hug them?

She tried to remember hugging her parents before, when she

was little. When she pushed her memories back to them, her mother was a pair of legs in the kitchen. It must have been summer because they were bare, and Emma remembers the softness of the skin against her cheek. And a hand that reached down to touch her hair. Of her father, she remembers a voice. A hard voice. Not shouting, exactly. Not angry, just hard. No words, nothing specific. Just hardness.

"Yes," she said at last. "I'd like to request contact." And so the woman promised to send her another form.

"We recommend that you write them a letter," the woman said. "They're more likely to agree to contact if there's a letter."

"What about my brother and sisters?" Emma asked. "Can I write to them, too?"

"I'm afraid not," the woman replied. "Contact requests are strictly between parents and children."

"Can I talk to the social workers?"

"What social workers?"

"The ones who…" *who took me.* "Who were there when I was taken into care. Or the one who came to check on me at my parents'. At the Weavers'. I think her name was Dorothy."

"That won't be possible." The woman's voice had suddenly gone curt. "The privacy of our employees—"

"Maybe I could just send an email, then, and you could forward it?"

"Miss Weaver," the voice said, softening a little, "I can count on one hand the number of social workers who worked for us back in 1991 and still do now. It's not a profession that a lot of people can manage to do long-term. I can't give you any specific information on the case workers involved with your family, but I can say that none of them still work with the department today."

"Right," Emma said. "Okay. Just the forms, then."

"And will you be writing a letter?"

"Yeah. I'll write a letter."

IT HAD TAKEN EMMA TWO DAYS TO OPEN THE ENVELOPE WHEN IT arrived at her apartment. Another to read through it. By then, her trip to Nova Scotia had been scheduled, arranged, booked. Confirmed. She told her parents that she would be researching her family history—her former family history—for her thesis.

"And you've thought this through?" Mike had asked, giving her a measured look. "You've considered the consequences?"

"Yeah, I might get a worthless Master's degree to go with my worthless Bachelor's degree," Emma quipped.

Julia shook her head. "I think you should take some time before you commit. Maybe a gap year—"

"No," Emma interrupted. "One more gap year like the last one and I'll be ready to retire by the time I finish school."

So there it was. Her parents told, her course of action confirmed, the information requested. And now, received.

With the forms was a notice; some information could not be disclosed, it said, because the biological mother had not provided consent. The adoption search clerk had requested a medical history, but the biological mother had not provided that, either. So that was that. Nothing further to be requested, nothing at all to be given.

The biological father, however, was deceased. Gary Gaugin, born in Windsor, Nova Scotia, November 27, 1962, died April 12, 1999. He was still alive when Emma was placed into permanent care and custody, but his parental rights had been terminated the previous year. He was not present at that hearing, and so his consent, it seemed, was neither needed nor desired.

Emma told herself she should be relieved. She wouldn't have to see them, interview them, ask them why she had been taken away, why she hadn't been returned. Because her biological father was dead. Because her biological mother hadn't filled out the form on her end.

Why not?

Because she didn't want to see her? Emma thought about the letter she had sent. It felt so formal, so distant. Maybe she should have tried to be more affectionate, more pleading. Was her ambivalence, her resistance, palpable? She would have liked to re-read it now, but she hadn't kept a copy. When her mother had sent word through the bureaucracy of the Community Services department, Emma had immediately deleted the file from her laptop. Gone for good.

Maybe she really had wanted to see Emma, but the letter had never reached her. Maybe no one had been able to find her, to ask her to fill out the form. Maybe that's why the contact form was not returned.

Maybe she had filled it out, but it had been lost. Or filed in the wrong place. Maybe she was waiting, wondering why Emma didn't reach out, call her, email her, come see her.

Maybe she was in prison. It was possible. Perhaps even probable. Knowing what she knew about her parents, Emma told herself she should feel relieved that she wouldn't have to meet them, to confirm the worst of what she thought might be true.

But she wasn't. Instead, she felt a dull sorrow. It was like suddenly pressing on a bruise that had been there all along, but that she'd protected so long she'd forgotten about, until now.

ⵧ

EMMA HADN'T FELT MUCH WHEN SHE HEARD HER FATHER WAS DEAD, but since that phone call, since the search clerk had said the words "I am very sorry to inform you that your father has passed away," the thought kept fluttering back to her unbidden, at the strangest times.

When she was grocery shopping, choosing Roma tomatoes, and she'd suddenly become aware of that void in the world—her father was dead. He wasn't somewhere, he wasn't thinking about her, he was gone. She was washing dishes with her dad after supper at her parents', and the awareness of his tall, lanky frame next to her reminded her that there wasn't another pair of hands dipping in and out of a soapy sink, or tapping the buttons on a remote control, or sliding a steering wheel under his palms that belonged to her other father, her first father. That father, that being, that shape and soul, the flesh and the blood, the genes she shared, were gone, had been gone nearly twenty years. No more. He had died when she was twelve. Just as she was in her final months of elementary school, already nervous to start attending Castle Downs Junior High in the fall, her father—biological father—was dying, and she'd known nothing about it then.

She realized she hadn't thought about him much in all that time, not personally or directly. She'd thought about them, the Gaugins, but as a sort of mass. But it was only now that her father was gone that she really thought about him as an individual, a distinct person. A person who might have shaped her life and who she was, except that he was gone, and had been for most of her own life. Only a space now, a nothing, a reminder that slid in and out of her consciousness with its own will in a way that a thought and a memory of him never had in the time before he died, or in that other time after he was dead and before she'd known it.

Heather turned off into a tidy neighbourhood past the traffic circle. The houses here were like those they'd passed earlier—small and neat—but this neighbourhood was laid out more regularly. Straight streets meeting in four-way stops. Squares of lawn and flower beds, even driveways slicing between properties. Heather turned again and pulled up to a white duplex. It had brown-painted wooden steps leading to the set of doors at its centre.

Heather stopped on the road in front of the house. "Here we are."

The bifurcated front yard had a small picket fence running all around it and up its centre. On one side, a slightly weedy lawn stretched between the fence boards. On the other side, shrubs and perennials bordered a small stone patio with a pretty wrought-iron table and chair. Heather led Emma up this side to the front door. Heather knocked smartly, and Emma didn't even really have time to be nervous before the door opened, revealing a woman in her fifties. Her hair was dyed blonde and pulled into a neat braid. She wasn't big, but she was built solidly. She gathered Heather into a big hug before she turned her eyes on Emma.

It was the gaze that was familiar. Those soft, steady eyes under the fine, dark eyebrows.

A ghost of a smile passed over Helen's face, there and gone so quickly that Emma wasn't really sure she'd seen it at all.

"Come in, you're soaked," Helen said at last. She moved into the front hall, and Emma followed Heather inside. Heather took off her raincoat and hung it on a hook behind the door. She held out her hand and Emma handed over her coat. She wished she'd worn a sweater—her jeans were even damper now, and she felt a chill settling into her bones.

"Have you got some tea on?" Heather asked.

"Yep," Helen replied.

Heather stepped through the hall and into the kitchen, at the back of the house. Helen turned to look at her youngest daughter. Emma stared back at her, not sure what to say.

"Emma," Helen said. She remembered Heather telling her that the first time she saw her mom as a teenager, she noticed that Helen was missing a tooth. Emma glanced involuntarily at Helen's mouth, but she couldn't tell. Embarrassed, she looked down. She could see the line on her jeans between the dry fabric that had been covered by her raincoat and the wet denim below.

"You're soaking wet," Helen said. "I can put your pants in the dryer if you want?"

"No, thank you," Emma replied quickly. Of the thousand ways she had imagined this meeting on the ride over, none of them involved her not wearing pants.

"Come on, the cold'll get into your bones. I'll get you a towel to wear." Helen squeezed past Emma and climbed the narrow staircase. Emma waited alone in the hall, listening to Helen open and close a cupboard upstairs and Heather pull cups out of a kitchen cupboard. She shivered.

"Here," Helen said, coming back down the stairs. She handed Emma a big, faded pink bath towel.

"Thanks," Emma said. She took the towel in her hand, not exactly sure what to do with it.

"Let's go have a sit," Helen said, heading into the kitchen. Emma waited awkwardly for a moment, then peeled the sodden jeans off the cold flesh of her legs. She wrapped the giant towel around herself like a skirt. It felt wonderfully warm and soft on her bare skin.

"Dryer's in here," Helen called. Emma followed her voice into the kitchen. There was a square wooden table under the window with three matching chairs. Helen held out her hand for the jeans and threw them into the dryer in the back corner. Heather had set three cups of tea out. She was pulling milk out of the fridge. She poured some into two of the cups, then looked at Emma. "Yes, please," Emma said, even though she didn't usually take anything in her tea, and Heather added milk to her cup, too. All three the same.

Emma waited for Helen and Heather to sit down before she took the last spot at the table. She sat by the wall, across from her mother and next to her sister. She tightened the towel around her waist before she sat down. The heavy fabric warmed her a little. So did the cup of tea in her hands. She looked at the mug. It had the green Sobeys logo on it. Heather's mug did, too, but Helen's advertised a radio station.

"Can I ask?" Emma started. Faltered. "Why you didn't answer the letter?"

"What letter?" Heather asked, frowning at Helen.

Helen shook her head, a slow, determined gesture, her eyes fixed on her mug. "Too much time, I thought. We're strangers by now."

Emma swallowed. "You didn't answer the letter, or let Community Services put me in touch with you. But...."

"But I let Heather bring you to me?"

"Our Heather, it's hard to tell her no," Helen said, hiding the ghost of a smile behind her teacup.

"What letter?" Heather repeated sharply.

Emma fidgeted, cast about for an answer. But Helen sat still, faintly smiling, not answering. Emma kept her gaze on her. "So you're writing a university essay on our family," Helen said at last.

"Master's thesis," Emma corrected. Helen nodded, her expression unchanged. Emma felt a little foolish. "But yeah."

"Am I gonna be in it?"

Emma stopped. She didn't know how to reply. "I guess," she

said at last. "I'm going to write what I remember. And I'm including some of the newspaper articles about. You know."

"Marian's stories?" Helen asked.

"Marian Rushdie's? Yeah. Did you know her?"

"Got to know her after Heather came to find me." She chuckled. "Gave her a piece of my mind. Didn't much like some of the things she said in the paper."

Emma looked at Heather, but Heather looked resolutely out of the window in front of her. "Can you tell me, when did that happen? Did you two become friends?"

"This for your essay?" Helen asked.

This time, Emma didn't correct her. "That depends on whether you want it to be or not."

Helen looked at Heather. Heather just shrugged. *Up to you*, she seemed to be saying.

"I don't got much choice about the newspaper stories and all going in, do I?"

Emma hesitated. She couldn't promise to leave Helen out, could she? But if Helen didn't *want* to be mentioned at all.…

Helen shook her head slightly. "Guess that part is up to you. I can't really stop you from putting any of this in, if you're really set on it. But maybe you don't write nothing about today, with us together?"

"Yes," Emma replied. "I won't share anything you tell me."

"Guess I'll have to take your word for it."

Emma wanted to tell her about ethics approval, to reassure her that she would need Helen's informed consent before she could officially interview her. But she suppressed the urge to start jabbering about the administrivia of academic research. She thought back to her Research Methods course. The instructor had been teaching about interview techniques. "Don't fill the silences by explaining or asking follow-up questions," he'd said. "If you want your subjects to open themselves up, to reveal themselves to you, let them be the ones to fill the silences." So she took a drink of her tea and kept her mouth shut.

Helen leaned back in her chair. "I didn't think I'd hear from Heather again after she took the bus out to my place that first time. Didn't exactly go great, did it?"

Heather smiled. "Nope."

"I probably wouldn't have, either, except then Marian Rushdie started phoning. First she called to tell me how Heather was doing in school. Bs in most classes, an A in math. Good for her, great, I said, but really I was thinking, why has this snooty bitch got to bother me? She's already got my kid, now she wants to rub my friggin' nose in it? But then she started calling to ask me how I was doing, how Kevin was. I didn't want to tell her nothing, even though Kevin got two years in prison and I was pretty down about it all. But I said to her, we're all right. And then one day, she asks if it's okay if she can get Heather to call me. Sure, I said, if Heather wants to talk to me, we'll talk. I didn't think she would, though. But sure enough, Heather starts calling once a week."

Helen glanced knowingly at Heather before continuing. "We didn't have much to say to each other at first. It's hard, getting to know each other all over again. But then this one time Marian calls me, asking how I am, and I get to thinking about those stories she wrote for the Lunenburg paper, and I think, This bitch probably doesn't think I even read them." She laughed then, a sharp cackle. "I don't remember what all I said to her, but I know I tore a strip off of her. And the crazy thing is, she just listened. She never said sorry, never told me off, even though I was some mad at her, she just listens, then she finally says something like, 'I'm glad you got that off your chest.' Then know what she does? She invites me over for dinner." Helen slapped her leg in mock-surprise. "Says her husband will drive all the way to Dartmouth to pick me up, then drive me home again after supper. And I'm still so mad and so surprised at how she took it all, I just say, 'Okay, sure, I'll come have dinner with youse.'" Helen laughed again and Heather smiled at her, the way you do when you hear a funny story you've heard a hundred times before.

"We were great friends by the end, Marian and me. It was a terrible hole in our lives when she passed." Helen reached out and squeezed Heather's hand. Heather was blinking hard. "Wish it could have gone the same way with me and the Weavers. The friendship, I mean."

"You never met them?" Emma asked. Of course she hadn't. Surely Mike and Julia would have told her—wouldn't they?

Helen shook her head. "Meant to. Saw her once. Pretty sure she knew it was me, too."

Emma felt a sudden spur of nervousness, as though she were caught in that moment, right now, as her mothers recognized each other across a distance. "What do you mean?"

"When the social workers told me the Weavers wanted to adopt you, I don't know. I got mad. Couldn't believe they wanted to take you away from me for good. Deep down I knew you'd probably be better off with them, but right then, when I heard they wanted you, all I could think was, no friggin way. They can't just take you like that, not for good. So I hitched all the way out to Lunenburg. Was going to show up at their place and tell them you were *my* kid, they couldn't just keep you. I was gonna wait until you got home from school. It was friggin stupid. I thought you'd see me, and you'd want to come home with me, that you wouldn't want to stay with them no more. Stupid. I was counting on you to cause a scene to get them to back off. But I didn't know what time your school let out, so I was just walking up and down your street, waiting. It was cold as hell, and I wasn't really dressed for the weather, but I didn't give a shit, I was gonna wait out there until I saw you. And the woman, Julia, she was home. She wasn't doing much of anything, but I could see her through the windows. She was just going round the house, tidying up, I guess, doing the same thing I was doing. Waiting for you."

Emma swallowed hard. She remembered how when she was little, first in Lunenburg, then in Edmonton, Julia would wait for her outside every day, no matter what the weather. Most other parents would wait inside for the school bus to pull up in front of the house, but not Julia.

"Then she put on her coat and boots and just came out to sit on the front step. That was it. She just sat out in the cold, watching for you up the street. Only she saw me instead. And the look on her face, it was so scared. Like I was a monster come to gobble her kid up. And I knew how she felt, no one who hasn't been through that could know, but I knew, and it was crazy. I wanted to go talk to her, tell her it was OK, I wouldn't take you away. She was safe, you were safe. Here she was, the woman who wanted to take my kid from me, and I felt bad for her. So I just turned around and hiked back out to the main road and hitched a ride straight back to Halifax."

Julia had never told Emma about seeing her mom. Of course, maybe Helen had it wrong. Maybe Julia hadn't recognized her at all. But Emma didn't think Helen had it wrong.

"What about our father?" Emma asked, her voice unsteady. "What happened to him? I mean, I know he—" She wanted to say *died*. She'd always hated the squinting way people said "passed away." It felt dishonest. But somehow, she couldn't say *died*. Not about her father. Not about Helen's husband.

Helen shook her head slowly. "He spent a few years in jail. The stolen property. Wasn't his first time, so it didn't go so good for him. He found me after, wanted me to come back to the farm with him, but I couldn't go back there without you kids. He said if we went back it would be easier to get you all back, but I knew that wasn't true. No way they'd send you back out there, not ever." Helen leaned back in her chair. She drained her teacup and poured herself another. Emma watched her stir milk into the amber liquid. "Anyway, he never did manage to get back out there. His dad, Big Kevin, passed away while Gary was in prison, and his mom was in a nursing home. Dementia. He took off. Landed up in St. John's after a while. Then I heard from my cousin, your auntie, that he died up there."

Emma felt disoriented, off-kilter, as though she'd fallen asleep on the bus then got off without knowing what neighbourhood she was in. She felt as though she still had questions, still wanted to know about the family, but didn't know how to form the words. The language from the newspapers—*adult family members, Kevin Gaugin, Gary Gaugin, minor children*—seemed stilted, inaccurate. An assault on Helen and Heather, her mother and sister, who sat at the table with her, remembering these people as their only family in a way that she could not. And the family words, the familiar and affectionate *Nanny and Poppy, Mom and Dad*, those were out of the question, too. Where did that leave her? Her and her questions, her research, and her life....

"You didn't ask about Kevin. Our brother Kevin," Heather said at last. Her voice was low and dull, as though she'd been carrying the heavy question around all day.

Emma looked at her and at Helen, but neither made eye contact. "What about Kevin? Does he still live here?" Would she meet him? When? Already, she began calculating whether she could afford to change her flight again.

Helen stood slowly. She turned to the fridge and plucked a piece of folded paper off the side, where it had been held by a flower-shaped magnet. She handed the paper to Emma. "It'll be a year in August," she said.

On one side of the paper was a photo of a heavy-set, dark-haired man with a tidy beard. He was smiling. The photo was taken outdoors, on the Halifax waterfront, by the look of it. He squinted a bit in the sun, giving him a slightly quizzical look. Underneath the photo, it read *Kevin Gary Gaugin, 1980–2016.*

Emma looked at Heather. "Fentanyl," Heather said. She sounded tired.

"I'm sorry," Emma said automatically, looking back and forth between Helen and Heather.

"Yeah," Helen replied, taking another sip of her tea. "Me too."

❧

HEATHER AND EMMA WERE QUIET MOST OF THE RIDE HOME. FINALLY, as they pulled into the commercial park on their way back to Emma's hotel, she was able to frame some of her thoughts into words.

She waited until Heather pulled up to a red light before she said anything. "Did you know him? Kevin?"

"Bit," Heather said. The light changed, and she turned the car down a side street that led toward the hotel. "He'd be around for a while, then he'd be gone, who knew where. Then back again. First time I saw him again, he gave me this great big hug, he was just grinning like crazy, and I thought, 'Wow, he really missed me.' She glanced over at Emma. The edge of her lip flicked up, but it wasn't really a smile. Emma resisted the impulse to smile back, an automatic gesture. Though she didn't feel much like smiling, either.

"Then next time we saw each other, same thing," Heather went on, pulling into the hotel parking lot. She drove up to the front door and stopped the car. Her hand remained on the gearshift after she'd put the car in park, poised to shift it back into drive. "And we'd run into friends of his, not even close friends, just people he knew, and he had these huge, happy hugs for them, too. It made me feel bad at first, like I wasn't so special after all. But it's just how he was. He loved people, everybody really. He was always giving people money, even if he didn't have any. Always buying sandwiches and coffee for homeless people and junkies, that kind of thing."

She'd let her hand drift off the gearshift as she talked. It was resting in her lap, the fingers turned upward. "But he had problems. Made stupid mistakes. He never thought anything through."

There was a silence after that, and Emma thought about the phrase her mother had used, *hole in our lives.* She thought about her dad and her brother Kevin. It was as though she'd just found a hole somewhere inside her she'd never notice before, and now she couldn't stop probing it, feeling the soft ache.

A man and a woman in business suits walked past their car, heading into the hotel. Emma sat, watching as the automatic doors opened and closed for them. She felt as though the words were blocked behind her tongue, as though they wouldn't take shape.

She looked back at Heather, not at her face but at her hand, still lying in her lap. It reminded Emma of a dead bird somehow. There was a pang in her chest, up just below her throat, and Emma suddenly had the impression that the ache was not her own, that it was Heather's pain she was feeling inside her own body.

"There was incest," she said at last, her voice sounding watery and faint to her own ears. "One of the journals I found, this woman in Lunenburg in the early 1900s, said that there was a Gaugin brother and sister who got married." There. She'd said it. She stared hard at the dash.

Heather shifted in the seat to look at her. "What the hell is wrong with you?" she snapped.

Emma turned, surprised. Heather was staring at her as though she'd just taken a shit on the passenger seat. "Me?" she asked.

"Honest to god. You've met our mom, you met me, you had dinner at my frigging *house* with my husband and my kids and the man who practically raised me, and you still think that's who we are? Some hill clan with a shallow gene pool?"

"I just wanted to know—"

"Why? Why do you need to go digging for muck? You could just be you, and I can be me, and that can be enough."

"But the journal—"

"Who the hell cares?" Heather said. "Out. I need some time on my own."

Emma took her bag and opened the car door. "I'm sorry," she said. Her throat tightened. She willed herself not to cry.

"Wait," Heather said. Her hands were still on the wheel, she was still staring right ahead. "Why the hell didn't you tell me you wrote to her?"

"She didn't answer."

"So?"

Emma had no answer. She hesitated as she got out of the car. What was she supposed to say? *Sorry? Thank you? I had a lovely time?* "Bye," she mumbled at last.

Heather raised a hand towards her. Emma couldn't tell whether it was a *goodbye* or a *no*. She pulled away without a word.

Emma made her way into the hotel, a deep heaviness in her chest. Not the tightness, the panic she was used to, but a weariness, a darkness.

She passed Glen on his way to the bar. He gave her a polite nod then seemed on the verge of turning away, but stopped when he saw her, his eyes darkening with concern.

"You okay?"

She shook her head, tears already spilling down her face. He followed her down the hall, and when the stairwell door clicked shut behind them he folded her in a hug.

She let herself sob once, twice, against his shoulder, then pulled her sorrow in. She straightened up. "Thanks," she said, not looking him in the face. "I have to go call my parents now." She felt him watching as she climbed the stairs to her floor.

"Emma," he called.

She stopped, but didn't turn.

"Can't you tell me anything?"

She just shook her head and kept climbing, not trusting herself to talk. She heard him sigh as she turned on the landing.

She tried Mike's cell first. As usual, he didn't answer it. She considered just leaving a voicemail—*Miss you, see you in a couple of days*—but she knew her quaking voice would give her away. As she held the phone in her hand, deciding whether she could handle Julia's concerned probing, the phone buzzed. Mike. Emma wondered where he'd left his phone this time.

"I'm having a bad day," was all she managed to say.

"Oh, Em. You'll be home soon. We'll figure something out soon," he murmured as she sobbed into the phone.

She let herself cry as he made vague plans, gestured toward solutions he promised they'd find together when she got home. She felt the darkness drain away from her chest.

Some of it anyway.

TWENTY-SEVEN

JACK HEARD THEM THREE AISLES OVER IN THE GROCERY STORE IN Chester. First, the wet smash of a jar landing on the institutional tile floors. Then Heather's voice, impatient, frustrated—not yelling, just a snapping command. Then Charlotte's thin, fussy wail. He set down his basket on the floor—nothing much in it, anyway, except a couple of cans of soup and some salted peanuts—and made his way over to the breakfast aisle.

Justin was standing next to a puddle of greyish applesauce. It had splattered his pants and his shoes. He was blinking fast. "I'm sorry, Mom," he said, not quite whining, not quite whispering, but somewhere in between.

"I *told* you not to touch, Justin."

"I just wanted to show you." He lost his fight against the tears, which splattered on his blue T-shirt.

"Yeah, and now look!" Heather crouched awkwardly, Charlotte slung to her chest in a carrier and, still whimpering and fussing, no doubt reacting to the tension in her mother's voice, in her rigid posture.

"Don't touch that, my girl, you'll cut yourself," Jack said, gently reaching for her elbow.

"Am I supposed to leave this mess for someone else to clean up?" Heather snapped. But she let Jack pull her to her feet.

"That you are, I'm afraid."

And, in fact, a teenaged stock boy had arrived at the end of the aisle with a cleaning cart. *One of Jan Harnish's boys*, Jack thought. Jan had been in his advanced drawing class years ago. She had a younger brother, Darren, about Heather's age. Jan still called him Professor Jack. Cheekily, though, always a wink in her voice now.

"Come on," Jack said. "I was wanting some breakfast, only I wanted some company even more."

"I haven't finished my shopping," Heather replied. She shot Justin an angry glare as the young Harnish boy started sweeping up the broken jar.

"Another time," he said. He reached for Charlotte and the baby held her arms out to him, letting herself be pulled free of the harness. She stopped fussing as she settled on his bony hip, twining her fingers in his wispy ponytail. He put his free hand on Justin's shoulder and guided him toward the exit, casting an apologetic look at the Harnish boy and at Jodie MacDonald, the cashier. Behind him, Heather harrumphed softly before she followed them out.

He led the way up the street toward the harbour and into the little bakery on the corner. He ordered a couple of cups of coffee and some Danishes.

"I have stuff to do, Jack," Heather grumbled. But she sat down and dumped a stream of sugar into her coffee nonetheless.

Justin scrambled onto the chair beside her and helped himself to a blueberry pastry from the plate Jack had set in the centre of the table.

"This about your sister?" Jack asked, stirring cream into his cup until the coffee reached the right shade of beige. He took a sip. Good as always, strong but not bitter.

"What?" Heather growled. But she didn't meet his gaze.

"She's going home soon, isn't she."

"I guess."

"Helen was okay meeting the girl?"

Heather snorted. "Oh, Helen's fine."

"Can I have some milk?" Justin asked. Heather shot him a glare. "Please." She stalked to the counter and bought him a tiny carton of whole milk. White. Justin gazed longingly at the chocolate milk in the display case but didn't say anything. Jack nudged the pastries toward him, and with a quick glance at his mother, the boy slipped another off the plate.

"Sometimes, I think on her at Marian's funeral. She's about the only reason I got myself through it."

"Helen is?" Heather asked.

Jack nodded. "We got to the funeral home, I don't know if you remember. And people were just starting to come. And you'd been up crying all the night before—you thought I couldn't hear you, but I could—but that day, you had a look on your face that said, *I'm not gonna cry, I won't.*"

"I did, though."

"You did, you did. But not then, not at the very beginning." Jack leaned back in his chair, settling into its plastic curve. "And all these people, good people, friends of ours, and folks from the paper, from the university, from around town, kept coming to tell me they were sorry, and I kept looking at the door, thinking, Christ, I've got to go, I can't keep this up." He stopped, pretending to take a sip of his coffee, but in reality he was trying to ease the tightness in his throat. Still, after all this time, it crept up on him sometimes.

Setting his coffee back down, he went on. "Then she came in, your mom. Helen. And she just kind of hovered next to the door. She had her coat on. It was one of Marian's old coats, actually, I don't know when Mar gave it to her, but she was wearing it all done up. And I remember thinking it's hot as hell in here, she must be suffering some in that winter coat. And I realized she was wearing the coat because she wanted to leave just as bad as I did, worse even. And she was crying, bawling like people don't do in public, and other than you and me, she didn't know anyone there."

Heather made a small noise, but Jack didn't dare look up to see if the sound was for him or for the kids. The tightness in his throat was still there, threatening him with sudden tears.

"But she stayed on through the service and the reception afterward," he said, steadying his voice, "looking sweaty and uncomfortable as hell in that coat. And she was doing it for Marian. She wanted more than anything to get the hell out, but she stayed on. And I saw her and thought, if she can do this, so can I." He took a slow swallow of his coffee, a real one this time. Even now, years later, it was hard to keep his voice steady when he talked about Marian's death. "I owe her a debt, I suppose."

"You should have just left," Heather replied. She stuck out her chin in that way she had when she was trying hard to sound sure. "If you wanted to go, there's no reason you shouldn't have."

"Yes there is, my girl," Jack replied. "There is."

"Well, what's any of this got to do with *Emma*?" Heather spat out the name. She kept her gaze fixed on her coffee cup.

"Oh nothing, I suppose. Just the way thoughts go sometimes."

Heather sighed. It was one of those unburdening breaths, the kind you make when you shuffle into the kitchen and drop two armloads of heavy groceries. She took a sip of her coffee, then reached over to touch the back of Justin's short, black hair. He slid his gaze over to her, tentative. She kept her hand on the back of his neck. His feet swung free of the bottom rung of the chair, tapping softly on the floor as he took another bite of his Danish.

"Suppose I'd better go back and get groceries, then."

"You go," Jack said. "Kids'll keep me company here."

"Yeah?"

Jack nodded as Charlotte stuck her chubby fingers into his mouth. He pretended to bite them and she squealed in delight.

Jack watched Heather cross the road on her way back to the grocery store. When she reached the sidewalk on the other side, she stopped to pull her phone out of her purse. She dialled and crossed her arms as she talked. Jack smiled. From here, she still looked like her sixteen-year-old self. All bravado.

TWENTY-EIGHT

THE WEEK THE FROZEN FISH STICK COMPANY OFFERED EMMA A FULL-time job as an Internal Support Analyst, Emma asked her mom to help her go through apartment listings. Julia had been working at home, revising their restaurant's menu. She always worked on the living room couch, her laptop balanced on a pillow. It took her a minute to process anything you said to her while her head was in her work.

"Mm," she said, typing away. Then she leaned back, blinked twice at the ceiling, and abruptly snapped her head toward Emma, as though she'd just realized she was standing there. "Wait, what? Why?"

"I...want to get my own place?" Emma replied. Why else?

"*Why?*" Julia asked again. She looked utterly aghast.

"Because it's time I moved out. I was considering this commune in California, but they'd make me give away all my possessions and become the Supreme Prophet's seventh wife and bear his children, and I really don't want to give up my iPod. So I thought maybe apartment instead."

"I thought you'd stay here through university!"

"I'm not going to university, Mom."

"But you might!"

"I'm not."

Julia's mouth scrunched up and tears spilled down her cheeks. She moved her laptop to the coffee table and held out her arms to Emma.

"Every day, I'm amazed by you. You are just so extraordinary, did you know that?"

Emma shook her head. "I'm pretty sure I'm not the first twenty-year-old to move out on her own," she said. But she sat down on the couch and let her mother pull her into a tight, weepy hug. Afterward, they sat side by side, scrolling through apartment listings that were close to Edmonton's downtown but not near the dodgier neighbour-hoods. Nothing near the Coliseum, nothing near Fort Road.

When Mike came home that evening, he insisted on sorting their short list into a spreadsheet. He scored each listing according to a complicated number of factors. His ranking was not far off of Emma's own preferences.

"I'll call them tomorrow and book some viewings," he said when they'd finished.

"No way," Emma replied. "I've got it from here." Even though she would much rather have let him handle it, the phone calls and the meetings and negotiating the lease details. All the kinds of things that made her stomach squirm when she thought about them. Still, no way she'd let her dad get her her first apartment.

∾

AS EMMA MADE HER WAY ONTO THE AIRPLANE AT THE HALIFAX airport, she thought about that spreadsheet, of the neat calculations that factored in cost, distance to work, shopping, and to the Weavers' North Edmonton house, age of the building, square footage, and amenities. She'd teased him about it. She always teased him about his desire to break every problem down into simple components, with mathematical solutions.

She wondered how he'd break down her current trip when he told her about it. How he'd calculate when and how often she'd come back to Nova Scotia for visits.

Monday night, after his shift, Emma assumed, Glen had knocked softly on Emma's hotel door. "Feel up to some company?" he'd called.

Emma opened the door. She was wearing the hotel bathrobe, and she knew her face was red and swollen from crying. She looked at the ground, not wanting Glen to see her looking like that, but also not wanting him to go.

"You didn't text me back," she said, hating the waver in her voice.

He frowned a little. "What is it you're wanting here?"

"I don't know. I'm going home tomorrow."

He nodded slowly. "Right." He moved backward, to go. As he moved out of the doorway, Emma suddenly felt as though he were taking the air out of the room with him.

"I do, though," she blurted.

He looked back at her questioningly.

"Want company."

"I'm not into, you know." He looked down at the carpet, blushing. "Hookups."

She felt her own cheeks flush red. "Me neither."

"You haven't ever said anything," he said, "about you."

What's there to say? You've seen me naked. The smirk was on her lips. But she didn't say it. Instead, she stood back, holding the door for him. He followed her into the room, and when she sat down on the unmade bed, he sat next to her. Took her hand in his and sat quietly, waiting for her to talk.

But she didn't say anything. Couldn't. What was there to tell, really? *I met my birth mom, found out my brother's dead, and pissed off my sister.* Somehow, the words were almost a lie; they were so incomplete, so short of being what had actually transpired. She kept swallowing, trying to hold the tears back. Wanting to say something, but not able to make the words form.

"I was really sick," she said at last. "After high school."

He looked at her face, his eyes so soft she had to look away. "Sick like...cancer?"

"Not like cancer." Forcing a hollow little laugh, she tapped her forehead with two fingers.

He nodded and didn't say anything. If he had, if he'd asked questions, she didn't know what she would have done. Probably said something shitty, something *crazy*. Something designed to repel him. But he didn't say anything, so she didn't have to.

When things got bad for her now, when the panic attacks hit her the worst, when she had the "panic poops"—that was what Julia called them—it was still a ghost of the feeling she'd had back then.

She didn't remember when it had first started coming on. She was working away in the coffee shop, and it was like going down a slope so gentle that you don't even realize you're on it until you're near the bottom. Every evening, she went to bed a little earlier. The later she stayed up, the more she thought about the next day.

That was the hardest. The subterranean, formless dread that seeped into her whenever she thought about the future. A year, a week, a day. It didn't matter. It all seemed dark.

If she tried to pin down what, exactly, she dreaded, that's when her legs would start quaking, her guts would churn and tighten. She wouldn't be able to sit still. She would start pacing around her room, then, if her parents weren't in the living room, between her and the front door, she'd head outside, walking, fast and aimless, until the tension in her face broke and she could cry. That was her signal to turn and head home. Because when the sobbing ended, she'd feel drained. Drained of energy, feeling, hope. The blackness would take over and she'd only feel the stark, overwhelming emptiness. She'd crawl into bed, no matter what time of day, and wait to be able to fall asleep.

If she couldn't sleep, she'd watch TV.

It was when she was watching TV that her mom came home unexpectedly. Emma had two days off work at the café. It was unusual for her to get a "weekend," even if it was in the middle of the week. Her days off were usually staggered—a Monday and a Thursday, or a Sunday and a Wednesday. But she'd worked opening on Sunday, and she didn't have to be back until five on Wednesday. She had two and a half days off. Two and a half days with nothing to do but sink into the blackness.

When she thinks back, she remembers making a sandwich. She could hardly see what she was doing—she'd been weeping since she woke up. She remembers whispering "help," even though there was no one in the house. She'd all but mashed up the tomato she was trying to slice because she was crying and she couldn't see what she was doing.

She took the sandwich with her to the computer and googled "help." She wanted the internet to suggest something, anything, to lift her out of this feeling. She half-laughed at herself as the sobs increased. The search results were less than helpful.

She went to the couch and found reruns of a '90s family sitcom. She turned it on and curled up under the blanket.

She doesn't remember bringing the knife with her.

Her mom came home from the deli and found her on the couch, curled under the blanket, clutching the kitchen knife like a child with a stuffed animal. Emma's quiet weeping had turned into a keening sound so loud that she hadn't heard Julia come in.

At the Emergency Room, the nurse told Julia they couldn't admit Emma because there just weren't enough beds for psychological patients.

"Do you have suicidal thoughts?" the nurse had asked. "Are you planning to hurt yourself?"

"No," Emma said. The knife had been a mistake. She'd forgotten to set it down. But she couldn't bring herself to form the words.

But Julia, Julia who used the words "acceptance" more than any person Emma had ever known, flew into a rage when they tried to discharge Emma. She smacked both hands down flat on the counter. "She had a knife!" Julia screamed. "A goddamn KNIFE!"

At that moment, Emma wished she didn't feel the weight of so much darkness so she could at least smile at hearing her mom swear.

In the end, they found an overnight bed for her, though not in the psych ward. Emma wasn't really sure where they had put her, and she didn't ask later. She had a bed, she was given something that sunk her into a weightless sleep, and when she woke up, Mike and Julia were curled up in wooden-armed recliners next to her. They went home with a prescription for a Selective Serotonin Reuptake Inhibitor and benzodiazepine.

The next day she met a counsellor, Aliyah, who insisted that she sit with her shoulders back and her eyes focused above the horizon. She taught her to meditate. Part of Emma wanted to make fun, but she wanted so badly for something that would lift the darkness that she would have eaten glass if Aliyah had suggested it.

And the thing was, she did start to feel better. Not all the time, not right away, but there were hours, and even days, that Emma marvelled at how it felt just to breathe without so much bleakness pressing in on her.

In those weeks and months, Julia kept trying to shore her up with positive affirmations. "You're smart and you're strong," she said as she walked her into the yoga class she'd enrolled the two of them in at the local rec centre. "You will get past this."

Mike, on the other hand, tried to plan her through it. "What do you need to do to get through this week?" he'd ask. "What do you want to be doing a month from now? What will make you happy?"

The odd thing was, that kind of planning would have absolutely sunk her before that day, the day she'd curled up on the couch with a kitchen knife. And really, nothing had materially changed. But somehow, the idea of looking ahead, of making plans for something better, lifted her now.

That month, she started researching IT programs at local colleges.

Glen sat, holding her hand, for a long time. Emma let herself lean into him, let him bear the weight of her.

"It's not who I am," she said when she could speak evenly.

"I know," he said. He squeezed her hand. "Well. I see three things happening here. Either we get some shitty room service and watch expensive pay-per-view in bed here, we go to my place for decent takeout and binge-watch something on my TV, or we go and see a movie that's so cheesy and so stupid you can't even think about anything else."

Emma couldn't help but smile a little. Her dad would like Glen. So would her mom. Julia, she meant. Hard to say what kind of person Helen liked.

"I don't want to go out," she said.

"Room service and pay-per-view it is."

"But I don't want to stay here, either."

Glen smiled. "That's a problem. What do you want less?"

"Stay here."

"Then let's go to mine and *not* go out from there."

Emma nodded. "I can do that."

He waited while she went to the bathroom to wash her face, smooth her hair into a ponytail, and put on some clothes. It was weird, she reflected—he'd seen her naked, but she felt too self-conscious to get dressed in front of him.

"Ready," she said as she emerged. Her face was still red, her nose and eyes puffy, but there was not much she could do about that. He smiled and kissed her gently.

They didn't talk as they drove to his apartment. As he parked the car he asked, "Do you feel like walking to get takeout, or should we order in?"

"Let's walk," she said. It felt good to be outside. It felt good to be with him.

They brought home shawarma and falafel, and a tall bottle of cider from a place half a block up from his apartment. He suggested streaming a new series, but she asked to see his movies instead. They ate lying on his bed as they watched his three short films—they were all funny, all about little kids, but they were kind of dark, too, and sad.

"I like them," she said honestly.

"Yeah?" he asked.

"I do."

When he smiled, it was as though she could see something release in his shoulders. He'd been nervous to show her his films, she realized.

That's when she began to talk. About who she was, who she'd been. About the Gaugins and the Weavers, about Edmonton and Halifax, about Heather and Jack and Helen and Kevin. About the farm, the old homestead. About the Inglis journal. He listened quietly. He didn't interrupt, he didn't recoil. And when she finally stopped talking, she felt lighter, cleaner. Her throat wasn't tight with tears anymore.

Afterward, they watched some other movies that had been filmed locally—he'd been the second assistant director on one, and the production manager on another. He explained the jobs to her, talked about working in the film industry, writing his feature film screenplay. She loved hearing him talk about his work, loved the light in his face, the way he punctuated his sentences by opening up his hands and gesturing. But she felt the weight of the day pressing down on her. She drifted off to sleep as he was explaining funding.

They woke up late the next morning. Ate breakfast. Had sex.

Then Heather called Emma's cell. Asked her to come spend the day with them. Justin was finished school, and Rafe had a day off work. There was nothing tentative in her tone, nothing resentful. Just, "Hey, feel like spending the day out here instead of in your hotel?"

"Can I bring a friend?" Emma asked impulsively.

"Sure, okay." Heather sounded surprised. No wonder.

She turned to Glen after she'd hung up the phone. She felt buoyed, as though she'd just dropped a bag of sand she'd been hauling around all day. "Feel like going out to Chester to meet my sister and her family?"

"Yeah, I'd like that."

"You don't have to."

"I want to."

As they drove along the highway in Emma's rental, Glen kept looking over at her. "So, when will you be back?"

"I don't know," she replied honestly. "When will you come visit Edmonton?"

"Soon as you invite me," he said.

It was a nice afternoon. Rafe made a small fire in the backyard firepit. Glen pretended he didn't know how to roast marshmallows so that Justin could show him how. Emma sat in a lawn chair with Charlotte in her lap, and the baby kept reaching out to touch Emma's nose and mouth with her chubby hands.

Heather didn't bring up their trip into Halifax—not their mother or their brother, not the stupid Inglis journal either. She didn't talk about Emma's research. They just talked about their lives. Like any two people catching up after a long absence. Heather told Emma about going to work as a secretary for a construction union and meeting Rafe there. Emma told Heather about the fish stick company and her slow ride through her undergraduate degree. Justin told them all about a dog who'd shown up to the park during one of his soccer matches and taken control of the ball, pushing it around the field with its snout, keeping it away from the kids and their coaches. Glen asked Justin if he could find the dog and get it to agree to be in his movie. An eager smile flashing across his face, Justin promised to look for it next soccer game.

As evening fell—a late June evening that still felt like soft afternoon—the kids snuggled sleepily into their parents' laps and drifted off. And the four adults, Heather and Rafe, Emma and Glen, sat and talked about nothing and everything, or lapsed into lazy silence and watched the fire.

As they sat, a yellow-flowering bush in the corner of the yard caught Emma's eye. "We had one of those at home," she said. "Caragana. You used to feed me the flowers."

Heather followed her gaze. "Not me," she replied. "That was Mom. She said the flowers tasted like bananas. They just tasted like grass to me, but you used to like them. At least, you said you did."

Emma nodded. She tried to re-form the memory in her mind, tried to make Helen younger, softer. Tried to put the little yellow flowers in Helen's hands as they landed on her tongue. She couldn't do it. She felt bereft, as though she had just realized she'd lost something precious—dropped an earring someone had given her at the beach, or thrown an old photograph in the garbage by mistake. She kept reaching for the memory and catching only its absence, aching and hollow.

Finally, Heather stood to bring her sleeping baby daughter to bed, and Emma and Glen helped to gather the ketchup, plates and cups, leftover hot-dog buns, and other mess. Justin, his eyes still closed and his head nestled into Rafe's shoulder, protested he wasn't sleepy.

Emma dropped kisses onto her niece's and nephew's heads, hugged them against their parents, and made promises to see them soon.

Back in the hotel parking lot, Glen hovered for a moment as he got out of Emma's car. "Should I come up?" he asked.

Emma shook her head. "I have to be at the airport early." She didn't want to say goodbye to him in a 5 A.M. rush to pack up and get out of the hotel.

They held each other for a long moment in the parking lot, foreheads pressed together. Finally, he kissed her and walked around to the employee parking lot at the back.

As Emma settled into her aisle seat on the plane, she replayed their goodbye briefly, wondering whether she should have explained why she didn't invite him to stay, whether she should have said more, whether she'd already said too much, done too much. Maybe, after all, she'd just been a fling for him. Maybe, despite what he'd said about not hooking up, this was what he did—date tourists, scores and scores of dewy-eyed tourists. Maybe he was already seeing someone else, someone on vacation from Toronto, or on a business trip from Montreal. Maybe he thought she was an idiot for crying on his shoulder in the stairwell, for hauling him out to hang out with her long-lost sister and her family. Maybe.

Emma leaned back in her seat. She closed her eyes and breathed in, then out, imagining that she was expelling her worries, her racing thoughts, with the breath. And in again, imagining the recycled air as fresh and clean. And out, taking the negative thoughts and feelings with it. So they could be recirculated to the other passengers in the sealed metal tube.

She opened her eyes. The middle-aged woman in the next seat gave her a sympathetic smile.

"Scared of flying?"

"Nah, but I'm fucking terrified of crashing," Emma replied, twisting the corner of her mouth upward. "Kidding," she added hastily. It was too late. The woman glared at her as she put in her headphones. Oh well. At least she wouldn't have to make small talk on the flight home.

She reached for her purse under the seat ahead to put her phone in airplane mode. Emails from Dr. Melnyk and Dr. Fuentes flashed across the lock screen.

Her stomach twisted. She was going to have to make some decisions. Soon. The night before, as she settled into the fluffy hotel linens one last time, she'd considered dropping out, or at least scrapping the project, going back to the Canada and World War I and Women thing. But that seemed stupid. After all, why not write about her family? Why not follow through on the research she'd already gathered? She could tell that story, even if it was only to her thesis committee. Her reasons for not wanting to put it down in her thesis—having to present it to her advisors with a convincing amount of unconcern, of swagger, seemed stupid. So she was a Gaugin. What was that to them? And anyway, what were they to her? Who cared what they thought of her family, or even of her.

And she could do a good job of this story. She'd do a better job than anyone else had—the reporters (even Marian Rushdie, who'd meant well), the families who suspected Gaugins of stealing their livestock or their pickles, or their daughters. Their stories were nothing to hers. They were nothing to Helen's or Heather's. Why shouldn't she tell that story, even if only to a handful of academics interested in obscure topics?

It wouldn't be the story she'd set out to tell. Or the one she'd expected. Certainly not the one she'd been afraid of.

What *had* she been so afraid of, anyway?

She wasn't sure how much she'd leave in. What she'd take out. Certainly, the Inglis journal would have to stay in. But she wasn't sure if it would *all* have to stay in. Perhaps it would be dishonest to leave out Grace's suspicions of incest. *Just gossip*, Heather had said. And maybe that's all it was. Maybe it wasn't. Did it matter? Who would care if it was true? Heather certainly hadn't.

The plane pushed back from the gate. It turned and began to taxi toward the runway. Next to her the woman was already dozing off, head lolling against the bulkhead. Her mouth dropped open and she snored softly.

What about the Gaugins today? Three weeks ago, Emma had half-expected she'd discover that the clan had re-established itself somewhere deeper in the woods, was haunting the local population, creeping into towns at night to sneak food and supplies and maybe even women. She felt her cheeks grow hot with shame. She'd need to decide if she'd write about Heather and her family. About Kevin. About her dad and her mom, about her grandmother dying in a nursing home. Would it be fair to them to leave them in? Would it be fair *not* to?

Emma's insides squirmed again. She closed her eyes. Focused on her breathing. On the weight of her legs on the airplane seat. Willed the tension in her guts to ease. She did *not* want to have to lock herself into the tiny airplane bathroom.

You can just be you, and I can just be me, and that can be enough, Heather had said. Could it, though?

Maybe it would have to be. If she could let it.

She breathed slowly.

Clean air in. Tensions out. And again.

There.

Certainly, she'd have to decide what story she would tell. And she'd have to decide soon. But not now. Not right now. Now, she just had to fly back home, and try to just be.

ACKNOWLEDGEMENTS

I AM SO GRATEFUL TO MY EDITOR, STEPHANIE DOMET, FOR HER WISE advice in helping me shape this story, and to Whitney Moran and Nimbus Publishing/Vagrant Press for their faith in me and my book.

Tremendous thanks to Sam Brannen, Bridgett Morgan, Lauren MacDougall, Linda Jensen, Mary Craig, Tina Jennings, Heather Fairbairn, Jennifer Allaby, Serena Lewis, and Sally Janes, who generously shared expert knowledge that guided my research. They helped me make my story real and true.

My love and thanks to Trent Soholt, for lending me strength and hope when I ran out.

CLAIRE FRASER

REBECCA BABCOCK IS AN AWARD-WINNING WRITER living in Halifax, Nova Scotia. She holds a Master's degree from the University of Alberta and a PhD from Dalhousie University. She often worries about being asked for medical help and having to explain she's not that kind of doctor. She has previously published a short story collection, *Every Second Weekend*, and her fiction has appeared in literary magazines in Canada and abroad. *One Who Has Been Here Before* is her first novel.